DOUBLE LIFE

Angela Pearse

clamp.pub

This is a work of fiction. Names, characters, places, and incidents either are the product of the author's imagination or are used fictitiously. Any resemblance to actual persons, living or dead, events, or locales is entirely coincidental.

First Paperback edition May 2022
Published by Clamp Ltd.

Set in Sabon, Dream Orphans and Garamond
Cover art by My Lan Khuc Valle

ISBN 978-1-914531-92-7 ePUB
ISBN 978-1-914531-93-4 Paperback (IngramSpark)
ISBN 978-1-914531-94-1 Paperback (KDP)

angelapearse.pub
clamp.pub

For Chris

CONTENTS

Chapter 1

CALLUM'S WEST END FLAT

⁕

'It's not exactly *sexy*, is it?' Callum surveys my comfortable beige bra with an expression of distaste.

I shrug. 'At least it's clean.'

Honestly, every time we're about to have sex lately, the subject of my underwear comes up. The man has lingerie on the brain. I'm not sure what the big deal is. My M&S bra is a functional piece of clothing. It keeps certain pieces of flesh where they're supposed to be. Besides, he usually whips it off me in five seconds flat, so why spend hard-earned money on expensive wisps of lace that aren't even supportive?

'Mmm, you smell nice, like the tropics,' he murmurs, sniffing at my neck. He slips a hand round to deftly unhook my offensive bra.

'It's Jamaican Delight body wash,' I say. (It was on sale at Superdrug. I thought it sounded exotic.)

A ridiculous urge comes over me to start singing 'I've Got a Lovely Bunch of Coconuts', but Callum isn't amused by silly stuff. Instead, I bite my lip and concentrate on undoing the lower buttons of his blue-and-white pinstripe shirt and unzipping his grey suit trousers. It's Tuesday night, and he has to work later. He hates the rigmarole of getting dressed after sex, hence why he's fully clothed and why I have my blouse unbuttoned, bra flapping loose, and skirt hiked up. Now with a quick series of hand movements, Callum edges my matching beige knickers down around my thighs, then checks his Apple Watch to make sure we're on schedule. Apparently, there's a new contract he wants to look over tonight . . .

Callum actually does have a great body, when he deigns to take his clothes off (that's usually reserved for Friday nights or the weekend, when he has more free time).

The fact that he's seriously built didn't escape my notice when I first met him two years ago. I'd taken a half-day off work to view some flats through Duncan Stratt, a letting and estate agency in the New Town. While I was waiting for the letting agent to appear, I noted the pop-up calendar of Antarctica on his desk—the only thing of interest in his sterile office. Idly, I picked it up. For September, there was a photo of a fluffy baby penguin alongside a dizzying number of scrawled appointment times.

Intrigued, I wondered, *Has he been there? Or does he want to go?* I assumed a man who had an Antarctica desk calendar must be an outdoorsy, adventurer type. Since I'd been expecting someone who was a bit rough around the edges, I was taken aback when he strolled in. Callum Stewart was the most well-groomed man I'd ever seen. He had short black hair gelled back hard into place, a clean-shaven jaw, salon-shaped eyebrows, and ice-blue eyes. He was wearing a black three-piece designer suit that fit him to perfection—not a speck of lint dared cling to it.

My face must've reflected my surprise because he flicked his eyes to mine, then to the calendar, and with remarkable perceptiveness, he said, 'A Secret Santa present. Too cold for me. I prefer going somewhere warm for my holidays.'

Callum took off his suit jacket, then unbuttoned and rolled up his white shirtsleeves. My eyes flicked over his lightly tanned, supremely muscular forearms, which suggested that he not only worked out but had also just returned from a holiday. He looked like the type of guy who'd stay in a five-star resort in the Bahamas.

His handsome, put-together presence was slightly intimidating, which irked me, so I replaced the calendar and couldn't resist a flippant, 'It looks like you have been somewhere warm recently, nice tan.'

The instant the words were out of my mouth I realised it was too familiar and flushed bright red. But Callum seemed amused, and I caught him giving me a once-over as he sat down. I was wearing my typical work outfit—cream silk blouse, grey pencil skirt, natural sheer stockings, and black three-inch heels. My long brown wavy hair was tied back in a bun, and I had on my black thick-rimmed, oversized glasses, several coats of long-lash mascara, and a generous slick of pink lipstick. I call it my 'sexy librarian' look, and since I am actually a librarian, I figure I can get away with it.

Leaning back in his chair, Callum fingered his blue silk tie and considered me carefully. Then he said in a low voice, with his eyes fixed on mine, 'So are you ready to see some flats, Ms McTavish?' I swear to God my insides turned to jelly.

Anyway, that was our first meeting. When I look back on it now, it seems strange to me that he didn't even say hello or introduce himself. It was like he didn't feel the need to bother with niceties.

I force my attention back to the present, and Callum is on top of me. He thrusts a few times, grunts, and then it's over. Sex with Callum is, shall we say, *perfunctory.* He thinks foreplay is a waste of time. The most I can hope for is the odd ear nibble or breast grope. That's when he's feeling particularly amorous. He mostly just wants to do the deed and then move on with whatever tasks are next on his list. He calls it 'pipe maintenance'.

The weird thing is it didn't start out like that. We used to have sex that lasted a normal length of time. But he started increasing the 'pipe maintenance' sex until it's pretty much become our go-to.

The first time it happened, about six months into our relationship, I was shocked beyond belief and seriously thought about dumping him right then and there. But Callum explained that it was just to save time and that he had some work to finish and that he still really liked me.

So I've gotten used to it. It's just the way he is. And all men have their foibles, don't they? Things you have to put up with?

Our sex life does tend to ramp up when we go away on weekend minibreaks. However, our last minibreak in the Lake District was a case of him thrusting three times in the morning and three times in the evening, which admittedly did leave us plenty of time for sightseeing.

Callum sighs and rolls off me, and I almost say sarcastically, 'Was it good for you?' But I just rehook my bra, button my blouse, pull up my knickers, lower my skirt, and head out to the kitchen, throwing 'Cup of tea?' over my shoulder as I go. Leaving him to sort himself out is my way of getting back at him. Why should I have to rebutton and zip up everything I undid exactly—I glance at my phone—four minutes ago?

Of all the rooms in Callum's three-bedroom flat, I love the kitchen the most. It's huge. All high-end appliances and black marble countertops. He has an Italian coffee maker, a blender with ten settings, and three ovens (not that he ever cooks anything). I could honestly just hang out here the whole time. One of the advantages of him moving into sales is that he has the pick of the bunch when it comes to lettings—he doesn't have to wait until something's advertised, which is why he moves flats every six months. He likes to live in different streets of central Edinburgh so he can provide 'local knowledge' for his clients.

His previous New Town flat had a Jacuzzi bathtub and a rooftop garden with views out to the Firth of Forth. I shed a few quiet tears when he handed in his notice. This current flat is in the West End in Palmerston Place, and he's been here five months. I know he's keeping an ear to the ground, so I've been using the blender as much as possible to make all kinds of smoothies before he leaves.

Maybe next time I'll suggest we have sex in here, I muse, flicking the switch on the gleaming chrome Dualit kettle. Callum could position himself behind me and thrust three times while I steep the tea. Then we can sip Earl Grey, and he can read the *Financial Times* and tell me what the share market's doing while I inspect my nails. He won't even need to see my underwear.

The scary thing is Callum might actually get on board with it. I glance at his fridge, where a weekly planner is held up by a couple of Duncan Stratt magnets. For Tuesday, September 9, he's written 'Emma' in the 7 p.m. slot—fitting me neatly in between 'meeting with Simon' at 6 p.m. and 'work on Harpington contract' at 8 p.m. Yes, he's all about efficiency.

I know I'm making Callum out to be a nightmare boyfriend, and you're probably thinking I'm a shallow bitch for going out with him only because he has a nice body and a shiny kitchen. There's much more to our relationship than that, of course. We actually have quite a bit in common.

For starters, we're both only children, and we both adore

Tesco sultana scones. We also like going for runs together on the weekend. Well, we start out together. He's much fitter than me, so I usually lag fifteen minutes behind and turn up red-faced and puffing. But still, it's a shared activity. Callum is also really good company when he's relaxed and not absorbed in his work, and we watch a lot of Netflix.

We get along famously with each other's families too. Callum's parents live in Jersey. I speak to his mum and dad on the phone when they ring, and they seem to like me. I also met his cousin, Robert (or Rabbie, as he told me to call him), who lives in Skye. We went up there one bank holiday weekend for a minibreak. Rabbie's unmarried and a farmer. He and I got on the whisky, and it was a brilliant laugh. It's a shame we haven't seen him since. Callum doesn't seem keen to go there again even though I've suggested it a few times.

He much prefers to visit my mum in Fort William. She adores him and always brings out the best china like he's royalty or something. She cooks his steak just the way he likes it too—so rare it's mooing—and fusses over him like he's the son she never had. Callum laps it up.

So you see, everything is all fine with us—it really is. I've just been dissatisfied with the physical side of our relationship lately. More so than usual. I just wish he'd make an effort to please me. Yes, I've tried talking to him. To be honest, things did improve after I did. He really seemed to get what I was saying about the sexual response cycle and listened intently when I was going on about the plateau phase. Well, he nodded a lot at least, and his eyes didn't glaze over. After *the talk,* he was very attentive, and we spent a few amazing evenings together. He didn't even open the *Financial Times.*

But it hasn't lasted. Callum's lapsed back into three-thrust Freddie, and I know if I say anything again, I'm going to come across as a nag.

The unfortunate part is that I've started looking at other guys on the street and wondering why I'm putting up with it. I'm thirty-two and in my prime, for God's sake!

The kettle finishes boiling, and I pour scalding water into our mugs and dunk the Earl Grey tea bags distractedly. Besides, what if we get married and he's so focused on his career that I don't have a baby until I'm forty? Is his swiftness in the sack going to be a problem? If he barely manages to get me aroused, then surely it's going to make it ten times harder to get pregnant at that age.

OK, he's never actually mentioned anything remotely along the lines of marriage or kids, so I could be completely barking up the wrong tree . . . Maybe I need to find out subtly before I get too ahead of myself.

Callum wanders into the kitchen, raking his hair back into place and tucking in his business shirt. He opens the fridge and peers in optimistically. He does it every time he comes into the kitchen. I can tell you exactly what's in there: a bottle of ketchup, a mouldy lemon, a bottle of milk, half a bottle of flat champagne, and a wilted bunch of lettuce.

I'm not sure what he's expecting to see if he doesn't go

food shopping. One of these days, I'm going to smuggle in a chocolate gâteau just to see the look on his face when he opens the fridge.

'Can you hand me the milk, please,' I say. He gives me the bottle, and I sniff it gingerly. It smells freshish. He leans against the counter, then flicks open today's copy of the *Financial Times* and starts reading an article. I bring over his tea and lean next to him, blowing on my own to cool it down.

'Callum?'

'Hmm?'

'Er . . . Do you want kids?' Whoops, so much for subtle. Callum jerks like I've prodded him with a red-hot poker.

'What?'

'Kids. Do you want them?' I repeat slowly.

'Uh, I haven't really thought about it.' He avoids my gaze and sips his tea.

'Well, you're thirty-six. Surely it's crossed your mind?'

'Perhaps. But not in a fully formed "I definitely want this" kind of way.'

'Oh.'

'Why? Don't tell me you're getting all clucky.' He sounds slightly panicked.

'Not especially.'

Callum puffs out a breath and smiles at me. 'We're all good, aren't we? No need to rush into things. We're just barely getting started.'

'We've been together two years,' I state pointedly.

'Shouldn't we be discussing things like this?'

He turns me around to face him and puts his hands on my shoulders. He's wearing his realtor expression, and I know what's coming.

'Having a baby isn't the answer to your problems, Em. You need to sort out your flat situation.'

'It's not my fault the landlord keeps putting up the rent!'

The shitty bastard's done it twice now. It's the main reason why I haven't been splashing out on sexy lingerie and why I've started buying discounted microwave meals. I'm always complaining to Callum, but he says the landlord is within his rights to do it as long as he gives me three months' notice.

He soothes me now with, 'I'll find you a cheaper flat. Just tell me where you want to live.'

'I want to stay where I am,' I state firmly. 'I just can't afford it.'

Callum drops his hands from my shoulders and returns to his newspaper. After a pause, he suggests casually, 'Why don't you get a flatmate?'

'A flatmate?'

'Yes, you've got two bedrooms, Em. Just rent out the other one. Problem solved.'

I shake my head slowly. 'I don't want a flatmate. They'll have friends over and be using my kitchen and lounge. And they'll want to *chat*.' I shudder. 'You know what I'm like. I'm an introvert. When I get home from work, I just want my own space—to read, watch Netflix, or think—without someone nattering in my ear. And I've got my library set up in the spare room.'

'Sorry, Em. Unless you move to a one-bedroom in a cheaper area or move in with me'—Callum shrugs his shoulders—'I don't think you've got any other choice.'

Chapter 2

STRIP 'N' STRAPS

✳

'It's all right for him,' I grumble to myself the next morning as I'm getting ready for work. 'He knows the owner, so he's paying cheap rent. He's not in touch with reality.' But neither am I, it seems, since I can no longer afford to keep living in Bruntsfield, one of the city's most expensive neighbourhoods.

The two-bedroom I'm renting was one of the handful that Callum showed me on the day we met. It's a top-floor flat in a four-storey stone-built tenement on Leven Terrace. It overlooks Bruntsfield Links, a sloping stretch of grass adjacent to the larger tree-lined expanse of the Meadows. The rent was slightly over my budget, but Callum saw I was smitten and encouraged me to take it. Then later, when we were back in his office going over the paperwork, he asked me out to dinner. After that, we went to his Marchmont flat for a nightcap and . . . well, you can guess what happened. At the time it felt like he was included in the lease agreement. I signed on the dotted line and got a flat *and* a boyfriend—it was a very productive day.

Opening the wardrobe, I flick through my collection of pencil skirts and blouses. I caught the bus back last night as I don't normally stay over at Callum's during the week. He doesn't like to be disturbed when he's working. Apparently, me padding across the polished marble floors in my bunny slippers is *very* disturbing to him. It's fine. I'd rather sleep in my own bed and have my own things around me anyway. His hard-edged furniture always makes me worried I'm going to whack a hip or stub a toe.

In contrast, my bedroom is an oasis of soft grey carpet, plump white pillows, and a snuggle-under flower-sprigged duvet—a 'run and hide from the world' haven, if you will. The walls are duck-shell blue, and the architraves are snowy white. I've hung up a few tasteful framed pictures (black-and-white prints of the Highlands and Edinburgh street scenes). My Art Deco dresser is from Gumtree, and my queen-sized bed with its black iron bedstead is from IKEA.

Before I moved in, I'd been living in a flat in the New Town with two other girls, and I was fed up with their drama. It was a relief to rent a place of my own and totally worth the extra money, or so I thought at the time.

Donning my beige bra and a clean pair of beige knickers, I look at myself critically in the full-length mirror hanging on the back of the wardrobe door. OK, maybe Callum has a point. It's not even remotely sexy. Perhaps if I make an effort in the underwear department, he might feel more inclined to indulge in foreplay instead of skipping it completely.

Inspired by the thought, I grab my phone off the dresser and check my bank balance. I've just been paid, so there's lots of lovely money sitting in my account. Before rent, utility bills, and council tax slash into it like an axe-wielding maniac and leave me with barely enough for food, that is.

I'll go shopping for cheap lingerie, I decide. How much could it be? Five or ten pounds at the most. I type in 'cheap underwear shops near me' and click on the closest one—a sex shop called Strip 'n' Straps. I flick through their selection. Ooh, they've got a sale on, up to forty percent off. Hmm . . . What about tartan crotchless knickers and a pair of nipple pasties? Callum won't know what's hit him. Right, that's my lunch break sorted.

Discreetly visiting the sex shop doesn't happen because I mention it to my colleague Sian when we're reshelving books in the non-fiction aisle, *J* to *L*, and she wants to come too.

'I'm only popping in for five minutes,' I whisper. 'Like, literally. I'm just picking up a few cheap items. I'm not going to spend half an hour trying things on.'

I know her. She's not a quick shopper.

'Oh, come on,' she whispers back in a pleading voice. 'I hate going into those places by myself. I always feel like a pervert. At least if you're there, they'll think we're lesbian lovers.'

I'm convinced Sian's in the closet with the door ajar. She's always saying stuff like that. I don't have a problem if she is a lesbian. I just wish she'd openly admit it instead of dropping hints all the time.

'Why do you want to go anyway? Got a hot date?' I ask, glancing at her.

Sian's sexy librarian look is even more extreme than mine. Today she's wearing glasses, pigtails, a tight-fitting black crop top with a push-up bra, a short pleated blue-and-black tartan skirt, black knee-high socks, black Doc Martens, and scarlet lipstick.

Her big hazel eyes fasten on mine, and she bats her expertly applied fake eyelashes. She twirls the end of a blonde pigtail. 'No, but I can give you my opinion if you want to try some things on. You know, tell you if it's sexy or not.'

I roll my eyes. 'We'll see,' I reply, checking the spine of the book in my hand and inserting it into its correct place on the shelf. I'm not sure I particularly want Sian ogling me as I model crotchless knickers.

The sex shop is in Cowgate, the street running underneath the Central Library. So we hotfoot it down there at noon, taking advantage of a break in the weather. It's been raining non-stop for the last five days, and my umbrella has become a permanent extension of my arm. The pavement is slick, but I've swapped my heels for trainers to mitigate the risk of slipping over and breaking a leg. We get only half an hour for lunch, so the quicker we can get down there and back up again, the better.

'What's all this in aid of anyway?' asks Sian as we power

walk along Chambers Street.

Sian's met Callum a few times. He drops by the library to collect me after work on the rare occasion he stays over at my place. The first time she saw him, her comment to me afterwards was 'He wears a suit well'. The next time, it was 'He's very confident'. That's all I've been able to get out of her. Not that I need her approval, but I'm curious to know if she finds him attractive. Most women do, so it will be a sure sign that she is batting for the other team if she doesn't. I'm sorely tempted to ask her outright if she prefers girls, but I'll bide my time until the right moment—namely, not in a small dressing room with my arse hanging out.

'It's just to spice things up,' I say vaguely. 'Keep Callum on his toes and all that.'

'Hmm.' Sian glances at me sideways, like she's not convinced. 'Are you having problems with him?'

'What makes you say that?' I ask, instantly on the defensive.

'No reason. He just seems a bit of a handful.'

We finish clattering down the steps and enter the small lane that leads into the narrow cobbled confines of Cowgate. I pull out my phone from my handbag to check the address again and to avoid having to reply. Callum *is* a handful, and most of the time, I really don't know how to manage him. He's got a very forceful personality. I found it incredibly attractive when we first started going out, but he can be quite overbearing. I have to constantly stand up for myself.

Otherwise, he'll squash me flat like an overripe strawberry.

'It should be somewhere round here. Keep a lookout for pink dildos in the window.' I show Sian the photo on Google, and she giggles. When we eventually find it, we scurry inside furtively, keeping our heads down. It's ridiculous. If we were guys, we'd be striding in confidently because everyone would know our willies were going to get a workout.

I'm relieved to see there's no one else in here. Just a woman behind the counter who glances up from her book. 'Can I help?'

'We're just after some lingerie,' I mutter.

She nods to the far wall. 'Let me know if you need a bigger size in anything.' Her eyes flick briefly over my chest. 'I've got some double-D and double-E stock out the back.'

Double-E! God, I'm not that big.

Sian's already flicking through the rack when I get there. 'Oh, Em, you have to buy this! And it's on sale too.' She's holding up a black harness BDSM number that's basically just a collection of elastic straps.

'Och, no! I haven't got a clue how to put that on. And even if I did, I'd have to be Houdini to try and get out of it.' I look through the crotchless knickers to see if they have them in my size.

'Well, I think it's hot. I'm going to try it on.'

She flounces into the changing room. I laugh to myself. If she can manage to get that contraption on in the next ten minutes *and* make it look hot, I'll be impressed.

After a few minutes, I hear agitated huffing and a muttered, 'Where the fuck does this bit go?'

I giggle quietly. Then Sian sticks her head round the curtain and beckons me over. 'Check it out!' Reluctantly, I put my head in, not sure what I'm going to see. 'Ta-da!'

Somehow, she's managed to get the whole thing on with all the straps in the right place. She's still wearing her bra and knickers, so nothing's showing. But I can see that with just bare flesh, it would look . . . quite revealing.

'Fuck! How the hell did you do that?'

'You just step in, pull it up, and fasten a few straps. It's easy. You should get it. Callum will salivate.'

I look at her doubtfully. 'Will he?'

'Trust me, he will.'

She sounds so certain that I find myself saying, 'OK. But can you just show me how you did it?'

Five minutes later, I'm at the counter paying for one in my size. I'm a bit worried that I haven't actually tried it on, but Sian's buying one too and has said she'll send me step-by-step photo instructions.

I tap my debit card against the machine and wait for the transaction to be approved. Even with the forty percent sale price, it's still more money than I should be spending.

Out of the corner of my eye, I see the words '£100 per sitting' displayed at the bottom of some flyers on the counter. Curious, I lean closer.

'What's that?' I ask the woman.

'Oh, life modelling. It's in Morningside. They're always looking for people. The money's pretty good.' She hands me a flyer.

'A hundred pounds!' I blurt out as I stare at it, flabbergasted. 'Just to sit there and do nothing?'

'Well, you have to be naked. I guess not many people are comfortable with that part.' She sniffs and eyes my chest again. 'You've got the body for it. It'd certainly give them something to draw.' She gives me a receipt, and I put it in my handbag along with the flyer.

'Enjoy your evening,' she says, nodding at the carrier bag.

I gulp. 'Thanks.'

This is either going to be the hottest night of my life or the most ridiculous.

We head back to the office, and I start cataloguing a pile of new stock that's come in while Sian carries on with the reshelving. But my mind keeps wandering to the flyer in my handbag. *One hundred pounds!* My broad-minded self is itching to do it.

But isn't it tantamount to prostitution? queries my prudish self.

Rubbish! counters Broad-minded. *It's not like you're having sex with anyone for money. It's purely posing for art. Look at the famous painters: Rubens, Klimt, Goya. They all used female nudes, and those women are now iconic.*

The likelihood of a painting of you in all your glory hanging in the National Gallery is extremely slim, Prude argues.

You never know! retorts Broad-minded.

I wrestle backwards and forwards with myself for the rest of the afternoon. I tend to do this a lot, especially if there's something I want to try that's a bit out there. One part of me is all 'Go for it! Do it!' The other part is horrified and wants to curl up on the couch with a cup of tea and a good book. Getting the two parts to shake hands and agree amicably is near impossible. Someone usually gets upset.

OK, I admit, taking your kit off and being drawn by a bunch of strangers is one of the more extreme ideas I've contemplated. And then there's Callum—how would he feel about it? I'm not entirely sure, but my gut instinctively says 'not happy'. He hardly likes me showing any skin when we go out for dinner, so I can't imagine he'd be overjoyed about me baring it all.

So, if I did it, I would need to keep it a secret. I'm not in the habit of keeping secrets from him. Yet, for some reason, a facet of my life that he has no clue about is instantly appealing. Besides, he doesn't tell me everything he gets up to. He might moonlight as a male stripper on Mondays and Wednesdays (the two nights I don't see him), and I'd be none the wiser.

Speaking of which, Thursday night is the night I've got planned for the sexy lingerie reveal. Callum's coming over to stay, so that gives me tonight to get to grips with figuring out how to actually put the thing on. It's been quite a while since we've had sex that lasts longer than four minutes, so I'm getting slightly desperate.

Just before 5 p.m., I check my phone and see that Callum's rung and left a message. Weird. He doesn't usually ring me at work.

'Hey, Em, can we swap Thursday night for tonight? There's a meeting I can't get out of. If I don't hear from you, I'll see you at five.'

Damn, it's that now, and he's always on time. I look over at Sian in the fiction aisle, *A* to *D*. I have to tell her she needs to send me the instructions, but then Callum comes striding in through the sliding glass door. Shit!

I plaster a smile on my face. 'Hi! I just got your message.'

'Hey.' He kisses me on the cheek. 'I didn't hear back from you, so I assumed swapping nights was OK.'

'It is! Absolutely. I'll just grab my stuff from the cloakroom.' I switch off my computer and get up from my chair. 'Ah, do you want to wait in the lobby?'

'Nah, I'll just sit at your desk.'

While he's settling himself, I look over at Sian in frustration, but she's got her back to me. I laugh loudly to try and get her attention.

Callum looks up, startled. 'Is something funny?'

'I just remembered a joke Sian told me at lunch.'

'Oh, sounds like it must be a good one. Tell it to me. I

need a laugh after the day I've had.'

Sian's now looking over and sees Callum sitting at my desk. She frowns, and I make a panicked face.

'Er . . . I can't quite remember it, but I'll get her to send it to me,' I say. I nod at Callum, raise my eyebrows, and make typing motions with my fingers at her. 'Help!' I mouth. I think the message gets through because she grins and gives me a thumbs up. I relax. Operation Lingerie is a go.

Chapter 3

CHICKEN CURRY SEDUCTION

✳

We walk through the Meadows in the rapidly descending dusk to reach my flat. My heels make pleasing tip-taps on the leaf-strewn path. Callum holds my hand, which he almost never does, so I'm feeling happy. Tonight will be great. I have visions of him keeling over with lust when he clocks me in the BDSM number. I smile to myself.

'Thinking about the joke again?'

'Maybe.'

'You're being very mysterious, Ms McTavish. I can't wait to hear this famous joke.'

He kisses the back of my hand and brushes it against his stubbled cheek. He's wearing his long dark-blue woollen coat over a grey suit, with the collar turned up against the frosty air. His delicious-smelling aftershave keeps assailing my nostrils; it's driving me wild. I don't know if I have the patience to deal with a hundred elastic straps. I take a deep breath. Easy, girl.

'By the way,' Callum continues. 'I had a chat to Shona in lettings. They're always getting enquiries about renting rooms in Bruntsfield, so she's going to forward her list of names to me. I'll do a pre-screen and weed out any undesirables.'

I feel a jolt of unease. This is moving a bit fast. After our conversation the other night about me renting out my spare room, I agreed to think about it. Now it seems he's taken the bull by the horns.

'I haven't had enough time to think about it,' I say petulantly.

'I know you. Your thinking could go on for weeks. You need to sort it out pronto.'

'There could be another option.'

'Like what?'

OK, this is where I tell Callum I'm considering being a life model. I open my mouth but then promptly shut it again. I can't. He'll flip his lid, and right now, I need him calm, relaxed, and receptive to being seduced.

'Uh, just a hobby that could bring in some extra cash.'

'What, selling your knitting creations on Etsy?' he scoffs. 'That's hardly going to bring in the big bucks.'

I quite like knitting. I find it relaxing, especially in winter, when the nights are so long and dark. But Callum has a deep distrust of arts and crafts. Once, I made him a very stylish black beanie. He just stared at it, aghast. If it doesn't have a designer label, he won't be caught dead in it.

'I could sell your beanie for starters,' I retort. 'That would fetch at least twenty pounds.'

'Hmm, I'm currently using it as a sock holder. You can't

have it.'

I think about the other option: his offer to move in with him. I'm incredibly tempted. After all, there's nothing more depressing than waiting for the ding of the microwave to finish cooking your reduced-price frozen lasagne. But I also know I'll just be doing it because of the money. Not because I really want to live with him. I enjoy *visiting* him, but I can't quite imagine actually living with him full time.

That's another thing that's a bit worrying. Because after two years, shouldn't you at least have a slight yearning to want to live with your boyfriend?

When we get to my flat, I put Callum in the lounge to read the latest issue of *House Beautiful*. (Interior design is another thing we have in common, not that we've ever even painted a wall together. But one day, we will, I'm sure.) I tell him to think about what to order for the takeaway. Then I head off to my bedroom to get changed.

As soon as the door's closed, I immediately message Sian: *Hi S, can you send me the instructions? Callum's staying tonight instead!*

I wait for a bit, but there's no reply. I ring her, but it goes straight to voicemail. It's OK. I'll just put on the contraption myself without her help. I feel confident. It's not rocket science, after all.

Soon, I'm red-faced and puffing and wondering if you do in fact need a PhD to figure it out. I've mostly got it right. I can at least see how it's supposed to look. I move a few straps sideways, adjust the leg garters, and do up the collar. It's so far removed from my usual M&S underwear that I'm pretty sure Callum is going to have a coronary. But when should I do the reveal? Maybe before dinner so we can work up an appetite. I put on stretchy black leggings and a black long-sleeved, polo-necked top to hide the collar. It makes me look like I'm off to burgle a house, but at least he won't think anything's going on.

Callum looks up from the magazine as I walk into the lounge. His eyes flick over my outfit. 'Why are you dressed like a sexy robber?' Damn, he doesn't miss a trick.

'No reason. Just in an all-black mood.'

I curl up next to him on the couch. He's loosened his red silk tie while he's been reading, and I reach over to undo it completely and pull the end so it slithers slowly from around his neck. I then drape it around my own and smooth my hands over the slippery silk of the tie, down over the curve of my breasts.

He looks at me and raises an eyebrow. 'We should order. What do you want?' he asks.

You, I think. *Stuff the takeaway.*

'I don't mind,' I reply huskily. 'You choose.'

'Indian?' He takes his phone out of his pants pocket and brings up the menu. 'The place around the corner is good.'

This isn't working. I'm going to have to be less subtle.

When the buzzer sounds, I go to let the delivery guy in

with the Indian. 'Hi, top floor,' I say into the entryphone. If it's my lucky day, he'll come right to the door. Lately, they can't be bothered to walk up the stairs and instead just leave it at the bottom. Soon, there's a knock at the door. Ooh, lucky day!

In the kitchen, I quickly take off my leggings and top and chuck them in the pantry. Then I open the foil containers and put everything on the table. The aroma of chicken curry and basmati rice permeates the air.

'It's ready!' I call. I'm at the counter with my back to Callum, stretching up to get down some plates, when he walks in. There's silence, and then comes a sound like steam escaping from a pressure cooker. I swivel around and, deliberately not looking at him, glide over to the table with the plates. I'm practically naked apart from a neck collar, an open cage bra, criss-crossing straps holding up a tiny triangle G-string, and further straps around my upper thighs. And that's just the front. The back is an even more complex web of black straps. I put the plates down and sashay slowly back to the cutlery drawer, so he gets a good eyeful of bare butt.

'Fork or spoon?' I ask seductively, looking at him over one shoulder.

The expression on his face is priceless. I so wish I could take a photo right now.

'Fuck, Em,' he chokes out.

'A fork it is,' I say smoothly and place one in his hand and guide him over to the table. He doesn't seem to be able to walk by himself.

'Wha . . . ?'

'It's just a little something for dessert. Now eat your dinner.' I resist the urge to add 'like a good little boy'.

I spoon some rice onto his plate and a helping of chicken curry. He forks some into his mouth automatically, but his eyes are fixated on my body. Thank God it's working.

'That's fucking hot,' he says finally.

'Oh, the curry?' I question innocently. I lean over with the spoon, take a mouthful from his plate, and chew slowly. Then I look at him and lick my lips, which are suddenly on fire. 'Mmm, spicy.'

Before I know what's happening, Callum's standing up from the table and yanking me into the bedroom. His clothes are coming off, and I'm being what can only be described as . . . *ravished.*

When we finally make it back out to the kitchen, the chicken curry is stone cold, so I pop it in the microwave. Callum is being super snugly and wants me to sit on his lap at the table. He's in his Calvin Kleins, and I'm in my blue bathrobe, and we eat off the same plate. I'm blissfully happy. It's pretty safe to say the kinky lingerie is definitely a hit.

'So are you going to tell me the joke?'

'Joke?' I'm lost.

'The one Sian told you.'

'Oh, that. Um, sure.' I rack my brain trying to think of a joke. The only one I can remember is one I saw online that made me giggle.

'Why do seagulls fly over the sea?'

'Why?'

'Because if they flew over the bay, they'd be bagels.'

He snorts. 'That's terrible!'

'I think it's funny.'

'You obviously have bad taste in jokes. And Sian too.'

'So what's your meeting tomorrow night?' I ask.

'Oh. Um, Camille Redfern has a property she wants to discuss. The owner lives in London and has been renting it out, but now he's decided to sell.'

My heart sinks. I can't stand Camille Redfern. She's a broker that Callum's agency partners with. She always insists on meeting him at a swanky bar and says she'll buy the drinks. I'm pretty sure she's hoping if she gets him drunk enough, he'll fall into her bed by the end of the evening. Callum's not stupid. He was on to her straightaway the first time and told me what happened. We had a bit of a laugh about it. She's harmless, but she is a pain. I sigh. 'Why does it have to be you? Surely there are plenty of *single* male real estate agents she can get her hooks into.'

He grins and shrugs. 'Maybe she wants the best man for the job.' I roll my eyes at him. 'You know I'm not interested in her, Em,' he tells me. 'She must be nearly fifty, maybe even sixty.'

'She's not that old! And she looks fantastic for her age, whatever it is,' I add grudgingly.

Callum slips a hand inside the front of my robe and pings one of the elastic straps. 'There's no way she could pull off this sexy little number.' He nuzzles my neck, and then his hand reaches farther inside my robe and cups my breast. I hardly dare to breathe. Surely not? He pulls my robe down and starts kissing my shoulder. It's definitely going to happen again. Twice in one night!

'Should we go to the bedroom?' I murmur.

'Let's just do it here,' Callum insists, taking my robe off completely and dropping it on the floor.

Having sex on the kitchen table amongst leftover chicken curry could quite possibly be the hottest thing ever. I love this man.

Later on, when we're in bed and Callum's fallen asleep, I lie awake, going over the evening in my head. It couldn't have gone any better. Funny how Sian was so spot on about what Callum would like.

My phone flashes repeatedly on the nightstand in the darkness, and I reach over and quickly put it under the covers so as not to wake him. Speak of the devil. Sian's in the process of sending through a series of instructional photos of her at various stages of putting on the lingerie. My eyes widen. This time, she's not wearing her bra and knickers, so everything's on show. *Jesus, that's X-rated!* I quickly delete the photos one by one, trying to mentally unsee what I've just seen and not giggle. What is she thinking? It's a bit late sending it through now!

Callum leaves early the next morning so he can shower at his flat and change into fresh clothes before work. Showing up in what he was wearing the day before will raise eyebrows, he says. And he doesn't want to look rumpled for his meeting with Camille. I bristle at that but don't say anything. After the night we've just had, I really can't complain. And he does smell slightly of chicken curry.

He kisses me at the door, and we have a brief cuddle. 'I'll see you Friday night,' he says. 'Do you want to go out somewhere? Or we could stay in, and you could wear that outfit again? Or a different one?'

A different one? How many pieces of BDSM lingerie does he think I own? The reality of what he's suggesting hits home. If I want decent sex from him, I'm going to have to dress up like this each time. That's going to cost money—money I don't really have. I almost say, 'Are you going to be funding all this lingerie?' But I clamp my lips shut. Callum's not stingy. He always pays when we go out for dinner or when we go away for the weekend. So he quite probably would fund it. But the thought of that makes me feel discomfited. I'm not sure why. So I just smile and say, 'I'll see what I can rustle up.' If worse comes to worst, I'm sure I can find a YouTube DIY video involving coat hanger wire, elastic bands, and cling film.

When he's gone, I have a shower in my en-suite bathroom and wash away the remnants of the evening with my Jamaican Delight body wash. The en suite just has a shower stall, a sink, and a loo, but the main bathroom is larger. It has a black-and-white tiled floor and a huge white enamel claw-foot bathtub with a rainfall showerhead. Oh, and a *Birth of Venus* shower curtain (that's my own touch—the original had a hideous green octopus). That's another reason I love living here. Coming home on a cold winter evening and sinking into a warm bubble bath surrounded by lighted candles is pure bliss.

I muse about Callum, as I usually do in the shower. On reflection, the thing that surprises me the most is how much he was turned on by the BDSM look. He hasn't given any indication of liking that kind of thing. We watched *Fifty Shades of Grey* together, and he didn't seem particularly impressed. In fact, I distinctly remember him falling asleep. Now it seems he's not completely immune, though there was no mention of trussing my limbs like a turkey or tying me to the bedpost with his red silk tie.

Back in my bedroom, with a towel wrapped round me, I can't resist taking the life modelling flyer out of my handbag and looking at it again. *One hundred pounds.* That could keep me in cheap BDSM lingerie for quite a while. It seems legit. It's glossy; there's a tasteful graphic of an artist at an easel and a phone number to ring. All I have to do is call and find out what's involved. There's no harm in that. If it sounds dodgy, I can just hang up. I drop the towel and look at my reflection in the mirror. Can I bear to have a bunch of strangers scrutinising my naked body with probing eyes? For one hundred pounds per sitting, I probably could.

Chapter 4

A MEETING AND A CHAT

⁂

By the time I reach the library on George IV Bridge, I've completely talked myself out of it. There's no way I'd be able to do that kind of thing. I'm not an exhibitionist. Last night was born out of desperation. No, what I'll do is set up a meeting with Blaire and demand that she promote me to senior librarian immediately, then I'll get more pay. OK, 'demand' may be too strong a word. I'll *gently suggest* that it's a good idea.

Blaire Munro is my boss and the director of the Central Library. I've asked for a promotion several times, but she keeps putting me off, saying I don't have the right qualifications. It's so frustrating. I'm an assistant librarian, but I'm practically doing everything a senior librarian does!

I stride through the double wooden doors of the intricately carved French Renaissance–style building that has been issuing book loans since 1890, thanks to Andrew Carnegie. Inside is more cheerful than the imposing stone exterior, especially the upper reference floor with its incredible domed ceiling. Mostly I work in lending on the ground floor. But sometimes I escape up top when I'm sick of answering questions.

Determinedly, I sit down at my desk, log in, and busily type an email to Blaire asking for a meeting with her this afternoon. She usually starts work at 8 a.m. sharp, so I know she's in her office on the first floor. Five minutes go by, then ten. Tendrils of tension emanate down through the floorboards as she tries to figure out how to put me off. I wait it out. My patience is rewarded fifteen minutes later with a brief email.

Emma. I can do 3pm. Blaire.

Yeesss! Ha ha. She couldn't think of a good-enough excuse. I've got one foot in the door. Now I just have to get her to promote me. Maybe I can bribe her with cakes from Patisserie Valerie.

Sian walks in just then and wanders over to my desk. 'Hi!' I say. 'What happened to you last night? Did you not get my message after work?'

She shoots me an anxious look and flushes bright red. 'I may have gone out. Got slightly sloshed, then sent you a whole load of really inappropriate photos.'

'It's OK. I deleted them. Don't worry about it.'

She breathes a sigh of relief and sits on the corner of my desk. 'Thanks, Em. Sorry about that. God. Hope you managed OK anyway. Was Callum surprised?'

I laugh. 'Let's just say he was a lot more interested in me than his chicken curry!'

Sian grins. 'I knew he'd go for it. He seems like he'd be more into whips and chains than lace and bows.'

She gets off my desk, and I notice then that she's wearing the exact same outfit she wore yesterday, like she hasn't actually been home. Her face is devoid of make-up apart from day-old mascara and clear lip gloss.

'I'll see you later,' she says. 'I've got to organise archive access for a woman who's researching the secret love affairs of Robbie Burns.'

Speaking of secret love affairs, I think, as I watch her walk over to the door to head upstairs.

Bemused, I sit there pondering what Sian said. Why does she think Callum's a 'whips and chains' type of guy? Does he come across as a sadist? He's just really confident, that's all. Confident and strong-willed.

As if I've summoned him or his ears have been burning, an email from callum@duncanstratt.co.uk pops into my inbox:

> *Hey Em, Shona's just sent me a list of at least ten people looking for a room in your area. I'll do a pre-screen and if they sound ok I'll set up some viewing times for the weekend. We're not doing anything Saturday afternoon, are we? – C*

I close the email and clench my teeth. Mentally, I scratch out 'strong-willed' and replace it with 'interfering'.

At 3 p.m., I knock on Blaire's door, armed with a selection of iced eclairs. I know she likes them. She routinely smuggles them into her office without offering us any. I've got my speech down pat, and I'm mentally prepared to do battle.

When I walk in, she looks up. 'Oh, Emma. Yes, our meeting. I'll just be a minute.' She tip-taps on her keyboard, so I sit down to wait and put the box of eclairs on her desk. I'm wearing the most conservative librarian outfit I own: a white shirt, a knee-length black pencil skirt, and a mustard-yellow cardigan. My hair is scraped back tightly into a neat bun. I've even donned my grandmother's long strand of pearls. It's a far cry from what I was wearing last night when I was being ravished on the kitchen table. Sometimes I feel like two very different people. Both are me, but they're opposite extremes.

'Right, Emma. Now what's this about?' Blaire pushes her horn-rimmed glasses back up her nose and swivels in her chair to face me.

Blaire is one of those women who have looked like an adult since they were ten years old. Unlike the rest of us dealing with the horrors of puberty, I'm sure she just calmly kept swapping her jumpers, skirts, and brown lace-up brogues for bigger sizes. Now in her early fifties, she has mousy brown hair, a pudding-basin haircut, and a kind of bland, featureless face. She never wears make-up or bothers plucking her eyebrows and is disdainful of anyone who does. I'm not against the natural look—far from it. But I get the feeling Blaire considers herself too intellectual to bother about such things. There was a rumour she was married once, but it's never been proven, and she doesn't talk about anything remotely personal to us underlings. I find her reticence intriguing, but not enough to pry. She scares me too much.

I clear my throat nervously. 'I wanted to speak to you about moving into a senior librarian role. It's something I've discussed with you previously . . .' I taper off as Blaire holds up a hand.

'I'll stop you there, Emma. As it happens, I have been considering revising staff roles and salaries recently. We've been given an increase in government funding for the next quarter.'

Ooh, that sounds promising. A handout to bolster the coffers. My face brightens. Maybe this isn't going to be as hard as I anticipated.

'But unfortunately, in your case, it isn't that easy,' she says. 'If you had a postgraduate qualification, I could promote you immediately. But you've only done an accredited short course, haven't you?' She smiles at me pityingly. 'I'm afraid that makes it more difficult to justify.'

My eyes narrow. I can't believe she's trotting out this old chestnut again. It's the same story every time. 'I'd like to, but really, it's not my fault that you don't have several suitable master's degrees or a PhD.' Blaire always makes me feel like I'm an impostor.

I agree that my educational journey into being a librarian has been somewhat haphazard. OK, I kind of fell into it. After a couple of years bumming around after high school, then waitressing and saving some money, I decided to study full-time. But the course had limited job prospects. It's a bit embarrassing. I haven't even told Callum the details; all he knows is that I did something in the arts. (OK, if you really want to know, it was dance and drama—fun, but highly impractical if you're trying to get a job in Edinburgh, the city of finance.) Anyway, because I love reading, I did a short course in librarianship, got a position here, and managed to work my way up from trainee to assistant level. That was before Blaire came on board. She seems to have made it her mission to prevent me from advancing. Maybe she's worried I'll try and steal her job, I don't know.

I try to keep calm and not get rattled. 'I have experience,' I state in a confident manner. 'I know the job inside out, and I've demonstrated I'm reliable. I can work evenings and during weekends too.'

She sighs. 'If it were up to me, Emma, I'd sign off on the paperwork tomorrow. But I know the board won't agree to it without you having the appropriate qualifications. Besides, the money could be put to better use, like upgrading the public computers.'

What is she on about? Those computers were upgraded last year! 'Isn't retaining quality staff more important?' I ask, trying not to show my annoyance.

She gives a small shrug. 'I'm sorry, there's really nothing I can do. Now was there anything else you wanted to talk about?'

Arrrgh! I really want to give her the finger right now. I'm so pissed off I can't actually speak. I shake my head mechanically and get up to leave.

'Don't forget your box—oh!' She's seen the Patisserie Valerie label. I open the lid and show her the four delectable glistening eclairs: two chocolate, one raspberry, and one pistachio. The sweet buttery smell of freshly baked pastry and cream wafts into the air. She looks at me expectantly.

I snap the lid shut and give her a grim smile. 'Afternoon tea for me and Sian. We've been working hard, so I thought we deserved a treat.'

I stomp down to the cloakroom with my Patisserie Valerie box and sit there amongst the coats, wallowing in self-pity and munching on eclairs. I knew it was a long shot, but she's so *unreasonable.* Agitated, I give the eclair I'm holding a squeeze for emphasis, and cream spurts out all over my hand. Scrambling for a tissue in my handbag, I touch the cool glossy paper of the flyer. For what seems like the hundredth time, I take it out and look at it. Without thinking, I reach for my phone and dial the number on the back. 'Hello,' I hear myself saying. 'Yes, I have your flyer. I'm interested in being a life model. Can you tell me more about it?'

Oh my *God.* Am I really going to do this?

I'm in Morningside, the well-to-do neighbourhood next to Bruntsfield, and hovering nervously outside a row of three-storey Georgian terraced flats. The woman I spoke to on the phone, Lorna Sutton, was really nice. Pleasant and *normal,* as if paying someone for being naked in front of a bunch of strangers was the most natural thing in the world. Apparently, her husband's an artist, and she set up this life modelling business a few years ago—first to find him subjects to paint and then later to help out the local artistic community. It seems there are lots of talented artists crying out for life models, but friends and family aren't too willing to take their clothes off for them.

By the end of our phone conversation, I still hadn't decided if I was brave enough to do it, but she invited me to come round after work anyway. She said most people don't make it past the 'cup of tea' stage and that it was perfectly fine if I decided not to do it. 'But there's no harm in just having a chat and seeing if it's right for you, dear.'

I take a deep breath and knock on the door. The woman who answers reminds me of my mother. She has a coiffured perm and is wearing a cream cashmere jumper, a tweed skirt, and very sensible shoes. For a minute, I think I've got the wrong address. I glance at my phone. 'Er . . . Lorna?'

Her blue eyes crinkle at the corners. 'Yes. Are you Emma? Oooh, come into the warm, dear. It's brisk out there.'

I quell the urge to giggle. She does have a slight touch of Mrs Doubtfire about her. Lorna ushers me into a spacious entranceway. Directly ahead, a flight of narrow dark wood stairs, fitted with a red-and-gold Turkish carpet runner, leads up to the second floor. I gather she and her husband own the entire end of the row.

'We can talk in here,' she says and ushers me into a room on the left. I gaze around in surprise. It's positively stuffed to the brim with antique furniture and knick-knacks. She gestures to a red velvet chaise longue, so we perch on there. There's a stack of china teacups positioned precariously by my ankle, and I keep thinking my leg is going to jerk out and send the lot crashing onto the polished wood floor.

Lorna glances at her watch. 'Unfortunately, Jack, my husband, is painting in his studio upstairs at the moment. Otherwise, you could've met him too. He's at his most productive at this time of day.'

'Oh, is he . . . with a life model?' I ask, glancing up at the ceiling.

She smiles at me patiently. 'Yes, dear.'

'And is she naked?' I blurt out. I can't help it—I have to know.

Lorna stares at me. 'Of course, dear. But *she* is a *he*. We actually have more men than women on our books at the moment.'

'Oh, right.' I feel like a bit of an idiot, but this whole set-up is throwing me. There's a naked man upstairs right this very minute. Getting his willy drawn.

'Can I get you a cup of tea?' Lorna offers. 'And perhaps a chocolate digestive?' She smiles kindly. 'It might help calm your nerves.'

God, is it that obvious? 'Yes, please.'

When we're settled with our cups of tea and a plate of biscuits between us, the interview as such begins.

'So tell me, Emma, why do you want to be a life model?'

'Ah, I don't know, really. I just saw the flyer, and it kind of spoke to me.' *It said 'one hundred pounds'.*

She nods. 'Are you interested in art?'

'Sure.' My Hairy Coo Highland print flashes into my mind.

'Are you comfortable with your body?'

'As much as anyone can be, I guess.'

She looks my outfit over. 'You seem very conservative.'

'Oh, this is just for work. I'm a librarian, and I had a meeting with my boss today. I'm usually a little more out there.'

Lorna's eyes shift to my pearls uncertainly, as if she doesn't believe me. 'Would you be OK wearing a wig or certain make-up?' A wig! That's a bit odd. What kind of wig? A curly red wig, like a clown's? Or a merkin?

'Oh, er . . . Sure, that sounds like fun. I did a degree in dance and drama at Edinburgh College, so that kind of thing is right up my alley.'

'Excellent! So I charge fifty pounds a head for the artists, and it's a sixty-forty split between us and the model. Sessions are five artists minimum, so you're guaranteed to earn a hundred pounds. But if it's a larger session, say ten artists, you can earn two hundred.'

I gulp. Ten? That sounds like a lot of people. Lorna sees my anxious expression and smiles reassuringly. 'If you're not comfortable with ten artists, we do have other models we can call on.'

'What kind of hours are involved?'

'A typical session is usually an hour and only on week nights or at the weekend. We take bookings well in advance, so you'd have plenty of notice.'

'Weekends are OK, but I can only do Monday and Wednesday evenings.'

'That should be fine. I can make a note of that.'

'And payment? How does that work?'

'Cash in hand at the end of the session.'

My heart is thudding. Who am I kidding? I know I'm going to do this. As soon as I picked up the flyer in the sex shop, I knew I was going to do it.

'When can I start?'

Lorna laughs. 'Whenever you like. We have a booking for a group of retirees on Saturday morning, if it's not too short notice for you? It's a nice easy one to start off with. Some of them can't see very well, but they're very enthusiastic.'

Chapter 5

THE JACK MYSTERY

✻

Callum's pretty chuffed that he's managed to line up three viewings for my spare room. It's the first thing he tells me when I walk through the door of his flat the next evening.

'I'm not expecting that you'll hit it off with anyone in this first round,' he says, taking my beige trench coat from me and hanging it on the coatrack. 'But it will give you a good idea of the kind of people looking. You want to make sure you're comfortable with the person you're living with.'

'Hmm,' I mutter, unwinding my pink cotton scarf and handing it to him. 'Are you sure the landlord agreed to it?'

'He's completely fine. We had a good chat, and he thinks it's a great idea.'

I pull a face and walk into the lounge. Callum follows me, still talking. 'Of course, being the lead tenant, you'll get the final say in who it is. And it might turn out to be fun. You can do each other's hair and watch rom-coms.'

'I'm not thirteen, for God's sake.' I roll my eyes. 'Anyway, why can't it be a guy?'

I sit on the couch and flick through Netflix. He's starting to really annoy me with his gung-ho attitude.

'Well, for obvious reasons.'

'What reasons?'

'You're going out with me.'

'I can still go out with you and have a male flatmate. You might hit it off with him and go golfing or whatever.'

Callum frowns. 'I don't think so. Not after Paul.'

I wince. 'Sorry.'

I forgot he's a bit sensitive about golfing mates. When Callum first started in sales, this experienced realtor, Paul McDonald, took him under his wing. They hung out together on the weekends and played golf. Then he found out Paul was poaching his buyers and steering them towards his own properties. Callum was pretty cut up about it. He hasn't tried to make friends with any other realtors since then. The friends he has now mostly work in IT, finance, or non-competing fields.

'I'm just not comfortable about you living with a guy,' he reiterates firmly, and I get the impression it's not up for debate.

'So all the people you're lining up for viewings are girls?'

'Yes.'

'That's sexist.'

He comes and sits beside me on the couch. 'You're an attractive woman, Em. I don't want some guy thinking he can get into your knickers.'

I snort. 'You go off and have drinks with Camille Redfern, who's dying to get into your Calvin Kleins.'

'That's different. You know it is. She's just after the money. If she manages to sleep with me, well, that's just icing on the cake for her.'

'Apart from the fact you're in a relationship, I still don't understand why she's making a play for you. Isn't she worried it will jeopardize you working together?'

Callum shrugs. 'It's just part of the game. Even if it did happen, it wouldn't mean anything to her. It'd just be like scratching an itch. She'd fuck me, discard me, then ring me up to sell a million-pound property the next week without blinking an eye.'

'Did she tell you all this?' I question, somewhat incredulously.

'She doesn't have to. I know how it works.'

I shake my head in disbelief. 'Sounds like real estate is a hotbed of intrigue.'

'Some people are very discreet. Others aren't. I could tell you things that would make your hair curl.' He winds a lock of my wavy brown hair around his finger, and tugs on it slightly so my scalp prickles. 'Most people in my line of work have something to hide. Apart from me, of course. I'm a model employee.'

He smiles at me, and I redden. I'm not one to talk. I do have a secret from him. It's not one that I think is a deal-breaker, but he might feel differently about it. I know I'm going to have to come clean at some point, but I want to see what it's like first before I say anything. The whole thing might turn out to be a big pile of nothing, and I don't want to put the cat amongst the pigeons if I don't have to. Callum hasn't asked me what I'm doing Saturday morning, and I'm not sure what I'll say if he does ask. *Oh, just the usual—a bit of cleaning, food shopping, taking my kit off for a bunch of age-challenged artists . . .*

'So Netflix and a takeaway?' I suggest brightly to change the subject. 'Or shall I slip into something more comfortable?'

He looks hopeful. 'That thing you wore the other night?'

'Ah . . . no, it's got curry sauce on it. I was thinking just me—au naturel.' I wave the remote with a flourish.

Callum takes the remote from my hand and starts searching through the movies. 'Netflix and a takeaway sound good.'

On Saturday morning, I wake up with a headache and a knot of dread in my stomach. We have toast and coffee in the kitchen, and then I get ready to head back to my flat. Callum's in his Puma shorts and sweat-wicking Nike T-shirt, limbering up in the hallway when I leave.

'So I'll see you just before three,' he says, kissing me on the lips. 'Sure you don't want to come for a run?'

'I'm sure.'

'You should be doing some kind of cardio three times a week, Em. It's great for getting rid of stress and toning up.'

'Mmhmm.'

We could be having a horizontal workout right now, I

think. *You're just not interested unless I'm wearing BDSM lingerie.* Yes, you guessed it. Last night's encounter was over pretty quickly, and I'm feeling grumpy and unloved.

Back at my flat, I shower, then check out my naked body in the full-length mirror. I suck in my stomach and poke the spongy tops of my thighs. Maybe Callum's trying to tell me something by his exercise comment. Plus if I'm going to do this life modelling thing, I want to look my best in the buff. Perhaps I should join a gym? Ugh, I hate gyms. I'd rather go for a walk around the Meadows. Besides, I don't have the cash for it at the moment. At least I'm neat and tidy *down there,* since Callum is very particular about personal grooming. When we first got together, he said pointedly, 'It's not the 1970s, Em.' Then he left me to draw my own conclusions on what *that* meant. Home waxing is a bitch, but it's cheaper than going to a salon.

I have no idea what to wear. So I settle for leggings and a sweatshirt. Plus no underwear, based on Lorna's advice. I assume it's so there will be no strap marks on my flesh. I leave my long hair loose, hoping it will give me a bit of camouflage.

On the bus to Morningside, I'm sure it's written all over my face what I'm going to be doing. Two girls whisper and giggle behind me, and my face burns. My palms start sweating. Maybe this is a really bad idea. But I can't seem to stop the momentum of my actions.

Lorna said to come round half an hour before the 11 a.m.

session so she can run through a few things with me. But just before I get to the flat, I receive a text from her saying: *Emma, I've had to pop out. Go around to the back door, it's open. I'll be there in 5.*

I scuttle down the side alley, feeling like an intruder. It leads into a small grassy yard with a garden shed and paved patio. On top of that is a cobwebby, rusted iron table, with two matching chairs and an old Princes tuna can with half a dozen stubbed-out cigarette butts.

Tentatively, I push down on the back door handle, and it opens easily. I step into a warm, bright kitchen and find myself face to face with a man who's noisily slicing up a block of cheddar on a wooden chopping board. A pile of oat crackers has spilled out of a packet. Watercress and tomatoes are piled up on another board.

He's wearing an old paint-stained grey business shirt and tatty blue jeans, and there's a streak of green paint on his forearm. *Who's this?* I wonder. *Lorna's son?* Painting must run in the family.

'Oh, sorry.' I hover on the doorstep uncertainly. 'Lorna said to come in.'

'Hello. You must be Emma. I'm Jack.' He smiles at me in a friendly way and gestures at the cheese. 'I'm just getting some snacks ready. Everyone's always ravenous after a session. Lorna will be back shortly, she's just gone to Waitrose to get some more milk for the copious cups of tea.'

Then it hits me. *Jack?* But . . . but this can't be Lorna's husband, surely. He's so young-looking! OK, he has greying hair, so he's definitely past his thirties, but not old and decrepit by a long shot. Perhaps late forties, early fifties? But she's in her seventies. I stare at him, rattled. I thought her husband would be a doddery old man in a tweed waistcoat, peering through bifocals at his canvas and needing help getting to the toilet. Even with his wild, grizzled hair and unkept beard, this guy has a faint Gerard Butler look about him. Woohoo, go Lorna! Camille Redfern, eat your heart out.

'Ah, nice to meet you,' I say at last.

'Likewise.' He goes back to slicing cheese. 'And great to have you on the books. Lorna said you were interested in giving life modelling a go. I take it you've not done it before?'

'No, never.'

'Ahh,' he says. I pick up scepticism in his tone.

'Surely it's not that hard?'

Lorna hasn't given me any indication that there will be any kind of effort involved. I'm hoping I can just strike a pose and zone out.

Jack pauses in his cheese slicing and leans a hip against the counter, studying me with a slight frown. I notice his eyes are almost the same shade of green as the streak of paint on his arm.

'I'm not trying to put you off. It's just that people think it's easy, but there's a certain amount of stamina involved. And you have to be quite flexible with some of the poses. But Lorna will start you off with the basics. If it's something you're serious about, you can always have a one-on-one session with me to try some more complicated moves.' He runs a practised eye over my body, as if sizing me up for a canvas.

Hmm, as professional as Jack sounds, something tells me that a one-on-one session with him trying out complicated moves is probably *not* a good idea. Before I can make an excuse, Lorna bustles in with a bulging Waitrose bag, and Jack immediately goes to help her.

'Hi, Emma. Sorry about that, but I see Jack has been holding the fort.'

She squeezes his arm fondly, and I try not to stare. I can't get my head around their relationship, especially after the offer he's just made.

Lorna gestures for me to come with her. 'I'll show you the studio before everyone arrives. There are just five artists today.'

'Great,' I say airily, trying to sound more confident than I feel.

We leave Jack assembling cheese and crackers and arranging teacups in the kitchen. Lorna escorts me upstairs. The second floor is similarly jam-packed with antiques and knick-knacks. She sees me peering at a gold elephant with a red-beaded saddle on a sideboard and says, 'It's Jack's hobby, collecting antiques and selling them online—when he can get around to it. He likes the buying more than the selling. We're getting a bit overrun at the moment, as you can see.'

'He has eclectic taste,' I comment, catching sight of a series of framed female nude sketches in rather erotic poses. I hastily avert my eyes. Did he buy those? Or were they the result of an inexperienced life model trying out some of his complicated moves?

The studio is set down a corridor at the back of the flat, like it's an extension. I ask Lorna if this is the case, and she nods. 'Yes, it was built in the early eighteen hundreds, and this part was extended in the Victorian era. Apparently, it was the owner's poolroom. It was quite dark initially, but we had skylights added.'

She opens the door and ushers me in. The contrast to the clutter of the rest of the house is so marked it takes my breath away. The room is completely devoid of furniture apart from a daybed with a black sheet and the chairs and easels set around it. The walls are painted a soft cream, with sketches and paintings propped up around the perimeter, and light is streaming in from three skylights. I can't explain it, but there's a creative energy in here. It's inspiring me to pick up a paintbrush and have a go myself, and I can't draw for peanuts.

'It's really warm,' I comment, surprised.

'Underfloor heating,' informs Lorna. 'We don't want you to freeze to death. Now, we usually get models to do four different poses for fifteen-minute slots, with a break in between each. How does that sound? I'll get you set up so you're ready when they come in. You don't have to talk to anyone if you don't want to, but some people are quite chatty and want to make conversation. It's their social activity of the week, after all. So expect to hear all about their grandkids, their dogs, and their hernias.'

Speaking of personal lives, I'm itching to ask her about Jack and how they met. I just *know* there's got to be an interesting story there. But I can't manage to segue into it. Has Jack had a hernia? How on earth did you two get together? So I just say, 'That sounds fine. Ah, where should I get changed?'

'Just through here.' She opens a door directly to our right, and inside is a small anteroom with cubbyholes and cotton robes in assorted colours hanging from hooks. Through another door, I glimpse a sink and a toilet. She looks at her watch. 'We've got about ten minutes. It would be a good idea to use the bathroom even if you don't need to. Just come out when you're ready.'

Before I can think too much about it, I take off my clothes and choose a blue cotton robe and tie it tightly. My breathing starts speeding up to the point that I feel light-headed. *It'll be fine,* I tell myself. *Just do one session. If you hate it, you don't have to come back again. You paraded around the kitchen in BDSM lingerie. This is nothing.*

Quite literally nothing, says Prude critically. *You're not even wearing a G-string for modesty.*

Taking a deep, calming breath, I walk out into the studio

and over to Lorna, who's standing by the daybed. *What the hell am I doing? If Callum could see me now, his jaw would be on the floor.* The thought makes me want to giggle. But I try to keep a straight face.

'So I thought we'd start you off with something easy. Can you take off your robe and sit on the daybed and try to assume this pose?' She shows me one of the sketches from around the wall. It's basically sitting upright with one leg drawn up across my body and the other bent at a right angle underneath. One arm is across my breasts, leaning on my knee, and the other is propped up against the side of my face. Phew, nothing is really on show at all. It's actually quite flattering and elegant.

Lorna walks around, adjusting my limbs slightly and moving my hair back from my face like I'm a life-size Barbie doll. 'How's that?' she asks. 'Do you think you can hold it for fifteen minutes?'

'Yes, of course,' I answer. Right at this moment, I'm completely and utterly sure of myself. It's going to be a doddle.

Chapter 6

TOE CRAMP AND WALKING STICKS

My left butt cheek is twitching madly. My right shoulder blade has an annoying itch. I have a cramp in my little toe, and I need to pee again. I swivel my eyes to the clock on the wall that is hung conveniently just across from my line of vision. I'm counting down, *Seven minutes to go*. Oh my God. This is unbelievably uncomfortable. Why did I think this was going to be easy?

Then there's a sharp tap on my ankle. Ow! This woman has moved her easel closer to me so she can see better. If she wants to get my attention, she periodically pokes me with her walking stick. If it weren't so painful, I'd laugh. In the last eight minutes, she's told me all about her five grandchildren (don't ask me their names); her dog, Daisy (a Scottish terrier); her gammy hip; and what she's been cross-stitching (three cats sitting on a wall).

The other artists don't seem to mind her going on, but it's trying my patience. I've just been muttering 'Uh-huh' and 'Mmhmm' and 'Is that right?' a lot. She seems to be doing more talking than sketching. I glance at the others in the group, who are busily working away. There are three women and a man. Apart from nodding and saying hello politely when they came in, they've just been either peering at me intently through their glasses or scratching on their paper with charcoal pencils. They appear more professional, at least. *Five minutes to go.*

The chatty woman is now trying to get personal information out of me. 'Are you married, dear? You're very pretty. Such a lovely voluptuous figure.' She eyes my hips and makes a couple of dramatic swoops on her paper. I quell the urge to giggle.

'Ah, no. I'm not married,' I reply.

'Shame. You have beautiful hair, so shiny.' She violently dashes off some jagged strokes, and I try to keep a straight face. I can't wait to see what she's drawing.

'I do have a boyfriend, though,' I explain. 'He works in real estate.' I almost add 'He likes it when I wear kinky lingerie' but bite my lip. *Two minutes to go.*

Finally, the first fifteen minutes is over, and I almost collapse in relief. My little toe is cramping so badly I wince in pain. While everyone's sorting out their sheets of paper, I shrug into my robe and hobble to the anteroom, aching all over and desperate for the toilet. Fuck me. I feel like a retiree myself. Lorna comes in as I'm bent over, hastily doing some leg stretches while massaging my toe.

'How was that, Emma? You did incredibly well for your first pose,' she says encouragingly.

I look at her doubtfully. 'Really?'

'Gosh, yes! We've had models who gave up after the first five minutes.'

Ahhh, probably from toe cramp or being beaten black and blue by women with walking sticks.

'Well, it wasn't particularly easy.' I flex my toes and arch my back, grimacing. 'What's with that woman and her walking stick?'

Lorna laughs merrily. 'Och, yes, Mrs Fraser is a bit *proddy*. Sorry about that. She doesn't get out much, I think.'

'The others seem very dedicated, though.'

'Yes, they've been coming for a while. They've improved markedly. Some of them could draw only stick figures when they started. Anyway, all set for your next pose? I'll give you one lying down so you can have a wee break.'

Thank God. I breathe a sigh of relief.

When I come out, the artists are ready, so I take off my robe with my back to them. Lorna has me lie face down on the daybed. She bends one of my legs at the knee so it's sticking up in the air and arranges one arm so my hand is placed on my head. I know she's deliberately trying to give me modest poses to start off with so I get used to being naked in front of people. I'm grateful, but it's nerve-racking to think my bits will be on show at some point. I mean, that's the purpose of life drawing, isn't it? They're not paying fifty pounds a class just to draw my leg sticking up in the air.

The next fifteen minutes go by relatively quickly, and before I know it, I'm back in the anteroom, doing more stretches and using the bathroom yet again. Mrs Fraser settled down because my head was facing away from her, so I couldn't really talk. All I heard was a lot of swooshing noises on the paper, which set me off into muffled giggles. I'm assuming she was drawing my butt cheeks.

I've been expecting Lorna to suggest less modest poses for the next two, and sure enough, she says, 'What do you think about standing up?'

I take a deep breath and say, 'OK.'

She positions me so I'm looking at the artists but my body is side on. My left leg is bent slightly and my right hand is on my hip and the other behind my neck. I'm half expecting someone to say, 'Oh my God! I can see that woman's tit!' But everyone just stares at me, then starts drawing. It's really weird. I feel about as sexy as a bowl of fruit. I guess they've seen it all before.

Time starts having less of a grip on me. Instead of watching the clock and counting down the minutes, I kind of space out and start thinking about other things—like what the flat viewings will be like, whether I should cook something for dinner, whether I should cook dinner wearing the strappy lingerie so Callum wants to have sex on the kitchen table again . . .

I'm so absorbed in my own thoughts that I jump when Lorna taps me on the elbow. She smiles at me and hands me my robe. 'Well done, Emma! Do you want to have a bit of a walk around and see the drawings?'

'Ooh, yes, please!'

They're really good! Even with my non-artistic eye, I can see that it's me captured on paper. Some sketches are just strokes and tasteful shading, but the man has drawn my face in quite a lot of detail. 'Gosh, that's brilliant!' I tell him, and he looks pleased.

'You're a lovely model,' he says. 'Very still, not fidgety like some of them.'

When we reach Mrs Fraser, I brace myself.

'What do you think, love?' she asks. 'Have I done you justice?'

To be honest, I'm not exactly sure what the hell she's drawn. Some vision in her head perhaps? It's all scribbles and slashes. It's like something an evil child who's been locked in an attic would produce. I look closer at a round circle beneath a mass of squiggles. It that my face? Has she actually given me vampire teeth? I glance at Lorna, whose mouth is twitching.

'It's great . . . very abstract,' I say. Hopefully, she's not planning on hanging that in her lounge. It will scare Daisy, the Scottish terrier, to death.

'I'll work on *contouring* with you, Mrs Fraser,' Lorna tells her kindly. She nods at me. 'Ready, Emma?'

The last pose is another one lying down—but this time, on my back. I'm propped up on my elbows, staring straight ahead, with my legs crossed at the ankles. There's no modesty for this pose. They can basically see everything. But again, there's that strange sense of disconnect. I might as well be a bunch of white grapes on a black tablecloth.

Then before I know it, the fifteen minutes are up, and I'm getting dressed in the anteroom. Next, we're all trooping downstairs to the kitchen for a cup of tea. Jack isn't there. Lorna starts doling out plates and asking if people take milk and sugar in their tea. When the tea is steeping in a large brown teapot in the middle of the table and the artists are all chattering away, she beckons me aside.

'I was really impressed with your efforts today, Emma. You're a natural. Jack agrees. He said you looked very professional—he popped his head in at one point,' she adds when she sees my querying look.

I'm surprised and pleased at hearing they thought I did well, but I'm a bit disconcerted Jack saw me. Which pose exactly? The one not showing much? Or the one showing everything?

'Um, thanks,' I say, blushing hotly. From the praise or the fact Jack saw me starkers, I'm not sure.

'So do you think you might want to do another session?'

'Oh, well, I do. But the thing is I have a boyfriend, and he doesn't know I'm doing this. He might be OK with it, or he might freak out completely. I'll just have to see how it goes.'

Lorna smiles and nods. 'Understandable. He's welcome to come round and meet us and see the set-up if it would make him more comfortable. He might like to try it himself.'

An image of Callum wearing only his blue silk tie as Mrs

Fraser whacks his bare butt with her walking stick flits into my mind. I bite my lip hard.

'Ah, I'll mention it to him. Speaking of which, I should head off now.'

'You don't want to stay for a cuppa? You're more than welcome.'

'Oh, I can't, I'm afraid. I'm interviewing potential flatmates.' Ugh. The sooner I tell Callum, the better, so I don't have to get a pesky flatmate.

'Right. Well, this is for you.' She discreetly hands me a rectangular white envelope. 'I'll be in touch as soon as we have anything else. And well done again. Everyone produced some lovely work today, thanks to your modelling.'

I raise an eyebrow, and she laughs a little, knowing I'm thinking of Mrs Fraser. 'Yes, well, not *everyone*. But she's improved a lot!' God, what was she like before?

I wave goodbye to the artists, who are busily pouring tea and demolishing the cheese and crackers. They wave back and call out 'goodbye' and 'thanks, Emma'. I almost wish I could stay and have a cup of tea and join in.

But I've got to handwash the lingerie, clean the bathroom, tidy up the kitchen, and hoover the whole flat before the interviews this afternoon . . . and then somehow break it to Callum about my new side gig.

I'm running late with everything, of course. So when Callum arrives just before 3 p.m., I'm still frantically cleaning. He takes over hoovering the lounge while I clean the loo and scrub the bath.

I'm not used to being this disorganised. The events of the morning have thrown me completely. I still can't believe I did it. I'm riding a wave of euphoria like I've just gone skydiving or sung karaoke (two things on my bucket list I'm shit-scared of doing, but pretty sure I could do now since I've just done this).

The envelope Lorna gave me contained five crisp twenty-pound notes, which I instantly hid in my dresser drawer. Not that Callum would ever go through my handbag, but I don't want to take any chances. Not until I tell him—which, to be honest, I'm dreading more than being naked. He's never going to be OK with it. Deep down, I know that.

Just as I finish plumping the couch cushions, the buzzer sounds. I look at Callum, and he switches off the Hoover and grins at me. 'Victim number one.'

For the first time, I notice that his hair is slicked back and he's wearing his grey suit, a white business shirt, and a black silk tie. He's in full real estate mode. He even has a clipboard.

I, on the other hand, am dishevelled. My hair is puffed out like a bird's nest, I'm perspiring madly and I'm still in leggings and a sweatshirt—and no underwear.

Callum runs a critical eye over me. 'Are you going to get changed? Maybe put on a bra at least. What have you been doing this morning, yoga or something?'

'Er . . . yeah.'

I run to my bedroom and quickly put on a bra, drag a brush through my hair, tie it back, and wipe my sweaty face with a tissue. I hear talking in the hall: a girl's high-pitched tone and Callum, in his realtor voice, saying, 'Come through into the lounge. You'll see it has an excellent view over Bruntsfield Links.'

I'm about to join them when I remember I've left the freshly washed BDSM lingerie in the main bathroom to air-dry. I have a body shape display hanger for dresses, so I arranged it over that, and hooked it up on the shower rail. Fuck.

I step into the hallway in an attempt to reach the bathroom, but Callum sees me and calls out, 'Emma, come and meet June!'

So I have no choice but to go in with a smile and make polite conversation. June seems nice enough. Slim, pale, light-brown hair tied back in a ponytail, wearing jeans and a grey hoodie. She's quite young, twenty-two, and works as a waitress in a local cafe. I see Callum note both of these points down carefully on his clipboard.

I can tell June loves the flat. She's looking around the lounge animatedly, and Callum encourages her by enthusing over the seafoam-green walls and intricate snow-white cornicing. Then he tells her that the modern L-shaped couch, matching easy chairs, and coffee table are brand new. Funnily enough, it's exactly the same spiel he gave when he showed *me* round the flat. Except that we hit it off and ended up rolling around on his super king-sized bed later that same evening. As I said before, Callum's all about efficiency. When he knows what he wants, he doesn't beat around the bush, so to speak.

We move to the kitchen, which doesn't have three ovens, a blender with ten settings, or any mod cons actually. But it's warm and cosy, with a window looking down onto a communal garden. 'Feel free to check out the walk-in pantry,' says Callum. 'Of course you can do your own thing. But Emma loves cooking, so perhaps you can have dinners together a couple of nights a week.'

What? Now I'm cooking for her too? But June laps it up and says she can bring home leftovers from the cafe to share.

When her back is turned to check out the pantry, I hiss at Callum, 'I need to get to the bathroom!'

'Just hold it in!' he hisses back.

June overhears and looks at us with a frown. 'Is everything OK?' she asks.

I nod quickly, and Callum moves forward to show her the cooker. 'It's a gas hob, which is brilliant if you want to whip up a quick stir-fry.' He lights one of the burners, and I stifle a laugh. He's never cooked a quick stir-fry or any other kind of meal on my hob!

I edge my way to the door, but it's too late—they're following right behind me. 'The bathroom's this way,' Callum says engagingly. 'It's got an awesome claw-foot tub.'

'Oooh, great.' June is nodding enthusiastically. 'I love

those baths. They're so cool.'

He swings open the door. 'After you,' he says politely.

Oh God.

June stops in her tracks, and there's a shocked silence. We all stare at the dripping BDSM lingerie swaying gently on the hanger. I risk a glance at Callum. His face has gone bright red, and his jaw is working, but no words are coming out. Finally, he turns to me and says in a clipped tone, 'Ah, Emma, would you be so kind as to . . . ?'

I hastily unhook the lingerie and hurry out of the bathroom with it clasped under my arm. But the damage is done. June is strangely quiet, and Callum desperately talks a mile a minute to fill the silence. We move to the bedrooms, but June barely glances at them. She keeps staring at me wide-eyed, like I'm some kind of sex fiend.

When she's gone, I collapse on the couch, laughing so hard I can barely breathe. Callum is appalled.

'Emma! What the actual fuck?'

'I forgot it! I was trying to get to the bathroom, but you called me into the lounge!'

'That was mortifying!' He takes a deep breath, straightens his tie, and rakes his gelled hair back into place with both hands. 'I'm glad you think it was funny. I hope you realise I'm doing you a favour here.'

'Oh come on, loosen up. It was hilarious.' I grab his clipboard and strike a line through June's name. 'Next!'

Chapter 7

PAY RISE AND PIZZA

✳

I mean to tell Callum. I really do. But it just never seems like the right moment. After the lingerie incident with June, he's tetchy with me, so I'm on my best behaviour for the next two viewings. Thankfully, neither is suitable—one is only working part time, and the other has such a long list of demands before she moves in that Callum doesn't even bother to ask my opinion. He just crosses her off the list, muttering 'Seriously?' under his breath.

Afterwards, I make us both a cup of tea. Callum ditches his suit jacket, takes off his tie, and slumps onto the couch. He looks exhausted. 'Now I know why I moved into sales. Lettings is a nightmare.'

'I thought you did a pre-screening?'

'I did, but they always just tell you what you want to hear. That June girl was probably the pick of the bunch, but somehow, I don't think she's going to say yes.'

He catches my eye, and I look away hastily, feeling a giggle rise.

'Never mind,' I say soothingly. 'Here, put your feet up and relax. Have a nap if you want. I'll go and start dinner.'

'Mmm, you're a wee star.'

In the kitchen, I have an attack of the guilts. I know he's just trying to help me keep my head above water. He doesn't deserve to have me keeping things from him. But when I go back into the lounge to come clean, he's fallen asleep.

Then the evening takes a passionate turn when I put on the lingerie after dinner, and he's supremely happy about that. So I keep quiet because I don't want to ruin his good mood. You can see how this is going.

By Monday morning, I've pretty much shelved the idea of telling him altogether. Besides, the forty percent sale at Strip 'n' Straps is still on. I have cash to burn, so I tell Sian I'm going down at lunchtime to get a few more things. In fact, if you think about it, I'm spending my earnings from life modelling on Callum to fund his taste in kinky underwear. So surely it evens out?

That's what I tell myself anyway as we head down to Cowgate. Sian is in a particularly good mood and chattering away. I'm surprised her lips aren't numb. It's a fine day, but it's freezing. She's wearing only a red short-sleeved crop top, a black-and-white polka-dot miniskirt, sparkly white tights, and black patent leather wedge-heeled shoes. No coat.

'Aren't you cold?'

'Nah . . . OK, well, a bit. Let's walk faster.' She hooks her arm through mine and snuggles against my black parka trimmed with grey faux fur for warmth. I can see my breath hanging in puffs in front of me. It's unseasonably chilly for September.

When we reach the shop, the woman waves us through to the lingerie section like we're becoming regulars.

'So what are you going to buy this time?' Sian asks, flipping through the rack.

'Dunno. It's going to be difficult to top that strappy thing. I've become quite an expert at putting it on too. I've got it down to three minutes flat.'

She giggles. 'And you don't even have to take it off to handwash it. I've been wearing mine in the shower, soaping it and rinsing it off.'

I stare at her. 'God, brilliant! I didn't think of that.'

'It's good timing with the pay rise too,' she remarks. 'You can buy a few more so you've got them on standby.'

I stop rifling through harness bras. 'What pay rise?' This is news to me.

'The one we've just been given.' She takes out a black mesh bodysuit to inspect it.

'I had a meeting with Blaire last Thursday, and she mentioned something about salary increases, but I assumed it was way off down the track.'

Sian shakes her head. 'I got an email this morning about a five percent pay rise effective in next month's pay. Did you not get it?'

'No.'

My head is ringing with alarm bells, and I've got a hot

stabbing feeling in my chest. My fist closes unconsciously around a bra I'm holding, but it's covered in sharp metal spikes, and they dig painfully into my hand. Ouch!

Maybe I'm being premature. It's probably just taking a while to come through.

'What time did you get the email?'

'Uh . . . first thing. It was there when I logged in.' Sian is looking distressed. 'I'm sorry, Em. I just assumed you got it too.'

Fucking Blaire! She's such a bitch. She's passed me over for a pay rise and given it to Sian instead!

Sian is gabbling away guiltily. 'And after tax and NHS, it's really only a piddly amount. Hardly worth bothering about, really . . .'

No, it's more the principle of the thing. Surely this isn't because I didn't give her an eclair? Even she wouldn't be that petty!

'It's OK, Sian. Don't worry about it. I'm probably going to get a flatmate anyway. That's going to be more of a help.' Dumb Blaire. Dumb pay rise. I replace the bra back on the rack and resume rifling.

'Have you found anyone yet?'

'Nah, I had a few people around to view it on Saturday, but they weren't right.'

'Well, a friend of mine has a nephew who's looking for a room,' she says offhandedly.

'If it were her niece, it would be fine.'

'Why can't you have a male flatmate?' Sian looks at me curiously.

'Callum's very against the idea. He's adamant a guy's going to try and get into my knickers.'

'I didn't think he was the insecure type.'

'Well, I guess even Callum has his insecurities,' I reply. 'How old is this nephew anyway?'

'He's thirty-three. He's from New Zealand and has been dossing on her living room couch for the last couple of months. She's getting desperate.'

'God, really? What does he do?'

'I'm not sure, but he's got a job. I think he's been cooking dinner for her most nights. And he leaves the toilet seat down.'

'Who is this friend of yours?'

'Oh, no one you know.' She pulls out a black T-shirt with strategically placed nipple holes and studies it intently. 'Anyway, should I give her your details? She can pass it on to him.'

'Go on then.' I sigh. 'I guess it's good to have a backup, just in case. It's a hundred and twenty per week, including bills.'

Sian nods and hands me the nipple hole T-shirt. She smirks. 'Just wear this when you tell Callum you're getting a male flatmate. I bet you fifty pounds he'll agree to it.'

In the end, I do end up buying the nipple hole T-shirt, the

spiky bra, *and* the mesh bodysuit. My budget has flown out the window, but fuck it. I'm still smarting about Blaire giving Sian a pay rise, so I'm attempting to plaster over my annoyance by shopping. It doesn't make me feel any better. Should I confront her again? Is it even worth it? She'll just bring up some bullshit about Sian being an exemplary employee and working weekends without complaint. Which is true—she does.

Disheartened, I'm like a bear with a sore head all afternoon, tapping so loudly on my keyboard that I get disconcerted looks from browsers in the crime fiction aisle. But by the end of the day, I've resigned myself to the fact.

On the dot of 5 p.m., I say bye to Sian and head down to Grassmarket to meet up with a few uni girlfriends. My friend Julie sent an email last week saying it was her birthday and that, rather than slit her wrists at turning thirty-five, she might as well go out and do something. So we're having pizza and a drink after work. Initially, I wasn't keen on going out on a Monday night, but now I'm glad of the distraction.

At the restaurant, I tell the server, 'Julie Campbell'. He points out the reserved table. I'm the first one here. I check my phone. No messages from Callum, but that's to be expected. I don't normally see him on Mondays, and we had quite a full-on Sunday morning since I was still wearing the strappy thing from Saturday night. An image of his pleased (and extremely aroused) face flicks into my mind. I'm not sure he's going to like this new collection of items as much.

Julie suddenly arrives in a flurry of outdoor cold and scoots into the booth beside me. 'Em! Great, you're here first. Tell me, honestly, what do you think?'

She whips off her dark-blue cable-knit beanie, and I gawp.

Julie's hair makes girls green with envy. It's golden and shiny and ripples in luscious flowing waves down her back. It's so captivating she has random people stopping her on the street and giving her compliments. My hair's pretty good, but even I get pangs of jealousy whenever I see hers. We started calling her Rapunzel at uni until she put a stop to it. But now I can't believe my eyes.

It's been chopped into a chin-length blunt bob with a fringe, and *dyed black*.

'Oh my fucking God!'

'I know, it's a bit drastic.'

'But . . . but why? Your lovely hair!'

Julie wrinkles her nose. 'I was so sick of hearing about it. All the time. Everyone always goes on and on. Blah blah blah. It's like that's all they see. I woke up this morning and thought, "Right, it's my birthday. Time for a change." So I went to my hairdresser and told her to cut it off and colour it. She was a bit reluctant at first.'

'I can imagine!'

'I practically had to put the scissors in her hand and force them towards my head.'

I look her over; it is actually very flattering. She has a small pert face with high cheekbones, so she can pull it off. 'I like it. It makes your eyes look really blue.'

Two more of the group arrive, Davita and Lilidh—leggy twins with long red curly hair, pale skin and just the right amount of freckles to look cute rather than splotchy. They're more Julie's friends than mine, but I get on OK with them. After saying hi to me, they stare at Julie blankly. Then as recognition dawns, they scream. Loudly. Then there are exclamations and 'Oh my Gods' and hands flying to mouths. To be honest, Julie's attempt at trying not to draw attention to herself is having the opposite effect. The final member of the group, Alana, arrives; and we go through the whole performance again. 'Oh my God, your hair!'

Finally, everyone gets over the shock, and we're ready to order drinks. The male server waits patiently as we confer and decide, then change our minds. He's in his twenties and rather easy on the eye. Alana swishes her shoulder-length ash-blonde hair, bats her heavily mascaraed eyelashes, and comments on his forearm tattoo—an intricate inking of an intertwined Celtic cross and a snake. He doesn't seem to mind, though. She has flirting down to a fine art, so it never comes across as tacky.

All of us did the same dance and drama degree and ended up in a variety of jobs. Julie is in PR, Davita is a burlesque dancer, and Lilidh is a catalogue model. Alana is the only one who's actually working in theatre. She's a casting director for some of the major playhouses in Edinburgh. It's such a fabulous job, and it suits her flamboyant personality down to the ground.

The server finally heads off with our orders, and Alana switches her attentive gaze to me.

'Emma, how are you? I've been meaning to get in touch, but you know how it is—busy, busy. We're in the middle of casting for a production at the Lyceum, so I've been run off my feet with auditions.'

'What's the play?' I ask curiously.

She rolls her eyes. 'A modern remake of Oscar Wilde's *An Ideal Husband*. It's good, but frankly, there are too many gay euphemisms for my liking.' She leans in and whispers, '"Pillow biters" and "shirtlifters".' I giggle. 'Speaking of ideal husbands, when are you tying the knot with that delicious Callum? I take it you're still together?'

Davita overhears, and her head immediately swivels round. She has a bit of a thing for Callum and doesn't mind everyone knowing it. Funnily enough, Lilidh can't stand him, which is completely bizarre as they usually like exactly the same things.

'Ah, yes, we're still together. But no plans on tying the knot just yet,' I say.

A look of relief crosses Davita's face, and annoyance flickers through me.

'He's in sales at Duncan Stratt, isn't he?' she pipes up. 'Lil and I are looking to buy a flat. Maybe he can advise us.'

Why do I get the feeling she's been up late at night drooling over his work profile?

The server arrives with our drinks and dishes of olives, so I don't reply to her. It's nice to think that my boyfriend is desirable even if he could be whipped out from under my nose at a moment's notice.

'We actually saw him the other night.' She nudges her sister on the arm. 'Didn't we, Lil? At Le Monde.'

I sip my house white, unperturbed. Yes, yes, he was out with Camille Redfern discussing million-pound properties. I know all about it.

Then Lilidh says something that makes the hair on the back of my neck stand up. 'Oh yeah. He was at the bar with a blonde. Petite, pretty.' She shrugs, not impressed, and continues looking at the menu.

Blonde? Petite? Camille's not blonde. She's brunette, and she's tall. Definitely not petite.

'Who was that?' Davita enquires, her eyes bright with interest. 'We're not getting him into trouble, are we?'

'Of course not. He was having drinks with a broker, that's all. It's part of his job,' I tell her breezily. But my heart is pounding. How can I get more information without seeming paranoid? 'Er . . . So did you say hello?'

'No, they looked very involved in their conversation. We didn't want to interrupt.'

I gulp. *Very involved!* Was she whispering in his ear? Did he have his hand on her butt? I take a large sip of wine and choke on it a little.

Julie glances at me. 'You OK, Em?'

Out of everyone in the group, Julie's the only one who knows about my frustration with Callum in the bedroom. We have catch-ups every few weeks, and during our last one, I accidentally mentioned it because I'd had too much red wine. In vino veritas and all that. But she was instantly sympathetic, and I trust her not to spread it around. If Davita knew, she'd think we were on the rocks, and she'd up her game.

I widen my eyes at Julie, and she immediately starts talking about how she's starving and tries to attract the waiter's attention so we can order our mains. The distraction works. Alana perks up, and the twins drop the subject. I stare at the menu, but I'm not hungry. All I can think is *Why did Callum tell me he was seeing Camille Redfern? And who the hell was he really with?*

Chapter 8

THE LAST INTERVIEW

⁕

The next morning, Lorna sends me a text asking if I'm free to do another session on Sunday at 2 p.m. The chance to get another hundred pounds is tempting, but I still haven't told Callum. Since I'm seeing him tonight, I make a bet with myself. If he tells me about the blonde he was with on Thursday night, then I'll tell him about my life modelling. Then everything will be out in the open. Trust and transparency: the two cornerstones of a healthy relationship.

Of course, there are a couple of things that could go wrong with this plan: First, Callum is having an affair with the blonde and will break up with me. Second, he'll break up with me when he finds out about my life modelling and go off with the blonde. Either way, it seems the blonde wins out, which doesn't seem entirely fair.

Luckily, he's just concluded missives on a New Town apartment he's been working on for a month with a fussy client, so he's in a jovial mood. He passes through the lounge on the way to the kitchen, and I see he's even changed out of his suit and is in Ralph Lauren jeans and a white Lacoste polo shirt. Unheard of for Callum on a Tuesday night.

'You're not working this evening?' I comment from the couch where I'm sitting with my legs curled under me, watching the news on BBC One.

He gives me a roguish grin. 'No, I'm taking the night off. You have my undivided attention.' He wanders into the kitchen and, moments later, comes back into the lounge again. 'Did you put that stuff in the fridge?'

'Maybe it was the Waitrose genie. I've heard if you shut your eyes and rub your iPhone three times, food and alcohol magically appear.'

'Hmm . . . More likely, it was a generous girlfriend who's been spending her hard-earned pay on me. I thought you were skint?'

I swallow. 'It wasn't that much. Just a few essentials I got on the way over.'

Callum sits down next to me on the couch and puts his hand on my ankle. 'A Black Forest gâteau and champagne are essential, huh?'

'Definitely.' I nod. 'We're celebrating your sale going through. You've done a great job.'

He smiles and rubs my ankle with his thumb. 'Thanks, Em. I almost tore my hair out at one point. But I'm glad it's finalised.'

'So, how was your meeting with Camille the other night?' I ask nonchalantly, flicking through the channels. 'You never said.'

He shrugs. 'Just the usual. I didn't want to bore you.'

'I'm interested. How many dirty martinis did she buy you?'

He chuckles. 'Just the one. She couldn't stay for long, so I just got the property spiel without the buttering up. Sounds like a good prospect, though.'

'That's great. Was it just Camille or did she come with another broker?'

Callum glances at me. 'No, just her. Why would she bring another broker? She's not going to share her finder's fee.'

My brain is rapidly processing this information. So the blonde has nothing to do with Camille. He must've met her after she left and had a *very involved* conversation. Unless it wasn't him and the twins got it completely wrong. I give a hollow laugh. 'Yeah, true. Why would she do that? So which bar did you go to?'

'Le Monde in George Street, as usual,' he replies, taking his hand from my ankle and scratching his neck. 'She always wants to go there.'

'It's a nice place . . .' I take a deep breath. 'So did you stay long after she left?'

'No, I just came home.'

'You didn't meet up with anyone else? Bump into someone from another agency?'

'No, I came back here.'

Callum is now staring me straight in the eye. There's no blinking. No twitching. Either he's telling the truth, or he's a really good liar.

'This is turning into twenty questions, Em. Is everything OK?'

'Sure, just keeping tabs on my man. There are a lot of women out there who want to get their claws into you.' I pick up the remote and start flicking through the channels.

But he takes the remote out of my hand and pulls me into a hug instead. 'You have nothing to worry about, Em. The only claws I want in me are yours.'

I close my eyes and rest my head on his shoulder. 'So you keep telling me.'

When Callum's gone off to collect the Thai we've ordered for our dinner, I take out my phone and look at Lorna's text. After a moment's hesitation, I type: *Hi, yes, I can do Sunday at 2pm.*

Trust and transparency—I'm not doing too well with either of those things at the moment.

It's not the first time it's cropped up. My doubting Callum, I mean. There was an incident a year into our relationship when he was working late almost every night for two weeks. It was some big multimillion-pound sale that had a long list of conditions, and the colleague he was working late with just happened to be a pretty female. I got really paranoid something was going on. But he was constantly reassuring me all the time and sending lovey-dovey WhatsApp messages.

As I still didn't believe he was being faithful and was on

the brink of breaking up with him, he then instigated the Tuesday and Thursday rule, so we now see each other those two nights a week. Guaranteed. Even if a big sale is going down. He said that he loved me, that I was important to him, and that he didn't want to lose me over a trivial work thing. Then he took me out to dinner to a flash restaurant and gave me a gorgeous silver pendant with two interlocking hearts. I guess I felt wooed and wanted, and it did boost my trust levels. So now because Callum made such a big song and dance about being trustworthy, it's *really* difficult for me to consider the possibility that he's lying to my face—and because I love him and don't want to believe it. But still, I can't help having a niggling little doubt.

The next day at work, when I'm supposed to be going through the lost stock catalogue, I check to make sure no one's around and bring up Google. We're not meant to surf the Net during work hours, but since I'm not getting a promotion or a pay rise, I figure no one's too bothered about what I do.

First, I do a scan of Duncan Stratt's team profiles to see if there's any new blonde realtor on board. Nada. Then Camille's team of brokers. Nothing there either. I'm just about to click off when I see a blonde on the edge of the group photo on the 'Our Team' page. She's definitely petite and pretty, but not a broker. Maybe admin? I check out the names at the very bottom of the page. There are two for admin: Samantha Gordon and Aisla Kennedy. No photos. Taking a deep breath, I bring up Facebook, type in 'Samantha Gordon', and go down the list of profile photos, trying to match them with anyone in the team photo. I spot Samantha on the third try. But she's brunette, not blonde.

Next, I type in 'Aisla Kennedy' and go through the same process. I see her straightaway—wide-set blue eyes, shoulder-length straight blonde hair with a layered fringe, and a small snub nose. She looks younger than me. Clicking on her profile, I'm surprised to see it's public and not locked down to friends only. She's a very active user, at least two or three posts a day. My hand is shaking on my mouse as I scroll down to last Thursday. I know I'm going to see something. Call it female intuition. Sure enough, a check-in at Le Monde and a photo of a frothy pink cocktail and a caption saying 'After work drinks with Camille Redfern.' I'm impressed. It's a pretty boring post, and she's had ten likes and five comments. But there's nothing else. No selfies of her and Callum or anything like that.

I check out a few more of Aisla's posts and the rest of her profile. She's been working with Camille for a couple of months, her relationship status is single, and she seems to like cupcakes a lot—eating and baking them.

I click out of Facebook and stare at my screen. Is it something? Or nothing? There's only a vague comment by the twins linking them together. Plus he didn't lie exactly because an admin staff member isn't a broker. But he still didn't mention her. That's the bit that's got me worried. A simple 'I stayed on and chatted with Aisla. She's in Camille's admin department' would've been enough to allay my fears. But now it's like I'm diving down a rabbit hole that has no resolution. Because the one question I really need an answer to won't be found on Facebook: Did he sleep with her?

Sian wants to hang out after work and see a movie, but I can't tonight. Callum's lined up five more flatmate viewings. I'm locked in for the whole evening when I could've been doing something productive. Like sitting on the couch, painting my toenails, and wondering if he's fucking someone else.

Instead, I find myself clutching the clipboard and supplying answers to all sorts of inane questions: 'No, I can't move my books out and bring in a double bed.' 'Yes, houseplants are fine . . . oh, you have *ten!* I guess that's OK.' 'Sorry, no, I don't want a cat.' 'So you're an early riser, and you want to do cardio workouts in the lounge at 5 a.m.? Um . . . no.'

By the time it's nearing 8 p.m., I'm lying on the couch, completely whacked. How Callum ever did this on a daily basis is beyond me. Everyone's just so caught up in what they want and trying to make me change to fit their lifestyle. What about *my* lifestyle?

I lift the clipboard and defiantly put a strike through each of the names of the five girls I've just interviewed. I really don't want to live with any of them.

There's just one more name on the list: Nathan Ellington, Sian's friend's nephew. He sent a text yesterday saying he was 'keen as', so I gave him the address and told him to drop by at eight tonight. But I can barely manage to open my eyes when the buzzer sounds. I can't deal with anyone else. Maybe I'll just pretend to be out. I shut my eyes and keep lying there. It goes again. Sighing, I get up to let him in. Sian will want to know how it went, so I'd better interview him at least. I can always say he wasn't suitable and that I chose one of the earlier ones. The houseplant girl wasn't too bad, and besides, houseplants are good for cleansing the lungs.

When I open the door and see the guy that's standing there, my first thought is *This has to be a joke.* Sian's set me up somehow. I stare at him, unspeaking, until he frowns.

'This is flat six, right? Emma?'

'Yes. Hi, I'm Emma,' I manage.

'Nathan.' He gives me a nod.

'Uh, come in.'

I open the door wider, and he saunters past me into the hallway.

Jesus. I should've got more details from Sian. *He's . . .* But I can't form a coherent thought because I have to immediately give him the tour.

'So this is the hallway.'

'Ah, yep.' He looks around. There's not much to see. It's pretty boring. I need to hang up some art or something.

'Yes, well, anyway . . . Through here is the k-k-kitchen.' I can't believe it. I actually stuttered. That hasn't happened since I was six years old! I need to get a grip. OK, he's good-looking. But so what? Callum is good-looking, and I don't stutter around him.

We enter the kitchen, and I trot out the usual 'There's a gas hob, and this is the walk-in pantry.' Opening the pantry door, I flick on the light so he can go in.

'You like oats,' is his only comment after observing my half a dozen one-kilo bags nestled on the top shelf.

'Well, I *am* Scottish,' I say defensively from the doorway. 'And it's good to be prepared in case of a pandemic.'

Nathan grins at me. 'I'm more of a Weet-Bix fella, so you wouldn't have to worry about me stealing your porridge.'

I relax and smile back. 'That's a relief.' He seems really friendly and has a sense of humour too, along with rugged good looks, which I can't help but keep noticing. Short dark hair, slightly dishevelled as if he's run to get here on time; perfectly symmetrical features; grey-green eyes that seem to sear right through me; and smooth olive skin.

I tear my gaze away. 'So that's the pantry.'

'Yep.' He walks out, and his glance falls on the solid oak kitchen table, which takes up most of the space. 'That's a decent size. Not a flimsy IKEA job.'

'Oh, yes, it's sturdy. Good for . . . er . . .' All I can see in my mind's eye is Callum and me having frantic sex amidst chicken curry containers. My face flushes. 'Entertaining.'

Nathan looks at me and quirks an eyebrow as if sensing there's more to the table than I'm letting on.

'I hear you like cooking?' I venture.

He shrugs. 'It's OK.'

'So you've been living with your aunt?'

'Yeah, she's been great putting me up, but I'm a bit over her couch.'

'You are quite tall. I bet that hasn't been comfortable,' I comment before I can stop myself.

'Yeah-nah, I'm starting to walk with a hunch.'

He stretches his hands above his head, and several vertebrae click back into place. The black T-shirt he's wearing under his jacket also rides up past the top of his jeans, and I catch a glimpse of tanned, muscled stomach and a smattering of dark hair.

Desire prickles in my midriff and I shift slightly in surprise. Shit. Is this guy being my flatmate a wise move?

'Ah, you might want to see if the bed is suitable as it's a single,' I say hastily, averting my eyes. Maybe he'll get put off by that and it'll all be a moot point.

I lead the way to the spare bedroom, which is down the other end of the hallway from mine. *Perhaps mention this,* Prude suggests, *so he knows they're not next to each other. Definitely,* says Broad-minded, *that way he'll know exactly where your bedroom is.* I keep my mouth shut, flick the light switch and let him go in.

'Wow,' Nathan says in surprise upon seeing the bookshelf. It's hard to miss since it covers the entire side wall. If it wasn't there, I could quite probably fit in a double bed. I wait for him to suggest moving out my books and bringing in a double, but he seems more interested in checking out the spines, running a finger along them.

'You have heaps of books.'

'I'm a librarian. It comes with the territory,' I say, leaning casually against the door frame.

'So you pinched all these from the library?' he asks.

'Uh, no. I . . .'

Nathan turns his head to look at me, and I see he's smiling. 'Just jokes,' he says.

'So is the bed OK?'

He sits on it, and does an experimental bounce. 'Yep. Way better than a couch for sure.'

'It's a single, though.' I can't seem to stop going on about the bed.

He shrugs. 'It's fine. I'm not looking to hook up with anyone. I guess if I did, I'd just go to theirs.'

'Oh, er . . . OK.' After the small talk, this admission feels like way too much information. Unless he's trying to test the water.

Nathan does another bounce and catches my eye ever so slightly. Oh, this is bad. Very bad. I need to bring up Callum.

I clear my throat. 'So, the thing is, I'm not sure if you

know, but I have a boyfriend. And he's been lining up female flatmates for viewings. You're kind of a—' I grapple for the right word not wanting to offend him.

'Backup?'

'Yes,' I admit reluctantly.

He nods. 'I get it. I probably wouldn't want a guy living with my girlfriend either. But I'm a good flattie. I've got references. I've got a job. I don't have weird quirks, none that I know of anyway. You won't even know I'm here. I even leave—'

'The toilet seat down,' I finish for him.

'Yep.' Nathan grins at me.

'Well, you'd have the main bathroom to yourself. I've got an en suite.'

'My own bathroom? Aw man, that's sweet.' He sticks his arms behind his head and lies back on the bed, staring up at the ceiling rose, a small contented smile on his lips.

OK, time to get the hot guy, who's starting to look extremely comfortable and at home, off the bed.

'Anyway, I guess I should show you the lounge.'

'Sure.'

He jumps up and follows me into the lounge. I do the usual Callum spiel and end with 'There's a view over the Links, and you can just see Arthur's Seat in the distance. It's nice in summer, being so close to the Meadows, though it does get a bit smoky with people's barbecues.'

'Sounds great.'

I invite him to sit down but then see the clipboard lying on the couch with all the names crossed out apart from his. I pick it up hastily, but he's noticed it.

'That's a lot of names you crossed out.'

'I know. To be honest, they were doing my head in. So demanding.'

Nathan stares at the clipboard in my hand. 'I'm very undemanding.'

'I'm sure you are. It's just . . .'

'The boyfriend. Right.' He looks dejected.

'So how come you're here?' I venture. 'I mean, in Edinburgh.'

'Work mainly. I got a contract on a building site. But it's been difficult to find a flat.'

'Oh, you work in construction?' I enquire. That would explain his . . . physique.

'Amongst other things. I guess I've got my fingers in a few pies.'

'Ah, OK.'

I can't quite get to grips with his personality. One minute, he's brazenly open; the next, he's shut up tight like a Swiss army knife.

Nathan looks at his phone. 'Anyway I should go. I've taken up enough of your time. Thanks for the tour. I do love the flat. It's kind of perfect, and the price is fine. But no worries if you want to go with a chick.'

He seems resigned that I'm going to say no. We move

towards the hallway.

'I'll let you know either way,' I say, opening the door.

He nods and gives me a smile. 'Thanks, Emma. It was great to meet you.'

'Likewise.'

Then he's gone, taking the stairs two steps at a time. I hear him let himself out into the street below. Killing the lights, I stand by the window in the lounge, watching out for him in the darkness. I see him pass under the street light, then head across Bruntsfield Links with long, loping strides until he's just a smudge in the distance and I can't make him out anymore.

Chapter 9

BIKER BOOTS AND ROAST LAMB

❊

Thou shalt not choose the hunky Antipodean.
Thou shalt not choose the hunky Antipodean.

I repeat the eleventh commandment over and over the next morning as I'm walking through the Meadows. It's a stunning day. There's blue sky peeking through the russet and green treetops, a low mist slowly dissipating across the dew-covered grass, and so many joggers out on the paths that it's Lycra gridlock. It's a pity I have to go to work.

Thou shalt not choose the hunky Antipodean.

The meeting with Nathan last night has me all a quiver. I was expecting to be able to cross his name off the list quite easily. I know I should and keep interviewing. But I'm wrestling with the two parts of myself again: Prude is convinced it's a bad idea and that there's no way Callum will be happy about it. Broad-minded is relishing the fact that Nathan is kind of intriguing and extremely easy on the eye.

As soon as I get into work, I bail up Sian in the sci-fi aisle,

R to *T*. She's up a ladder to reach the top shelves. I study her outfit with interest. Today she's wearing a white shirt, a tight black V-neck sweater vest, and a short red-and-black tartan skirt with red heels. Her blonde hair is pulled back into a bun, and she's wearing red-framed glasses and matching cherry-red lip gloss. She's been showing up in some very sexy librarian outfits recently. It's strange she never gets hauled over the coals for them.

'Hey! So Nathan came round last night to view my flat. You look nice too, by the way.'

'Thanks!' She smiles down at me, then pouts her glossy lips. 'Er . . . Who's Nathan?'

'Nathan Ellington. Your friend's nephew?'

'Oh! Sorry, yes. I forgot that was his name. My friend just refers to him as "the nephew". Pass me that yellow book, will you?'

I hand it up to her. 'Oh, you've not met him?'

'No. Just acting as the middlewoman, helping out two friends.'

I take a book from the trolley and shelve it in the middle section.

'So how did it go?' Sian asks.

'Fine. He just wasn't what I expected.'

'In what way?'

I can't say he was so good-looking that he knocked my knee-high socks off. Sian might tell her friend, and it will probably get back to Nathan. Tricky. In the end, I avoid all reference to his looks and settle for 'He was nice. Very easy-going and didn't seem to mind anything I told him about the flat.'

Sian shrugs. 'He's a Kiwi. They're pretty laid-back. If I were you, I'd snap him up. I told you he cooks, eh?'

'Yeah, I asked him about that, and he just kind of shrugged.'

'Probably being modest.'

'So why is your friend desperate for him to leave again?'

'Oh . . . Ah, she's only got a one-bedroom, and she's started dating someone. So it's not exactly ideal, him being on the couch, if you get my drift.'

'Who is this friend of yours? Have I met her?' I've had drinks with quite a few of Sian's friends since we started working together. She hangs out with an eclectic bunch of people. But if this woman is Nathan's aunt, she must be quite a bit older than us.

'I don't think so, but you may have.'

'What's her name?'

She comes down the ladder and grabs an armful of books. 'Anna,' she mumbles.

'Anna . . . Hmm . . . doesn't ring any bells.'

'You can't go wrong with Nathan, Em. You should choose him.'

'He seems really nice, and he's very keen. But . . .'

'But what?'

'Callum. He's going to have to meet him first.'

'Ah, methinks you're going to be wearing sexy underwear tonight.'

'He's not that easily swayed.'

Sian arches an eyebrow. 'He's a guy. If you give him a hard-on, he'll agree to anything.'

However, Callum's keen to go out tonight rather than stay in for a takeaway. He suggests our favourite Italian restaurant down the road from his flat. But this is good. I'll wait until he's had a few wines, then drop Nathan casually into the conversation. My paranoia about blonde Aisla is still there too. So maybe if he has enough wines, he'll let his guard down completely, and I'll kill a lot of birds with a couple of bottles.

'Do you know what you want?' he asks when we've been perusing the menu for about five minutes. It's still early, so there are hardly any other diners here. Callum likes to come before six so we get our meals faster.

'Yes. The prawns, the fettuccine, and the *insalata mista.*'

He tsks. 'You always have that, Em. Get something different.'

'Fine. I'll have the *tagliata di filetto*. No fettuccine.'

He balks slightly. The beef fillet is the most expensive thing on the menu. But he smooths his face into a smile. 'I'll have that too. Why not live a little?'

I clink my glass of wine with his. 'Hear, hear.' He takes a sip and I top him up generously. We're halfway through the bottle already, and we haven't even ordered. Callum nods at the waiter, who comes to take our orders, and he asks for another bottle of red. Excellent.

'So I interviewed those potential flatmates last night,' I begin as I break off a small piece of bread and dunk it in olive oil. 'Thanks for setting that up.'

'Not a problem. There were five, as I recall. You must've found someone suitable in that lot.'

'Ah, there were actually six on my list. Someone I heard about through Sian.'

He taps his fingers on the table and looks around. 'Well, they're probably not going to be any good. Sian's friends are a bit kooky, aren't they? Have they even got a job?'

'Yes, they do.'

'What?'

'They're a construction worker.'

Callum snorts and takes a gulp of wine. 'A construction worker? I bet she's butch then.'

I cough and pour more wine into his glass. '*She* is a *he*. It's Sian's friend's nephew.'

His eyebrows instantly draw together.

'Before you say anything, just listen. His name's Nathan, and he's from New Zealand. He's been sleeping on a couch for two months. He has references, a job, and he's perfectly normal. There was no list of demands as long as my arm. I told him about you and that you preferred me living with a girl, and he understood. But really, none of the girls I interviewed were anyone I could live with. I think I should choose him.'

Callum has been listening to me without saying anything. 'Well, it's ultimately your decision, Em. But I just worry for your safety, that's all. One glimpse of your knickers drying on the rack and he might turn feral.'

Here we go, I think.

'He seemed perfectly fine. Anyway, I have a sneaking suspicion he might be gay. Apparently, he likes cooking.'

Callum looks amused. 'A gay construction worker from New Zealand who cooks? This gets even better.'

God, why did I have to go and say that? I suppose Nathan could be gay, but something tells me he's very much not. Now Callum seems to have latched on to it.

'Anyway,' I continue, 'I was thinking I could invite him round tomorrow night to the flat for dinner, and he could meet you.'

He nods enthusiastically. 'That's a great idea. What did you say his name was?'

'Nathan.'

'Definitely sounds gay.'

'Callum . . .'

'Well, you said it, not me. By all means, invite him round. Maybe he could even cook us a meal if he likes wearing a pinny that much.'

Oh God, what have I done?

Callum and I spend an enjoyable evening conversing, eating

medium-rare steak, sharing a chocolate gelato, and even having mediocre au naturel sex later when we're back at his flat. All the while, I'm racking my brain trying to come up with a suitable text to send to Nathan. I'm worried I'm going to scare him off. It all sounds slightly ludicrous.

Thou shalt ask the hunky Antipodean to cook and be gay.

In the end, I ring him on the way to work the next morning.

'Hi, Nathan? It's Emma, from the flat in Bruntsfield.'

'Hey, Emma. How's it?'

'Great. Can you talk?'

'Sure.'

'Sooo, there's good news and bad news. Which do you want first?'

'The good news.'

'I've chosen you.'

I hear him let out a breath. 'Awesome!'

'But there's a catch.'

'Lay it on me.'

'Callum, my boyfriend, wants to meet you. Are you free tonight?'

'Yeah, I can do tonight. Is that the bad news?'

'Not exactly. How would you feel about cooking us dinner?'

'Uh, it's kind of random, but I can go with.'

'I can help,' I say hurriedly. 'And it doesn't have to be

anything involved. A stir-fry is fine.'

'It's OK, Emma, I don't mind. Though I feel I'm getting a reputation about my cooking skills. They're pretty average.'

'Great, thanks.' I take a deep breath and plunge in. 'Also, do you happen to have any gay pride clothing?'

'Uh, not last time I looked. Any particular reason?'

'Callum may have got the impression you're that way inclined. And now he's slightly more on board with you moving in. So I just thought you could maybe, er, go along with it . . .'

There's a stunned silence at the other end of the phone. I know I've totally crossed the line. I pull off to the side of the path and perch on the arm of a dew-covered iron bench, feeling a bit sick.

'I'm not gay, Emma,' comes Nathan's firm reply.

'Yes, I figured,' I state overly brightly. 'I've got a pretty good gaydar, and you didn't register at all.'

'Why does he think I'm gay?'

'I guess I was trying to make him more comfortable about us living together because I know he's weird about it. So I said that you may be gay because you like cooking . . .' I trail off lamely.

There's another silence. 'It's kind of out there. I'm not really comfortable pretending to be gay,' Nathan says at last.

To be honest, it's a relief.

'I know, it's stupid. I'm sorry for asking.'

'But I really like the flat, and I thought we got on well.'

'Me too,' I say quickly.

'So should I still cook dinner? Or just forget it?'

I sigh in relief that he's not running for the hills and start walking again. 'Please do. If you still want to, that is. Callum will just have to deal with you not being gay.'

I can sense him shaking his head in disbelief. 'I was told Scots were a bit mad, but being asked to pretend I'm gay is one of the stranger requests I've had since I've been here.'

'Er . . . Yes, I'm sure it is. So, um, just come round any time after six!'

I'm starting to wonder if the houseplant girl is the easier choice. But I do like Nathan. And the fact that he's willing to take on Callum as a straight man makes me like him even more.

After work, I'm at the Sainsbury's in Simpson Loan, gathering ingredients for the stir-fry, when my phone starts ringing. Nathan.

He's changed his mind. I'm too crazy. He'd rather keep sleeping on his aunt's couch than live with me.

'Hi,' I answer hesitantly, bracing myself.

'Hi, again. You haven't bought the stir-fry ingredients, have you?'

I stare at my basket. 'Not yet. I was just about to.'

'I thought I might do a roast.'

'A . . . roast?'

'Yeah, I've got all the ingredients. It won't take long if I can bung it in the oven soonish. I'm heading to yours now.'

Shit. I dump the plastic packages of stir-fry veggies and chicken breast and tell him I'm ten minutes away. Since I haven't changed out of my heels, I run as fast as I can through the Meadows, trying not to break an ankle.

When I arrive, after hiking it up the stairs like a hill runner, I'm totally out of breath. I head to the kitchen and quickly wash my cereal bowl and mug from breakfast, wipe the counter with kitchen spray and a damp cloth. In the lounge, I rip an armful of freshly washed underwear off the drying rack, run down the hallway to my bedroom, and biff it onto the bed.

I catch sight of my reflection in my bedroom mirror. Jesus, I look like I've been pulled through a bush backwards. So much for a leisurely forty-five minutes to get ready! The buzzer goes and I know, once I let him in, I have exactly two to four minutes, give or take—depending on how fit he is—to make myself look presentable. I buzz him in and hastily redo my hair into its bun, adjust my glasses, apply some lipstick, and pull the wrinkles out of my stockings before there's a knock at the door. Fuck. He's fit.

'Hey.' Nathan grins at me when I open the door, and it's like a kick to my stomach. He's even better-looking than I remembered. There's just something about the way he smiles genuinely and how his grey-green eyes crinkle at the corners. And also something exotic and edgy about him that I can't put my finger on.

'Come in,' I say faintly.

'I like the librarian look,' he comments, giving me a nod. When he came round on Wednesday, I'd changed into jeans and a top, so he hasn't seen the pencil skirt and blouse ensemble.

Nathan walks past me holding a canvas shopping bag, and I notice he's got on tall black chunky biker boots with studs and buckles. Interesting. When we get to the kitchen, he takes his jacket off, and I gape. What the hell? He's wearing a tight black tank top and ultra-skinny black jeans. There are several gold chains looped around his neck and a gold band ring adorns each of his thumbs. With difficulty, I remove my eyes from his tanned bulging biceps and swallow hard. 'Please don't tell me you're trying to look gay.'

'Gay? No, this is what I normally wear on a Friday night when I'm cooking a roast.' He cocks his hip and adds 'Darling.'

'Oh God.'

'Too much?'

'But I thought—'

'Trust me, I'm not gay. But if someone thinks that what I'm wearing is gay, I can't stop them thinking that can I?'

'I meant just a "Gay Lives Matter" T-shirt. Not dressing up like you're in the Village People!'

Nathan's mouth twitches. 'I knew I should've worn my tool belt and construction helmet.'

I groan.

'Look, don't stress; if he asks me, I'll say, "No, I prefer chicks". Now please can you turn the oven on to 190 degrees? I need to get the lamb in. Otherwise, we'll be eating at eight o'clock.'

Obediently I turn the oven on, trying not to laugh as he clunks around in his boots getting ingredients out of the shopping bag. I hand him the roasting pan.

'Foil?' I pass it over. Nathan lines the pan and gently places the lamb in, rubs it with oil, and starts studding bits of garlic over it.

I can't help staring at him. 'Is all that get-up yours?'

'The tank top and the jeans are mine, but I raided my aunt's storage cupboard for the rest. The boots are her ex-husband's. He was a biker with the same-size feet as me, as it turns out, and there was a box of her costume jewellery from the 1980s.'

I'm a bit overwhelmed that he's gone to all this effort.

'Thank you. It was stupid even suggesting it. And cooking a roast . . . you didn't have to.'

He winks at me and smiles. 'I really like the flat.'

I quickly look away and open the oven door, but my face is red from more than just the heat. What am I doing contemplating living with this guy? There's obviously some kind of attraction between us. But again, weirdly, I can't seem to stop the momentum of my actions.

'Oven's hot enough,' I mumble.

'Great.'

'I might just leave you to it for a bit,' I say, 'and go and get some wine from the bottle shop. Unless you want beer? Or cider?'

'Wine is beaut,' Nathan says.

So I leave him peeling potatoes, put on my trainers, and let myself out of the flat. I check my phone. Half an hour until Callum arrives. My stomach is starting to clench nervously. I can't predict at all how this is going to go. It's weird having a guy who's not my boyfriend cooking in the flat. But it's kind of nice too.

Chapter 10

DINNER FOR THREE

✻

I dither around at the bottle shop trying to choose the best wine to complement the lamb. I don't want to buy something cheap and nasty since Nathan's going to all this trouble. I've still got some life modelling money, so I can afford to splash out on a few mid-range-priced bottles of red. But then I end up in a queue, so it takes a good fifteen minutes before I get back to the flat. I'm fishing about in my handbag for my keys when someone pinches my bum. I let out a screech and jump a mile in the air. I pivot around to find Callum laughing at me.

'Do you mind? I almost stabbed you in the eye with my key!'

'Did you not get my message?' he asks.

'No.'

'I left work drinks early. I'm starving. How long until the stir-fry's ready?'

'You might have to wait a bit longer. He's cooking us a roast.'

'A roast! Fuck. He's going all out.'

I open the door and walk into the entranceway. Callum

has obviously had a few because he's very handsy, groping my butt as I walk up the stairs in front of him. God. He chooses *now* to be amorous? I hope he doesn't do or say anything inappropriate. Who am I kidding? This is Callum. When we get to the top floor, I drag him back from the door and hiss, 'Please behave! For me. No groping in front of Nathan.'

He shrugs. 'I can be affectionate with my girlfriend if I want. Besides, if he's gay, is he really going to care?'

'It's just not appropriate,' I counter, primly straightening my skirt. 'It's kind of an interview. You wouldn't grope me at an open home, would you?'

Callum raises his eyebrows. 'Depends on what you were wearing.' He hooks a finger in the neckline of my blouse and peers down at my breasts. 'Hmm . . . probably not with that bra.'

Thank God for dowdy underwear. Maybe the thought of my beige bra and knickers will sober him up.

I open the door to the flat and give Callum a warning glare as he walks past, but he ignores me and goes into the kitchen. I follow, hot on his heels, and almost bump into him when he stops suddenly in the doorway. He lets out a breath. Yikes. Hopefully, Nathan hasn't taken off his tank top or anything. I peer tentatively over his shoulder and almost laugh out loud.

Nathan, wearing my pink-and-white-checked apron over his tank top and jeans, is standing at the counter and busily assembling what looks to be a plate of pre-dinner snacks.

'Gidday, mate,' he says to Callum and holds out the plate. 'I'm Nathan. Carrot stick and hummus?'

Callum silently takes a carrot stick and dips it in the pot of hummus. I walk past and try not to look at him. I know the expression on his face is going to make me start laughing hysterically.

'Nathan, this is Callum. How's everything going?' I ask, depositing the wine on the counter. 'What's the ETA on the lamb?'

Nathan checks his phone. 'About forty minutes, I'd say. Everything's in the oven. I thought we could have drinks and snacks and'—he looks at Callum meaningfully—'get to know each other.'

Callum backs towards the doorway. 'Uh . . . I'll just be in the lounge watching the news,' he says and quickly exits the room.

When he's gone, I lean against the counter, weak with suppressed laughter.

'You might want to tone down the flirting a little. You're coming on pretty strong,' I tell Nathan, tearing off a piece of kitchen towel and wiping my eyes.

He grins mischievously. 'He's an attractive guy. If I was gay, I'd be all over him like a rash.'

I take a deep shuddering breath, trying to control myself. 'I was worried about *him* being inappropriate. Now I'm worried about *you!*'

'I know. I should probably come clean before it totally gets out of hand.'

Nathan takes off the apron and carries the plate of snacks while I grab a bottle of wine and three glasses. Callum looks up warily as we enter the lounge and clicks off the TV. I sit next to him on the couch, set up the wine and glasses on the side table, and start pouring. I'm glad that I bought four bottles. I'm going to need many glasses to get me through this evening.

'So, Nathan, Emma tells me you're a construction worker,' Callum says when Nathan's sat down in the armchair opposite the couch. He's so rangy; his legs go on for miles.

'Yeah,' Nathan replies, taking the glass of wine I hand him. 'It's something I did back home, and they're short of skilled workers here.'

'What project are you working on at the moment?'

'A new retail development in Haymarket. So the flat is beaut as it's just a fifteen minute trot to work.'

'Must be difficult to keep your eyes to yourself.'

'Huh?'

Callum raises his eyebrows and flexes his bicep muscle. 'You know, the other workers.'

Nathan looks at me. 'Yeah, so the thing is—'

But Callum is on a roll. 'How come you're living up here in Edinburgh? Most Kiwis usually gravitate towards London, don't they? And the nightlife is much better down there for your scene.'

Oh God, 'your scene'. I'm going to have to say something.

I open my mouth, but Nathan beats me to it.

'I *was* living in London, as it happens. But the relationship I was in ended, and it all got a bit ugly. I decided to make a fresh start up here.'

'Sorry to hear that. Break-ups are hard.' Callum nods sympathetically as though he can relate. However, from what he's told me, he's always been the dumper, not the dumpee.

'Yeah, it was even harder as we've got a kid together,' adds Nathan quietly.

I almost choke on my carrot stick. He has a kid!

Callum looks dumbfounded. 'But how?'

'It's complicated,' says Nathan. 'I don't want to bore you with the details. Hey, I should probably just check on the lamb. I won't be a minute.' He gets up and lopes out of the room.

Callum is opening and shutting his mouth like a goldfish. 'I'm so confused right now,' he says. 'Surrogate? Adoption? But poor guy . . . Not only has he been through a bad break-up, but it also sounds like there are paternity issues with the other father.' He shakes his head sadly.

At that moment, we pass the point of no return. I want Callum to be OK with Nathan living here, and after hearing Nathan's story, he's totally on his side now. It's not like they're going to be best mates and hanging out together anyway. Callum hardly ever stays over. And if he does, it's going to be 'hey' and a nod in the hallway as they pass like ships in the night.

'Yeah, it doesn't sound good . . . I'll just go see if Nathan wants any help. We can't be too far off,' I say getting up, eager to avoid any more of Callum's conjecturing.

But he grabs my hand. 'Just to let you know, I'm OK with him moving in, Em. I mean, Jesus. He sounds like he really needs some good luck in his life. Though just be careful you don't get too involved. You could end up being a shoulder for him to cry on.'

In the kitchen, Nathan is at the counter poking a skewer into the lamb.

'Smells good,' I comment to fill the silence.

'Yeah, I think another ten minutes and we should be OK to go.'

I'm not sure what to say to him now after the clanger he's just dropped.

'I'm sorry about . . . everything. It must be hard for you.'

'Yeah, it's a long story. But Naomi—that's my ex—and I weren't married. So it's making things more complicated where my daughter is concerned. We're still working through things.'

'How old is your daughter?'

'She's three.'

'What's her name?'

Nathan looks at me, and his eyes soften. 'Katie.'

He obviously adores her. God, what a nightmare for him. My throat tightens, and I well up slightly. He notices my watery eyes and looks away from me quickly. He bends down to put the lamb back in the oven.

I take a breath. 'So do you want the good news or the bad news?'

'The good news,' he answers, straightening up.

'Callum just told me he's totally fine with you moving in.'

Nathan grins. 'Awesome. And the bad news?'

'He still thinks you're gay and that you either adopted or used a surrogate mother. And now I don't have the heart to tell him otherwise.'

'Ahhh,' he says in a despondent tone. But there's a slight smile playing around his lips, and I'm wondering if he's as contrite as he's making out. 'I guess he's going to have to know at some point, isn't he? Sorry, I shouldn't have come round dressed up like this. I was just in a weird mood. Sometimes I do things without thinking.'

'I know exactly what you mean! It's like you know what you should be doing, but then you end up doing the exact thing you shouldn't.'

Nathan leans against the counter with his arms folded and surveys me. 'Anything you want to tell Uncle Nathan about?'

I turn bright red and pull out the cutlery drawer abruptly. 'No.'

'I mean it, Emma. You can talk to me. If you ever need a sounding board, that is. I'm a good listener.'

Oh God, somehow this is all about me now. I'm fine. I don't have any issues. I now have a side gig and a flatmate, so I've got plenty of money to buy proper food *and* enough kinky lingerie to satisfy Callum's desires. Everything's just hunky-dory.

I smile at him and say brightly, 'I can't wait to try the lamb. I'll just go and get Callum so we can eat.'

Then I walk out of the kitchen, feeling Nathan's eyes trained on my back.

After he's on his third helping of lamb and starting his fourth glass of wine, Callum drunkenly declares that Nathan is moving in tomorrow. And that he'll help him. OK, I wanted him to be all right with Nathan moving in, *not* be his best mate.

'Is tomorrow OK with you, Emma?' asks Nathan.

I'm pretty sloshed myself, so I wave my fork in the air. 'Of course! We'll both help you! Where's your aunt's place? I don't think I actually asked you.'

'It's in Stockbridge.'

'Very nice,' purrs Callum. 'So you're giving up Stockbridge to slum it in Bruntsfield.'

'Hardly!' I scoff. 'Bruntsfield is just as upmarket as Stockbridge, and it's better connected for transport.'

'I know that, Emma. I'm just joking. God, you're so sensitive sometimes,' Callum retorts.

Nathan is watching us curiously. After our discussion in the kitchen, he's probably wondering if everything is quite as it seems.

'So how did you two meet?' he asks, pouring himself some more wine. 'If you don't mind me asking.'

'He seduced me on the job,' I reply immediately. 'He showed me some flats, then that same evening asked me up to see his etchings.'

Callum pokes me in the shoulder with his forefinger. 'Hey, you're making it sound sordid! I'm very profesh . . . professional.' He's having a bit of trouble getting the word out.

I watch Nathan's mouth twist in amusement. I'm not sure how he's still relatively sober. Either he's had less than we've had, or he's got a much stronger constitution.

'I'm sure you are very professional, Callum,' says Nathan seriously.

'I am! But I mean, look at her!' He gestures at me. 'I couldn't help myself. I had to ask her out, and one thing led to another.'

'Yes, she's very pretty indeed. I can see why you lost all self-control,' Nathan says, and I realise with a start that the way he's giving me a once-over is definitely not gay.

Callum sees him doing it and narrows his eyes suspiciously. I can almost hear the cogs in his wine-fugged brain churning as he tries to work out whether a gay man would look at me like that.

'Pretty in an objective way, you mean? Like appreciating a piece of artwork?' he enquires.

Nathan stares at him and smiles slowly. 'Of course. Emma

is right up there with the *Mona Lisa.*'

'Hello?' I interrupt loudly. 'I am still here, you know! A living, breathing person—not the bloody *Mona Lisa!* Getting back to tomorrow, how much stuff have you got to move?'

Callum is still looking at Nathan with narrowed eyes but eventually drags his attention to me. 'Yes, I don't want to strain my back. Are we talking about two suitcases or boxes of things?'

Nathan laughs. 'I've got very little. Thanks for the offer, but I'm sure I can manage. Most of my stuff is back in London. I kind of left in a hurry.'

'Ah.' Callum looks at me knowingly.

Nathan gets up to clear the plates. When he's over at the sink rinsing them under the tap, Callum taps me on the arm, makes a clenched fist, and grimaces. Huh? Oh, right. He thinks Nathan's ex-partner is physically abusive, and that's why he's done a runner.

'Are you still OK with this, Emma?' he hisses. 'What if the ex shows up on the doorstep and starts throwing his weight around?'

'You don't know that's why he left. Stop making things up!' I hiss back. I call out to Nathan, 'Hey, leave those! You cooked dinner. We'll sort them.'

'Well, OK, if you're sure?' Nathan looks around the kitchen doubtfully. The counter is covered in pots and pans, and I think he may have used every piece of crockery I own.

'Definitely!' I say firmly.

'I should probably head off soon anyway. It's getting late.'

'We can share an Uber if you like,' Callum suggests. 'I'm heading down to the West End.'

'Oh, are you not staying over?' I ask him, surprised.

'I want to get up early and go for a run.' He pats his middle. 'Got to keep in shape.'

Callum running on a Saturday morning after a night of heavy drinking? That's a first. I notice he hasn't offered to help clean up the kitchen, and that's more likely the reason he's not staying over. I push down my annoyance and ignore him.

'Thanks again for cooking, Nathan. The lamb was delicious, and those roast potatoes were divine.'

'You're very welcome. What time should I come round tomorrow?'

'Noon?'

'Sweet.'

Callum has whipped his phone out and is ordering an Uber. 'It's three minutes away, Em, so we better leave now.'

Nathan shrugs into his jacket in the hallway, where I've hung it up on the coatrack. Callum has already put his on and given me a kiss on the cheek and is waiting in the corridor. Typical. He's escaping before I can guilt him into tidying up.

'Thanks, Emma. I feel stink about all the dishes. If you're too tired, just leave them, and I can fix it tomorrow,' says Nathan, lingering on the doorstep.

'Don't be daft. It's fine.'

They head off, and the last thing I hear before I shut the door is Callum's voice floating up from the stairwell asking Nathan if he plays golf.

Sighing, I change out of my work clothes and into an old T-shirt and trackpants. It takes me at least another hour to clean up the kitchen. But, even though Nathan made all the mess, it's Callum's face I picture as I scrub angrily at the roasting pan.

Chapter 11

THE SAVILE ROW SUITS

❊

I have good intentions of cleaning the whole flat in readiness for Nathan's move in. But instead, I end up lazing in bed until 10 a.m. To be honest, I'm glad Callum didn't stay over. At least this way, he's not in the flat when Nathan does show up. I remember the 'Do you play golf?' comment and shudder. The less time they spend together, the better. Nathan's like a new toy I want to keep all to myself. For what purpose, I don't know. I just don't want Callum muscling in on him.

When I eventually get up, I do a quick hoover in the spare room and dust my books. Then I make up the bed with fresh sheets, pillowcase, and duvet cover. The spare room has a small wardrobe, but it's full of my old coats, which I've been meaning to donate to charity. I transfer them in one big armful to my wardrobe and shove them in the bottom. As noon draws nearer, I get nervous. What if he's changed his mind? Hopefully, Callum didn't say anything obnoxious in the taxi last night.

The buzzer goes, and I let out a small squawk. Be cool, Emma. Opening the door, I hear scrapes, rustles, and grunts coming from downstairs. I descend and find Nathan standing in the entranceway, surrounded by bags. He's holding a small green leafy plant.

'Hi!' I say.

'Gidday.'

I glance at all the bags. 'I thought you didn't have much stuff?'

'I didn't think I did. This is for you, by the way. A "Thanks for choosing me" present. I bought it at the market this morning.'

'Oh, thanks. That's nice of you.'

I eye his bags, worried we're blocking the entranceway. 'Shall we . . . ?'

It takes three trips, but Nathan's six full bags of various sizes are now ensconced in the lounge. I'm not quite sure how everything's going to fit in the spare room. As much as I love my flat, the storage aspect is sadly lacking, so there's no extra space I can offer him.

I stand with my arms folded, considering. 'Perhaps you could get some of those vacuum pack bags, and we could slide them under the bed?'

'Nah, I just need to declutter. It's London stuff. I don't need it anymore. I should just donate it to charity. Do you know any places around here? Stockbridge has a few, but I don't want to traipse all the way back down there again.'

Before I can stop myself, I say, 'There are tons of charity shops in Morningside. I'm going there tomorrow afternoon, if you want to come with me. I have some coats I need to donate too.' *It's fine,* I think. *I'll just say I'm visiting a friend.*

'That would be cool, thanks. I actually have an appointment in Morningside tomorrow afternoon, so that works. Shall we just see what's in my room in the way of storage so I know how much to keep?'

We head to his bedroom and stare in silence at the tiny three-drawer dresser, and then at the slim inset wardrobe with its metal railing and half a dozen hangers. Why didn't we talk about this the other night? *Because you were too busy watching him bounce on the bed,* Prude chides. I realise now that the set-up is ridiculous for a guy his size. It's like offering him dolls' furniture.

'The wardrobe is bigger than it looks,' I state encouragingly. 'You could fit quite a lot of things if you pack them in tightly. Though if you did want to buy some kind of free-standing wardrobe or dresser, I'd completely understand.'

He nods. 'IKEA then?'

'Definitely IKEA.'

We spend a pleasant afternoon getting Nathan settled in. Well, *my* part is pleasant. I lie on the couch with my laptop, browsing through possible IKEA options for his room, while he sits cross-legged on the floor and sifts through his bags. A mound of clothes grows in the corner. Mostly shirts and jeans, from what I can gather from my surreptitious noseying. No handcuffs, posing pouches, or sex toys, so far. Though a black leather journal with a gold ribbon has piqued my curiosity. Does he keep a diary?

Callum messages, wanting to know how it's all going. I send him a brief reply: *He's here and unpacking.*

I'm still annoyed at him for skiving off last night. I haven't asked Nathan what they talked about in the Uber. I'm not sure I want to know. As I say, he's here and unpacking. That's good enough.

I happen to glance up when Nathan pulls a bunch of expensive-looking dark suits out of one of the larger bags. 'They're nice!'

He shrugs and says, 'They can go.' Then he dumps them in the pile.

Curiously, I get up and check the labels. 'Oh my God, they're Savile Row! You can't throw them out. They're worth a fortune! Why have you got Savile Row suits anyway? Surely . . .' I trail off.

'A construction worker wouldn't need a designer suit?' He finishes my sentence for me.

'I wasn't thinking that!' Actually, I was.

He brushes the sleeve of one of them. 'So slight confession: these are work suits.'

'Huh?' I'm confused.

'In London, I wasn't doing construction.'

My heart starts pounding. What the hell? This guy is full of surprises. Don't tell me he's a stockbroker moonlighting as a construction worker.

'What did you do?' I ask, wide-eyed.

'I was an architect.'

'Really?' I breathe, trying to take it in. 'But how? Why? What the fuck?'

'It's not a big deal, Emma. People change jobs all the time.'

'Yeah, but usually to advance themselves, not slip down the ladder!'

'I guess.'

'How many years' experience have you got?'

'About eight.'

I grab my laptop and type in 'architect salaries London' and discover he'd be pulling in at least six figures. I shake my head. 'Are you absolutely crazy?'

Nathan smiles at my gobsmacked face. 'Possibly. There's more to life than money, though.'

'But . . . but it's a shitload of money!'

'You sound like Naomi. She wasn't too happy when I wanted to give it up.'

'I can kind of understand her thinking. I take it you didn't like it, though?'

'Nah, I didn't. It isn't me. I got railroaded into it by my father. It was his dream. He wanted me to have the opportunities that he didn't have, so it was either study architecture or get kicked out of home. In hindsight, I should've just left. But I was young, and I didn't want to live on the streets of West Auckland. I probably would've ended up a druggie or dead.'

'And your mum?'

'Stepmum. She didn't give a rat's ass about me.'

'Oh.'

'I thought I'd just study, get my degree to keep him happy, and then escape to the UK. But I met Naomi at uni. We moved to London, and I found myself working sixty-hour weeks and hating every minute of it. I wanted to be doing something . . . quite different. I never cared about the money or a professional career, really. I just wanted to be happy.

'Anyway, that's why I have Savile Row suits. And why I'm getting rid of them. They're just a reminder of that part of my life, which is now over.'

'You quitting architecture . . . Is that why you and Naomi broke up?'

'It's part of the reason, yes.' A guarded look comes over Nathan's handsome face, and I sense I shouldn't push it. But I can't help it. It's like he's throwing away a winning lottery ticket. I don't understand.

'So you came to Edinburgh to pursue your dream of being . . . a construction worker?'

'Amongst other things.' Again, the guarded look.

I let out a breath. Callum is going to flip when he hears this, though I realise I probably can't say anything without the ex-girlfriend featuring largely in the story. Somehow, Nathan and I are now stranded together on a fabricated island of our own making.

I look at the suits. 'Maybe you should keep one, just in case you go out somewhere nice or get invited to a wedding?'

He grins. 'If you and Callum get hitched, I can wear it to yours.'

I look away quickly. 'I don't think so.'

'Do you not want to get married?'

'I do, but . . .'

'He's not the marrying type?'

I shrug. 'Every time I bring up anything remotely to do with the future, he shuts it down. I'm getting to the point where I'm wondering why I'm even bothering.'

As painful as it is, it's the closest I've come to admitting to anyone, apart from Julie, that Callum and I are having issues.

But Nathan doesn't overreact. He just says, 'Sometimes these things have a way of working themselves out. And you don't have to do anything.'

Uncannily, as if he knows we're talking about him, my phone beeps with another message from Callum: *Are you coming over tonight?*

The thought of trying to tempt him to have sex with me is suddenly exhausting. Why do I have to wear kinky lingerie? Why can't he just want me as I am? So I type: *Not tonight, sorry.* Then I wait, looking at my phone with trepidation. I usually never say no, especially not on a Saturday night.

He messages back with: *Fine, I know when I'm not wanted. Enjoy your girly bonding session lol.*

Suddenly, I'm relieved that Callum thinks Nathan is gay and surprised to find that I don't care if he never finds out the truth.

The next day, after lunch, Nathan and I catch the bus into Morningside. I rang a few of the charity shops, and they all said they're interested in taking new stock. Nathan chose his favourite of the Savile Row suits to keep, so he has three to donate, as well as a selection of business shirts. I think he's nuts not trying to get money for them on eBay, Gumtree, or some second-hand designer suit shop. But he says he doesn't want the hassle. I was itching for him to try one on, but I managed to stop myself from asking.

There's a pair of empty seats together at the front of the bus, and we squash in with all our bags of clothes (I've got two old coats, multiple scarves, and a handbag I never use). 'It looks like we're running away from home,' I say with a giggle.

'I kind of am,' he says soberly.

'Oh, sorry, yes. Well, just think of all the extra room you'll have to buy new clothes,' I point out, trying to be cheerful. 'We'll have to do an online shop!'

'Yeah, I'm not earning what I used to, so we might have to go easy on the online shopping. Buying a free-standing dresser is enough for now,' Nathan says wryly. I note he doesn't seem to mind me offering, though. Already, we've settled into a kind of harmonious coexistence in the flat, though it was slightly disconcerting hearing him walk around this morning.

'What time are you meeting your friend?' he asks.

My face flushes. 'Oh. Half one.' Lorna asked me to come round early again. I've told Nathan I'm meeting up with a uni friend, which is a big fat lie. But I can't exactly tell him the truth, can I?

'And your appointment's at two?'

'Yep.'

He hasn't disclosed what it is, and I haven't asked. The fact that he's called it an 'appointment' suggests something vaguely medical. However, any kind of medical appointment on a Sunday is odd. It could be a shrink to deal with his break-up, perhaps?

The clothing drop-off goes surprisingly well. My coats are snapped up by the British Red Cross, and the woman at Chest Heart & Stroke Scotland almost keels over at the sight of Nathan's suits. In fact, I wonder if she is having a heart attack and a stroke combined. She whips everything from his arms quickly with an 'Oooh, lovely! Thank you!' before he can say anything.

We look at each other when we get outside, and I laugh. 'I *knew* they'd snap them up!' I exclaim triumphantly.

But Nathan doesn't look that happy about it, and I feel a bit sorry for him.

'You can still change your mind, you know. I'll cause a distraction, and you nip out the back. I'm sure she hasn't got the price labels on them just yet.'

'What will you do?'

'I don't know. Knock over a display stand of hats or something.'

For a moment, he looks unsure. 'I'm actually tempted by that idea. Maybe we should just walk.'

'Do you want to grab a coffee or something? I've got twenty minutes before I meet . . . Alana.'

I feel a pang of guilt. Alana does live in Morningside, but the last time we met up here was about six months ago. She's always so busy.

'Oh, aren't you meeting her for a coffee?'

'No, I'm going to her flat.' I cross my fingers in my coat pocket.

'Ah, sure then. Where's good?'

'Blackwood Coffee. It's just down the road.' And it's just up from Jordan Lane, where Jack and Lorna live.

After ordering at the cafe, we perch on bar stools at the window. Nathan has to contort his legs to manoeuvre himself in. I watch, fascinated.

'We can sit at a table if it's easier.'

'Nah, it's all good. Just the usual dilemma of being the size of the Incredible Hulk.'

I open my mouth to say something suitably complimentary, but out of the corner of my eye, I see Alana about to cross the road and head our way. Oh shit. Hastily, I swivel around on my bar stool so my back is to the window.

I'd have to be really unlucky if she comes in here to grab a coffee. If she's meeting a friend, I'm doubly screwed. It's highly likely, as this is the place where I met her last time.

Nathan is still going on about his height issues, but I can't concentrate. The doorbell tinkles, and someone with blonde hair walks in. Arrrgh. Do I swivel back to the window or stay where I am? I'm frozen. Then I see with relief it isn't her. Thank God. Our coffees arrive, and I slowly swivel back around to peer out the window. Alana isn't outside either. I breathe more easily. That was a close call.

'All right there?' Nathan is observing me with a frown. 'You look like the woman with the suits, all white and shaky.'

'Hah! Yeah, I'm fine. Just need a caffeine fix,' I tell him and take a gulp of coffee.

Stupid. I should've just gone straight to Jack and Lorna's, not lingered around where I could be seen.

When we leave the cafe, I peer around cautiously, expecting Alana's voice to ring out with a 'Hey, Emma!' But the coast is clear.

'What are you going to do for half an hour?' I ask Nathan as we walk down the street.

'Dunno. Maybe hang out in the small park and enjoy the sun, what little of it there is.'

'Yeah, well, no one ever moved to Scotland for the weather.'

He smiles down at me. 'Cute. I'll have to remember that one.'

Just then, the door to a gallery opens in front of us. Two girls come spilling out onto the street, laughing hysterically. One of them is Alana. I'm standing right there, but she's doubled over and doesn't see me.

Without thinking, I grab Nathan's hand and yank him into the gallery. 'I just need to show you this!' I whisper urgently.

Somehow, we manage to get into the gallery without Alana even being aware that I'm there. I glance out the window, and she's moved off down the street with her friend, still laughing. I wonder what it was that was so funny.

Nathan is looking at me questioningly, and I realise we're still holding hands. I drop his like a hot potato. 'What did you want to show me?' he asks.

I look around the gallery, desperately trying to see something interesting.

'Perhaps it's this, dear?' The gallery owner, a middle-aged man with glasses and a tweed jacket, points behind me to the wall. Nathan and I both turn slowly to see a life-size portrait of a naked young man with an extremely large, erect penis reclining on a red velvet chaise longue.

'It's by a local artist, Jack Sutton. I prefer landscapes myself. But I've been getting a steady stream of people coming in ever since I've had it up. No pun intended!'

I stare at the painting wordlessly.

'Was this what you wanted to show me?' asks Nathan, deadpan.

'Ah . . . yes,' I answer slowly. 'I thought you might be interested in . . . uh . . .'

'A guy with a big dick? I thought we'd established I'm not gay?' I can hear the amusement in his voice. Shit.

'Let's just go,' I mutter and stumble out onto the pavement with Nathan following behind me. 'So I think I'll just head off now.' I can hardly look at him.

'Well, thank you for the artistic detour, Emma,' he says. I can tell he's trying not to laugh. 'It was *very* educational. Enjoy your catch-up with Alana. I'll see you later.'

He shakes his head as if to say 'mad Scots' and walks off towards the park. Oh God. How embarrassing. Now I know why Alana and her friend were cracking up. Even worse is that it's Jack's. Trust him to have a painting of a well-hung guy in the local gallery. After this, I'm even more determined to avoid his attempts to get me to pose for him. There's a very good chance I could end up in the gallery myself!

Chapter 12

I AM CLEOPATRA

*

After I leave Nathan, I walk to Jack and Lorna's, trying to get into a calm state of mind. Alana popping up like that was a bit too close for comfort. Imagine if she'd seen me. I would've had to introduce her to Nathan, and then he might've said something about us meeting up, and she would've been confused—I'm agitated just thinking about it. It's my own fault entirely for fibbing, I know that. But honestly, how can I tell him the truth about my life modelling gig? He thinks I'm mad enough already.

Lorna opens the door when I buzz and ushers me into the hallway. 'Hello there!' she intones cheerfully. 'How are you?'

'Great,' I reply.

She peers at me. 'You don't look it.'

'Let's just say I've had better days.'

'What's the problem?'

I sigh. 'I'm having to avoid certain conversations about what I'm doing here.'

'Oh? The boyfriend?'

'I still haven't told him. And now I've got a new flatmate, who I can't tell either.'

Lorna clicks her tongue. 'Being a life model is nothing to be ashamed of, Emma. It's actually very brave.'

The painting of the naked guy in the gallery floats into my mind. I bet he's cowering in his flat right this very moment, too scared to show his face in public in case someone recognises him.

As if reading my thoughts, Lorna says, 'Anyway, we've got a different group in today, so you might enjoy it a bit more. Less proddy.'

'Oh, so not the retirees?'

'No. Remember I mentioned wearing a wig and make-up at the interview?'

'Yes.'

'Well, it's an art history class. They want their life models dressed as famous historical figures.'

'Oh!' I perk up instantly; a disguise is much better! 'Who am I going to be?'

'You can choose. There's a chest of accessories upstairs if you want to come and have a look. Obviously, there won't be a costume since they need to draw your figure, but it's still fun to partly dress up.'

I follow her upstairs, keeping an eye out for Jack. He's probably in the kitchen, slicing up wads of cheese again. Best to try and avoid him at all costs. Walking into the studio immediately calms me down. I just find it a very peaceful space. I sit on the daybed, and Lorna drags over a large chest and flips open the lid. Wow! I've never seen so many wigs.

'So we have Lady Godiva, if you want to be her . . .' She draws out a long blonde wig. 'Or Cleopatra . . .' She takes out a short black wig with gold beaded ends and an accompanying gold headband. 'There's a gold neck collar that goes with it. I wore this to a Halloween party one year—with a black slinky tunic dress, though.' She tinkles with laughter.

'Definitely Cleopatra,' I say. 'That would be fantastic.'

'I'm pretty good at the eye make-up, if you want me to do it. I practised for ages with black eyeliner, went through about two tubes of the stuff.'

I nod. 'Yes, please.'

'OK. Well, I'll just go and get my make-up box if you want to get changed into a robe.'

'Thanks, Lorna.'

I feel a bit better. This will be fun.

In the anteroom, I undress and put on a white cotton robe and attempt to fit the wig. But it perches on top of my head and looks ridiculous. Lorna comes in with her make-up box and gently removes it. 'We'll do your make-up first and then put the wig on afterwards. Just tie your hair back for now.' She tells me to close my eyes, dabs on foundation, and lightly brushes on eyeshadow. Then she draws on eyeliner and pencils my eyebrows.

'Do you want to wear fake lashes as well?'

'Gosh, OK.'

She applies the lashes and sweeps some blush on my cheeks. Finally, she sits back. 'OK, now the wig.' She undoes my hair and reties it into a low looped ponytail. After asking me to bend my head forward, she fits the wig snugly, tucks in my hair evenly at the back and adjusts it. Then she puts the headband on and places the gold collar round my neck.

'What do you think?'

I gaze into the hand mirror she holds up. 'Oh my God, it's brilliant!' Lorna's literally just turned me into the Queen of the Nile. I don't look anything like myself. My eyebrows are arched and defined. I've got shimmering blue and gold eyeshadow on my lids and winged eyeliner sweeping out, making my eyes look huge. She's even done an Egyptian symbol under one eye. I flutter my false eyelashes.

'What about lips?' I ask.

'Ahh, yes! Just some nude lipstick so it doesn't detract from the eyes. Pucker up, dear!'

I purse my lips obediently. She applies some lipstick, blots it, and does another coat.

'Perfect. The transformation is complete. So we've got about five minutes. If you can get into the first pose that you did last week, I'll go down and shepherd everyone up.'

'How many are you expecting?'

'I think maybe six or seven artists today.'

I gulp. 'And what kind of ages?'

'Oh, varying. An eclectic bunch,' she answers vaguely.

I take one last look at myself and follow Lorna out into the studio. 'I'll see you in a bit,' she says. She rubs my shoulders briskly, and I realise how tense I am. 'Relax! You look amazing.'

I take off my robe and try to remember how the first pose went. That's right. Sitting down with my leg drawn up across my body and the other bent at a right angle underneath. Then one arm across my breasts, leaning on my knee, and the other propped up against the side of my face. The pose that doesn't show anything.

I've just settled into it when I hear footsteps outside and Lorna's voice saying, 'Come and meet your model for the day.'

I don't look round but just stare straight ahead, queen-like, as they file into the room. I can feel their eyes checking me out, though. There seems to be a general consensus of approval, and I hear a murmured 'Great make-up!'

Then as the group settle themselves behind the easels, I shift my eyes slowly around the room, looking at them. Lorna's right; it's an eclectic bunch. There's an older man with a grey beard; a girl with her hair in plaits, who has already started sketching; and . . .

Oh my *God*! Nathan is sitting to the extreme left of me. He's chatting with a woman wearing a red muslin top and a matching headscarf. Horrified, I check again in case it's a guy that looks similar. But, even though he's sitting down behind an easel, I can see it's definitely him by his height and what he's wearing. Fucking appointment, my arse! He's a construction worker, an architect, and now an artist too? What next—a Cirque du Soleil acrobat?

I swallow hard and inch my head around, slowly and carefully, away from him. *Shit shit shit.* If he recognises me, it's going to be mortifying. Never mind the fact that he's about to get an up-close and personal introduction to my naked body—not something I particularly want him to have, especially after only one day of living together! I mean, of course there's always the possibility of bumping into someone as they come out of the bathroom after a shower minus a towel, and it's terribly awkward for a few days. But this is completely different. This is going to be him staring intently at me, *every inch* of me—my breasts, my nipples, my crotch . . . drawing me . . .

I feel slightly nauseous. I can't possibly sit here and tolerate that. I'm going to have to try and leave early or make some kind of excuse. Maybe I can pretend to faint from the wig being too hot.

Lorna claps her hands. 'Welcome, everyone! So we've got a new girl with us today. She's done only one previous modelling session so far, but she's already a natural. This is—'

'Cleopatra!' I interject loudly in a deep, sultry voice. The group laughs, and I see out of the corner of my eye that Nathan is smiling. He doesn't seem to be reacting in any way that's out of the norm—namely, standing up and pointing at me in shock and crying out, 'Emma, I know it's you!'

Then I realise with surprise and relief that he's completely and utterly taken in. Unless Lorna accidentally says my name or I speak in my normal voice, he's going to think, for all intents and purposes, that I am Cleopatra.

This thought comforts me somewhat during the next fifteen minutes as I rack my brain trying to figure out what to do. The best and easiest option I can come up with is to say I'm feeling unwell and try to leave. I've thought about pretending to faint, but I'd have to do that in a modest way, like flat on my face. And there's always the chance Nathan will rush over to help, and the wig will come off. So I'm not sure that will work.

When the fifteen minutes is up, Lorna comes over to me and hands me my robe. 'Do you want to do some stretches?'

'Yes, thanks. Er, Lorna, can I talk to you about something in the other room?'

'Of course. I'll be right with you.'

I head to the anteroom, and once inside, I sit down on a chair and stick my head between my legs.

Lorna comes in and immediately rushes over.

'Are you OK?'

'Ah, I'm not feeling too good.'

'Oh no! Something you ate perhaps?'

'Possibly, I had sushi for lunch.'

'Do you feel like you might throw up?'

'Yes, I think so,' I utter weakly. I am starting to feel pretty sick to my stomach.

'Damn. They were paying extra as well.'

'Extra?'

'Yes, I charge this group more since they have a specific request for historical figures. But I won't be able to get anything from them if I cancel it after just one pose.'

I'm torn. I know I'm putting her in a difficult position.

'Well, it might be OK if I lie on my front,' I hear myself saying as I straighten up and look at her. 'It would help with the nausea.' What the hell am I doing? Am I seriously going back out there?

But Lorna is looking thoughtful. 'I guess that could work for the next one. Hopefully, you might start feeling better. You can just close your eyes and relax.'

Somehow, I'm following Lorna back in, and she arranges it so that I'm lying mostly on my front with my legs drawn up in a foetal position and my arms splayed out on either side. I know it probably looks a bit weird, but I'm so happy nothing is on show.

She announces to the group, 'Ah, so we've come up with something a little different for this pose due to Cleopatra not feeling herself at the moment.'

There's a silence as everyone digests this information.

'Has she been bitten by an asp perhaps?' suggests Nathan, and the class titters. My fists clench in annoyance. He's the reason I'm having to do dumb poses!

After the fifteen minutes are up, Lorna comes over and whispers, 'How are you feeling?'

'Much better, thanks,' I whisper back.

She brightens. 'Oh, good! Do you need a break or . . . ?'

'No, I can do the next one.' Fuck it. If they want a proper pose, let's just get this over with.

'OK, if you could just turn this way.'

After she's finished arranging me, I end up reclining on the daybed, propped up on one elbow and with one of my legs crossed in front of the other. I'm staring out at the room haughtily.

'Great, looks like Cleopatra has made a remarkable recovery,' chirps Nathan. God, he's being Mr Comedian all of a sudden. I stare at him witheringly, and he grins. His eyes travel the length of my body, assessing me, and goosebumps prickle over my skin. He notices and raises his eyebrows slightly. Yikes. Luckily, he shifts his attention back to his drawing and doesn't make any more comments. I try and tune him out. He seems pretty absorbed in what he's doing anyway, and I feel like a bowl of fruit again.

When I'm in the anteroom, doing some stretches and grabbing a cup of water before the next pose, Lorna comes in to check on me. 'Still feeling OK?' she enquires.

I smile feebly. 'Getting there, thanks.'

'So for the last pose, how would you feel about doing

this?' She demonstrates, and my mouth drops open. Oh dear God, please, no! 'It would definitely produce some fantastic drawings,' she enthuses.

'I don't suppose I could do something a little less . . . full bodied?'

Lorna smiles encouragingly. 'I think you can handle it. Trust me, you'll feel like you can do anything after you've done this. It's very empowering.'

Somehow, I feel more like I'm going to be sitting in a corner, rocking backwards and forwards. I take a deep breath. It's all just mind over matter. What's fifteen minutes in the scheme of things? Nothing. Besides, Nathan's practically seen everything now anyway.

I gulp. 'OK. I'll do it.'

Lorna beams. 'Good girl!'

Five minutes later, I'm watching the clock and counting down. I'm standing with my legs astride and my sweaty palms pressed together in a prayer position between my breasts. I can't look at Nathan. I just can't. As soon as the pose began, there was a general flurry of excitement as everyone started sketching madly. Lorna was right; it's definitely inspired them.

Finally, it's over, and I realise I'm going to have to hotfoot it home before Nathan gets there. I need to leave. Now. I put on my robe and try and catch Lorna's attention, but she's looking over Nathan's shoulder at his drawing. She glances up and beckons to me. 'Come and have a look!'

I shake my head hastily, tap my stomach, and make a mournful face. Her mouth twists in sympathy. I scurry to the anteroom, throw on my clothes, and yank off the wig. Thank God I've got my sunglasses. I can wear them to hide the eye make-up until I can get home and scrub my eyes. Lorna comes in.

'Sorry to rush off like this. I'm really not feeling well again,' I moan, clutching my abdomen.

'That's all right, I completely understand. Thanks so much for sticking it out, Emma. That last pose you did was just the ticket. I'm sorry you didn't get to see Nathan's drawing. It's quite impressive.'

'I'm sure it is,' I say, edging towards the door. 'I'll see you later!'

'I hope you feel better soon.'

She hands me my envelope, and I stuff it in my bag. I poke my head out the door. Everyone else is now gathered around Nathan and exclaiming over his drawing. Curiosity pricks at me. What on earth has he drawn? But I take the opportunity to make a run for the studio door while they're all distracted.

Unfortunately, Jack is lurking at the top of the stairs waiting for the session to finish, and I can't avoid him.

'Hey, Emma,' he greets me. 'Good timing. You really are showing a lot of promise. I wanted to chat about doing a one-on-one with me. Are you—'

'Sorry, Jack,' I interrupt. 'I really have to get going. Bit of an emergency. I may vomit without warning!' I grab my stomach and make a puking face at him.

'Oh, of course.' He steps back hastily. I fly past him, down the stairs, and out the door.

Chapter 13

CALLUM COOKS MAC AND CHEESE

⁂

I ring Callum on the bus and get his voicemail. So I message him and say I'm staying over. I don't give him a choice in the matter. He messages back five minutes later and says it's fine, but that he's at an open home for the million-pound property, so he'll be back by 4 p.m. at the latest.

Back at the flat, I run around like a woman possessed. I throw work clothes and underwear into an overnight bag while scrubbing furiously at my eyes with make-up remover. The eyeliner Lorna used must be heavy-duty waterproof. By the time I've managed to get it all off, I look like I've been crying for a week or chopped copious amounts of onions. But I can't fuss around. Nathan might walk in at any moment, depending on how many cups of tea and cheese and crackers he stays for.

If he sees my eyes looking like this, he may guess it was me at the studio. No. I need to be totally away from him tonight. It will be nice for him to have the flat to himself anyway. He can just relax and settle in. I write him a flatmate-type message on a pink Post-it Note then look at it critically.

Hi Nathan, I'm staying over at Callum's tonight. Help yourself to anything in the fridge and I have Netflix. See you tomorrow. Emma

It's a bit unfriendly. So I add an exclamation mark at the end and a couple of *x*s after my name. Hmm . . . Maybe it's too friendly now? I don't want him to think I'm coming on to him.

I attempt to change the *x*s into a smiley face. But that looks totally weird now. I screw up the note, dump it in the rubbish, and type a WhatsApp message instead. No *x*s and no smiley faces. I send it as I'm walking to the front door and instantly hear a muffled answering beep. Huh? I check my phone, but there are no messages. Then I realise Nathan's outside and just about to come into the flat. Frantically, I leap into my bedroom just as he unlocks the door.

Wow, that was close! He stands motionless in the hallway, reading the message right outside my bedroom door, while I'm positioned on the other side with my arms akimbo and my head cocked to one side like C-3PO, not daring to move a muscle. I can hear his breathing as he taps out a reply. Just in time, I quickly flick my ringer to 'Off' and his message flashes up on my screen: *Sweet. Enjoy your evening.* ☺

He gives a sigh and goes into his bedroom. *Great,* I think. *Now what?* Maybe I can message him and get him to go to the shops and buy something we're out of. All I can come up with is baking powder. Not exactly an emergency. Unless you're in the middle of making muffins.

Cautiously, I peer into the hallway, trying to see if his door is open or closed. Almost immediately, Nathan comes out of his room, and I see a flash of tanned skin. Quickly, I pull my head back in. Jesus, is he naked? It's too tempting not to look. Fair's fair. He's seen me naked. I peek out and catch a glimpse of his perfectly formed butt cheeks disappearing into the bathroom. Then the patter of the shower starts up. I let out a breath. I have to leave now. Otherwise, I'll be stuck in my room all evening. Pity, though, maybe he wouldn't be wearing a towel coming out of the bathroom either . . .

By the time I get down to the West End, it's nearing 4 p.m., but Callum still isn't home. I check my phone. No messages. I'll just have to camp out on the stoop until he gets here. I remember how Nathan and I talked about running away from home on the bus. Now I am. For tonight at least.

What a bizarre day. First, nearly bumping into Alana. Then Jack's portrait in the gallery. Then Nathan showing up at the life modelling session. Me posing as Cleopatra, then getting stuck in the flat and seeing him naked. I shake my head. I need to come up with a suitable response when Callum inevitably asks what I've been doing today. The truth sounds like something out of a soap opera. I'm busily concocting a believable story when he strolls up the path, looking sleek and businesslike in his coat and suit.

'Hey, stranger! It's been a while,' I say.

Callum stops in his tracks when he sees me. 'Hey, Em. Uh, I just saw you on Friday. It hasn't been that long?'

Hmm . . . weird. It feels like I haven't seen him for weeks. I open my mouth to say something but close it again. I think the less I say, the better.

I stand up, and he kisses my cheek. His face is flushed, and I notice he's sweating.

'Did you run to get here?' I ask.

'No.'

'Your face is all red and sweaty.'

'I didn't run, OK?'

'But—'

'Let's not argue about it on the front steps!' he snaps and opens the door. I follow him into the hallway, slightly stung.

'What's the big deal? Why are you all snippety?'

'I'm not. I just want to relax, and instead, I get harangued.' Harangued? That's a bit of an overreaction. I just asked him if he ran to get here.

'I didn't mean it to sound like that,' I say.

Callum sighs and looks down at me. 'I'm sorry. I've just had a trying day.'

'Oh, yuck. Did you get some annoying people at the open home?'

He rolls his eyes and takes off his coat. 'You could say that.'

I tug on his red silk tie, running it through my fingers. 'Poor you. We could go into the bedroom. I'll help you relax.'

For a minute, he looks tempted, then shakes his head. 'Maybe later on. I need to have a shower.'

Nathan's firm naked buttocks flash into my mind. All of a sudden, I really want to be in the shower with Callum. 'I could join you.'

'I'll just be five minutes. Give me your bag. I'll put it in the bedroom.'

I try not to mind. Callum's usually grouchy after an open home. But just this once, I wish he'd take me in his arms and murmur in my ear, 'Mmm, I'm very dirty. I want you to wash me all over.'

I flop on the couch and close my eyes. Suddenly, I'm immersed in a vivid fantasy of being in my flat and stepping into the shower behind Nathan. I press my wet naked body against his. He doesn't say anything, just hands me the body wash. I pour some out, lather it up, and start soaping his back. Then I run my hands down over the curve of his butt. As he turns around to rinse off, I pour out more gel, lather up again, and start on his chest . . .

I'm so caught up in the fantasy that I don't register Callum's come into the lounge and is asking me a question.

'Sorry, what?'

'I said, so how's it going with Mr Down Under?'

It's a very *clean* fantasy of sorts and hardly pornographic, but I still jump guiltily.

'Uh, fine. He seems to be settling in OK.'

'That's good. Do you want a wine or a snack?'

'You actually have food?'

'Yes, I went shopping.' He looks pleased with himself.

'What the hell?'

'I thought I might cook us something tonight.'

I stare at him in shock. 'You . . . cooking? Do you even know how?'

'Of course! It's not that hard. I just generally choose not to because I'm busy doing other things.'

He heads off to the kitchen and comes back with a couple of glasses of chilled white wine. Ah, OK, I see what's going on. He's got his nose out of joint because Nathan can cook. Now he has to prove himself. 'You don't have to cook, Callum. We can just get a takeaway.'

'I want to. Besides, it's not healthy having takeaways all the time.'

'What are you going to cook?' I ask tentatively. Oh God. Please don't let him tackle something cordon bleu. I don't want to be gnawing on something blackened and inedible at 10 p.m. just because he's trying to compete with Nathan.

'I thought maybe mac and cheese?'

I breathe a sigh of relief. At least Callum knows his limits. Even he can't go too wrong with that.

An hour later, we're in the kitchen. Callum is at the hob stirring what is meant to be a white sauce, and I'm sitting on a bar stool, grating the cheese at the island counter. I wonder idly what Nathan is up to. *Probably ordering a takeaway.*

How ironic. I need to stop thinking about him and heat things up in the West End.

'Phew, it's hot in here,' I comment and take my jumper off. Callum glances round, and his eyes almost fall out of his head.

'What the fuck are you wearing?' he splutters.

'What does it look like?' I reply as I continue grating the cheese. I am in actual fact wearing the tight black nipple hole T-shirt. When I put it on in the bedroom just before, I had to admit it looked pretty sexy. Sian's right. I could probably get him to agree to anything right now.

'You're coming out with some interesting outfits lately, Ms McTavish.' He seems to have forgotten about his white sauce and is staring intently at my bare nipples.

'Shall we have a quick interlude?' I suggest.

'Here or in the bedroom?'

'Here if you like.'

Callum grins and cuts the gas on the hob. He swivels me around, and I arch backwards over the counter so he can lavish my nipples with his tongue. I moan and bury my hands in his hair (being careful not to muss it too much—he hates that). But I'm so ready. I've been ready all day. He pulls my jeans and knickers down until they're completely off and spreads my legs. He unzips his jeans. It's just the right height and angle for him to thrust into me while I wrap my legs around him. I'm so turned on that I come almost immediately and before he does. Which is a first. He groans in my ear soon afterwards, though, and surfaces looking dazed.

'Fuck, that was good.'

'You're very welcome,' I say smugly. He hands me my jeans and knickers. I shimmy into them, still on the bar stool, while he watches. 'That top gave me an instant hard-on.'

I giggle. 'Sian said it would.'

Callum looks taken aback. 'Sian said that?'

'Yeah, she's got good taste in kinky lingerie. She instinctively seems to know what you'll like.' He doesn't say anything, just zips up his jeans and heads back to the hob.

'You don't mind us discussing that kind of stuff, do you? It's just girl talk,' I say, nibbling on some cheese.

'I guess not, as long as you don't go into intimate detail. And I don't want Mr Down Under knowing anything either.'

'We've hardly had time to discuss the food shopping, let alone our sex lives . . . But don't worry,' I add hurriedly, seeing the look on his face, 'I wouldn't say anything to Nathan!'

'Good. I was thinking actually, maybe we should throw him a house-warming party.'

'A . . . party?'

'Yes, to help him meet some more people. He said in the Uber the other night he didn't really know anyone here.'

'That's a nice thought. At my flat, though, not at yours?'

'Of course at your flat. I don't want your friends puking on my carpet.'

'They wouldn't do that!'

He raises his eyebrows. 'Julie?'

'OK, she got slightly hammered that time. But she did make it to your bathroom before she puked.'

'Just.'

'Well, I'll talk to Nathan. Are we thinking next Saturday?'

'Sure. It's a bit short notice, but we probably don't want too many people turning up since we'll have to provide the drinks.'

'Right.' One minute, he wants Nathan to meet people; the next, he doesn't want a large gathering. I can't keep up.

'As for tonight'—Callum holds up a spoonful of congealed white sauce—'I think we should order a takeaway.'

'What about all this cheese?'

He shrugs. 'The mice are going to get lucky.'

I send Nathan a WhatsApp message later that evening to test the water about the house-warming party.

He messages instantly: *Hey! Yeah, I'd be up for it.*

I message back: *Cool we'll send out the invite. What are you doing?*

He replies: *Nothing much. Just chatting with a friend from London. You?*

I type: *Had a takeaway, ate too much. Now slobbing on the couch.*

He comes back with: *Lol. I raided the fridge but only found oat milk and veggies. We need to shop for some real food. ☺☺*

I chuckle.

Callum looks up from his paper. 'Who're you messaging?'

'Oh, just Nathan, to ask him about the party. He's on board.'

'Great. I'll see if Josh and Alex are free.' He picks up his phone.

I screw up my nose. 'You know that Alex is going to be sniffing around Julie all night. She's not interested.'

'He won't. He got the hint well and truly that night we went out on a double date. Though I still think she should give him a chance and get to know him.'

I shudder. Callum's friend Alex works in IT. Since both he and Julie are single, about a month ago, we decided to set them up. The four of us went out to a Middle Eastern restaurant. At first, she was pleasantly surprised since Alex is quite good-looking—until he opened his mouth. Unfortunately, he has no idea how to talk to women and completely rubbed her up the wrong way, saying all kinds of inappropriate and sexist things. Callum insists that he's a really nice guy underneath and just shy around pretty girls. I disagree. I think he's intolerably arrogant and has a chip on his shoulder. Who knows why. Anyway, Julie took a real dislike to him and didn't want to give him her number. Which was fair enough, I thought. But apparently, he was really interested in her, and now he's offended. Go figure.

'Perhaps Josh would be more her type?' I suggest. Josh does something in finance. I've met him only a few times, but he seems nice.

'Maybe. He's been seeing someone at work. But I'm not sure if it's serious. When did you become Julie's fairy godmother anyway? I'm sure she can do all right without your help.'

'She's been single for a while, and there are a lot of frogs out there.'

Callum narrows his eyes. 'Are you saying Alex is a frog?'

'Well, he's hardly a prince! He needs to up his game. He's going to end up single for the rest of his life if he keeps up his "I'm shit-hot" attitude.'

'I'll tell him you said that,' he threatens.

'Don't you dare!'

Chapter 14

ROM-COM GIRL

⁂

In the end, both Alex and Josh are free on Saturday night, as are Julie, Davita, and Lilidh. It's kind of nice on the face of it. Like everyone's eager to convene at my flat to meet Nathan, though I know Davita's keen because of Callum and Alex is keen because of Julie. Callum is keen because he wants to catch up with Josh. Julie and Lilidh are keen because there'll be free food and booze.

Alana is going to be away in Spain for the weekend, and she sounds disappointed she's missing it. I promise that we'll catch up when she gets back. Even Sian said she'll put in an appearance since she hasn't met Nathan yet. I wonder if I should invite his aunt, but Nathan said she's not really into parties. I still haven't found out much about her, except she has an ex-husband who's a biker. I did ask him outright what she does, and he said she worked in an office doing admin or something. I gather he's not that close to her.

By the time Saturday rolls around, there's a core group of eight of us, with a few friends of friends saying they may turn up. I'm not usually a big party person, but I'm actually looking forward to it since I'll know everyone there. I just hate going to parties when you know only one person, and they take off to talk to other people, and you're left trying to make stilted conversation with complete strangers.

Nathan has offered to do the food and said he'll make some classic Kiwi party snacks. I'm not exactly sure what those are. On Saturday afternoon, he's busy in the kitchen, whipping up a bowl of home-made dip, rolling pastry, and baking things that are oozing cheese on trays. So I leave him to it and go round to the bottle shop. Lorna gave me one hundred and sixty pounds for the Cleopatra session. So I've got plenty to get in the basics—beer, red and white wine, cider, and a few bottles of whisky. Callum is also raiding his liquor cabinet. His clients always give him bottles of wine and spirits, which he never drinks, so he says it's a good chance to have a clean-out. If anyone wants anything special, then they can bring it themselves.

When I get back, I stow the whisky in the lounge, then take the rest to the kitchen. Nathan is still cooking madly and waves me away when I ask if he needs help.

Fine, I think, *I'll go and get ready.* But then as I start looking through my wardrobe, I realise that I have absolutely nothing to wear. This isn't strictly true as I have a whole wardrobe of clothes, but they're mainly work clothes and 'hanging round the flat' clothes. Not 'hosting a party' clothes.

In a panic, I message Sian: *Help! Have you got anything I can wear?! I want to look sexy but not slutty.*

She messages back: *Lol. I'm not the right person to ask*

then.

I reply: *You must have something!*

I wait for a while and figure she must be checking her wardrobe.

Sure enough, she says: *I've got a black dress that's slightly too big for me.*

I reply: *Can you send a pic?*

Sian sends through a photo of a black dress on a hanger. I can't exactly see it, but it doesn't look too raunchy, so I type: *OK. Do you want to come round at six and we can get ready together?*

She says: *Sounds fun! See you then – Sx*

I go through my wardrobe looking for a plan B outfit just in case (a) the dress doesn't fit and (b) it is too slutty.

At 5.30 p.m., I wander into the kitchen again and note there are no signs of cooking, and everything's been washed up and put away. Nathan is calmly having a cup of coffee at the kitchen table and reading one of my books. I told him when he moved in that they weren't off limits, and that he could borrow anything he liked.

'Are you OK out here? Is there anything I can do to help?'

'Nah, it's all done.'

I open the fridge and see plastic containers of small pies, mini quiches, cheese-and-bacon pastry swirls, and bowls of dip covered in cling film.

'Gosh, this all looks fantastic!'

'It's actually what I made for Katie's third birthday party, minus the lolly cake,' Nathan says with a short laugh. 'I kind of forgot it's for adults.'

'Don't worry, I'm sure it will all be gobbled up.' My stomach rumbles. 'I'm starving just looking at it.'

'Have some chips—sorry, *crisps*. I bought about ten bags.'

'OK. Oh, by the way, Sian's coming over at six to get ready.' I don't mention she's bringing something for me to wear.

He smiles. 'Cool, I finally get to meet the famous Sian.'

I rip open a packet of salt and vinegar crisps, and we sit there munching in companionable silence.

'What are you reading?'

'Uh . . .' He looks at the cover. '*The Undomestic Goddess*.'

'Oh, I love that! It's one of my favourites. So funny. Which bit are you up to?'

'She's just spent the night at the Giegers' and is in the kitchen freaking out about making lunch for them. The gardener is asking her about vegetables, and she's pretending to make a sauce out of wine.'

I snort. 'Keep reading. It gets funnier.'

'I didn't pick you for a rom-com girl,' he comments.

'Oh?'

'Well, you're a librarian, so . . .'

'So I can't have a sense of humour?'

'I just thought you'd be more into literature.'

'You can class any book as literature in the broadest sense,' I say loftily, taking a handful of crisps.

'I guess.' He doesn't look convinced.

'So why did you pick that one and not *War and Peace*? It's in the bookcase somewhere.'

'Oh, I read that last week.' He catches my eye, and we laugh.

'Sure.'

'What kind of books do you like?' I ask curiously.

'Me? I'll read anything, even girly romances.'

'Do you like happy endings?' I ask without thinking.

He looks at me and smirks. 'Yeah, I do.'

I realise what I've said and almost choke on my crisps. I swallow hard. *Do not react to the innuendo. Do* not *react!*

But I can't help it. A slow blush starts. I've been doing this on and off all week actually. I've noticed Nathan tends to jump on anything I say and twist it into something sexual, even innocuous things. I wouldn't mind usually. But because of the life modelling class and seeing him partly naked, not to mention that I find him extremely hot, well, let's just say it's making things a bit sexually charged.

He sees me looking flustered. 'Sorry, I shouldn't do that. It's a bad family habit. My dad did it, and I seem to have picked it up. It's not appropriate. I'll tone it down.'

'No, it's fine!' I protest. 'It's just hot in here with all the cooking. I think I'll open a window.' I get up, quickly push the nearest window ajar, and take a gulp of fresh air.

I've been on tenterhooks all week as well, worried he's going to have a light bulb moment and realise it was me posing as Cleopatra. I'm thinking he hasn't twigged because I usually wear my glasses around the flat, I have longer hair, and Lorna's make-up was so full-on. But it's still kind of funny and strange that he turned up there. I keep having flashbacks and cringing, then giggling to myself. I'm sorely tempted to go poking around in his room when he's out to find the drawings. But I've resisted so far due to the fact that if he caught me, I'd look like a total snoop.

The buzzer goes. Sian. Perfect timing. I mutter something about letting her in and escape from the kitchen. I poke my head out the door as she comes bounding up the stairs. She's wearing jeans, an emerald-green jersey, and a white puffer jacket. Her blonde hair is tucked up under a pink beanie with a white pom-pom. 'Hey, Em!' she enthuses.

'Hey, Sian.' Weirdly, her energy starts to make me feel drained and stressed, and I sense this party is going to be hard going. Suddenly all I want to do is go to bed early. I wish Callum was here. He's good at being the centre of attention. It means I can flit around the edges and not be noticed.

'Everything OK?' she asks, hearing my lacklustre tone.

'Yes, I'm fine. Just a bit tired after all the party prep. I'll perk up. Come and meet Nathan.' I smile and put an arm around her.

'Ooh, yes!'

We head to the kitchen, where Nathan is still reading. He

puts down the book and gets up immediately.

'Sian, this is Nathan. Nathan, Sian.'

'Gidday,' he says and holds out his hand.

I wait for Sian to have some kind of girly reaction, but she simply shakes his hand and says, 'Hello, nice to meet you finally.'

'Likewise. Thanks for putting me in touch with Emma about the flat.'

'You're very welcome.'

There's a bit more social chit-chat: 'Are you enjoying the flat? How do you like Edinburgh?' That sort of thing. Then we head to my bedroom to get ready.

'So what did you think?' I ask when we're in my room with the door firmly closed.

Sian shrugs and dumps her handbag on the bed. 'He seems nice, laid-back. Kind of what I pictured from what you said.'

OK, I wasn't expecting her to drop to her knees, but I thought she'd be a little more enthusiastic. Surely it's not just me who finds him incredibly hot? I look at her disbelievingly.

'What?' she asks.

'You don't think he's good-looking?'

She sits on my bed and considers. 'Sure,' she replies at last. 'But does it matter how he looks? It's more important he pays his rent on time.'

I take a deep breath, go over to my dresser, and start brushing my hair. She's right. I need to put the males in my life in their correct pigeonholes. Nathan is my *flatmate*.

Callum is my *boyfriend*. I need to keep a fixed solid line between them—not a blurred and wavering one. And I definitely need to exercise more self-control. I can't keep having fantasies about Nathan in the shower. To use his words, 'it's not appropriate'.

Sian nudges my leg with her foot. 'Hello? Earth to Emma.'

I smile feebly at her. 'Don't mind me. I'm just spacing out. It's been a long week. So go on, show me the dress. It better not have holes cut out anywhere dodgy.'

She snickers. 'Trust me, it's very conservative!'

When I put the dress on, I'm not so sure I trust Sian's opinion of what's conservative. It's black velvet, very short and tight with thin straps and a low-cut neckline. The back consists of two criss-crossing straps and an intricate corset-type panel holding it all together. When I come out of the en-suite bathroom, she wolf whistles. 'You really fill that out in all the right places! It always just looked saggy baggy on me.'

'Do you think so? I feel like I'm about to fall out of it. Maybe I should Sellotape it to my boobs or something?'

'It'll be fine. Just don't make any sudden twisting movements. Or bend over. Or walk . . .'

We look at each other and giggle. 'I'll just stand motionless in the corner all evening then. I can move my mouth at least.'

'What time's Callum coming over?' she asks. I check my phone.

'Half six, so he should be here soon.'

'Right.' Sian fiddles with the pom-pom of her beanie, which she's taken off, and I notice she hasn't gotten changed.

'What are you wearing?'

'Uh, I just thought I'd wear this. I'm not sure I'll stay that long.'

'Sian, you can't go casual if I'm wearing this! Put on one of my skirts and a pair of heels or something. Do a sexy librarian look.'

She shakes her head. 'No, honestly, I'm not really in the mood. But I'll do your make-up if you want.'

That's weird. I don't get it. Sian loves dressing up. Maybe it's her time of the month or something. She's just finishing my make-up when the buzzer goes.

'That'll be Callum.'

My stomach tenses as I look at myself in the mirror. I'm now seeing the dress through Callum's eyes, and I know he's going to suggest I change because it's too provocative. We've had discussions (well, more like arguments) about my outfits before. It seems he's fine if I wear BDSM lingerie in private, but he'd rather I dress conservatively in public. In his words, 'I don't want people to think you're a slapper. What you wear reflects on me.' But my flat isn't a public place, so really, why can't I wear what I want?

I hear Nathan let him in, then Callum's voice in the hallway and the clinking of bottles.

Callum knocks on my door. 'Em?'

'I'm just finishing getting ready. I'll be there in a sec!' I call out to him. 'Wish me luck,' I say to Sian. 'Callum's about to come down on me like a ton of bricks.'

'Why? You look hot, Em.'

'That's the problem,' I mutter. 'He wants a lady on the streets and a whore between the sheets.'

I put on my best black stilettos. Then with Sian trailing behind, I march out into the lounge, where Nathan and Callum are busy setting up a makeshift drinks table. 'Anything I can do to help?' I ask.

Both of them turn around, and I'm presented with two men checking me out, but in completely different ways. Nathan's eyes are roving appreciatively, while Callum's are beady with disapproval. 'You can't wear that,' he says immediately. 'There's too much on show.'

'I can wear what I want,' I state firmly. 'Besides, we're not out on the street. It's just a bunch of friends.'

'Emma looks great, Callum,' chimes in Nathan. 'Doesn't she, Sian?'

Wow, Nathan's sticking up for me. I think I may like him even more if that's possible. We all turn to look at Sian, and she nods, avoiding Callum's laser-like glare. Since he's completely outnumbered, Callum has no choice but to back down. His lips press together thinly, and he doesn't say anything. Nathan hands me a bottle of white wine. 'Would you be able to put this in the fridge, Emma, and switch the oven on low?'

'Sure,' I say and walk out of the lounge.

In the kitchen, I lean against the counter and take some deep breaths. Nathan comes in and sees me. 'Are you OK?'

'Yes, just trying to get into my happy place. I should probably go and smooth Callum's ruffled feathers,' I say with a sigh.

He nods, then gets the plastic containers out of the fridge and puts them on the counter. We stand there for a minute, not saying anything. 'Emma—' he begins, and I hear the tone of reproach in his voice.

'Don't say it,' I tell him defensively. 'It is what it is.'

He touches my arm briefly. 'OK. Just . . . please wear the dress. You look fantastic. In fact, if we're dressing up, I may go and put on my suit.'

I give him a cursory smile. 'Now you're talking. And . . . thanks.'

'All good. Remember, if you need to lighten the load, I'm just down the hallway. And I cost less than a registered psychologist.'

I giggle slightly at that, though him thinking that I need counselling because of Callum is a bit sobering. I'm hardly a battered woman!

When I go back out to the lounge again, I catch the last part of a conversation Callum's having with Sian, something about doing an open home tomorrow.

'Oh, is this another one for Camille's property?' I ask.

I haven't been keeping up with his open homes lately. He's been doing a few of them, weekdays and weekends. I haven't actually seen him since last Sunday night. So he's officially broken his rule of seeing me on Tuesdays and Thursdays. *I'm* the one who should be upset, not him.

'Yeah, from two to three tomorrow. I might stay over tonight, though, if that's OK.' He slides his hand into mine and gives it a squeeze, and I relax. I'm forgiven, it seems. But I'm sure the half-empty glass of red wine in his other hand is part of the reason.

'Of course. Sian, what do you want to drink? Did Callum offer you something?' I run my eye over the table. There's an eclectic mix of alcohol on there. I spy bourbon, gin, rum, even a bottle of cognac.

'Yes, he did. Maybe just a Coke?'

'Really? Not even a rum and Coke?'

Sian shakes her head. That's odd. She's never one to refuse a free drink. I glance at her. She's all nervous and twitchy. There's definitely something going on with her. Should I pull her into the bedroom before everyone gets here and ask her what's wrong? Or should I just leave it? The decision is made for me as my buzzer goes three times in quick succession. People are starting to turn up. I resolve to talk to Sian before she takes off, though. Something's not sitting right.

Chapter 15

THE HOUSEWARMING PARTY

⁂

By 7.30 p.m., most people are here apart from Julie, who's running late, and Nathan, who's popped out for a bag of ice at the bottle shop. Everyone's in small groups. Lilidh is telling me about Davita's latest burlesque show, a 1920s review involving feather boas and beaded flapper dresses. Callum is reluctantly talking with Davita and trying to catch my eye to rescue him, and Sian's chatting with Josh and Alex. My buzzer goes again. I open the door for Julie, who hands me her coat and a bottle of wine. She's wearing a white high-necked Victorian blouse, black pants, and red heels. I still can't get used to her hair. It's so different.

'Hi,' she says, then sees my dress and does a double take. 'You look amazing!'

I'm glad I didn't kowtow to Callum. I've been getting a steady stream of compliments since the party started, so I've cheered up. 'Thanks.' I give her a gracious host smile. 'Come and have a drink.'

Julie looks around the lounge, and her nose wrinkles slightly when she sees Alex. He glances over but doesn't recognise her. Maybe she's safe if he's not into brunettes. We head over to the drinks table.

'Where's the Kiwi flatmate?' she asks.

'Oh, he's just gone out to get some ice. He'll be back soon. What would you like?'

She gazes at all the bottles. 'Gosh, that's quite a collection of spirits. Just a red wine for now, thanks. I might save the hard stuff for later.'

I pour a glass for her and one for myself. 'Yeah, you can thank Callum's clients for all that. He's had a clean-out. Hopefully, he's left something in his liquor cabinet for medicinal purposes.'

We start chatting about what she's been up to. She's partway through telling me a work story when she glances over my shoulder and stops mid-sentence. My back is to the door, so I can't see what Julie's looking at. But by the way her mouth is hanging open, I've got a pretty good idea.

'Holy Mary, Mother of God,' she says in a hushed tone. 'Is that him?'

I surreptitiously glance behind me to see Nathan talking with Sian, Alex, and Josh. True to his word, he's wearing his Savile Row suit and a white shirt. My insides do a slow cartwheel.

'Yes, that's Nathan,' I manage.

'How on earth did you convince Callum to let *him* live with you?' She sounds incredulous.

OK, it's not just me. Julie is definitely on the same page when it comes to Nathan's hotness.

'Ah, it's a long story, but Callum may have got the impression that he's gay.'

'Please tell me he's not.'

'He's not,' I answer.

'Is he single?'

'Yes, but . . .'

She lets out a long, slow breath. 'Introduce me.'

'Jules—'

'Shh, he's coming over.'

Nathan approaches, looking like some kind of male model, and I can practically hear Julie's hormones kicking into overdrive. To be honest, I'm having trouble controlling my own. He nods at Julie. 'Gidday.'

'Nathan, this is my good friend Julie Campbell from uni. Julie, Nathan Ellington, my *flatmate,*' I say, emphasising 'flatmate' in the hope that she'll get the hint that Nathan is off limits. But Julie is in serious flirt mode and starts teasing him about his accent. Worse, Nathan, by the way he's grinning amiably, seems to be enjoying it.

I clutch my wine glass so hard I'm surprised it doesn't shatter. Draining what's left, I say I'm going to the kitchen for some water. They don't take any notice, so I sigh and leave them to it. I shouldn't mind. They're both single. So why do I suddenly feel my life isn't worth living?

In the kitchen, I pour myself a large glass of water and gulp it down with a shaking hand. My head is pounding. I desperately need a quick reset before I go back out to the lounge, so I nip into the pantry and shut the door (I'm sure Nigella does this all the time for a zen moment). If anyone discovers me, I'll say I was looking for cocktail ingredients.

I'm doing some deep breathing and trying to be OK with Nathan and Julie hooking up when someone comes into the kitchen and says, 'She's not in here.' It's Sian, obviously looking for me.

I nearly push open the door and cry out, 'Yes, I am! I'm in the pantry!'

But then I hear Callum say, 'Are you coming tomorrow?' So I stand there, listening intently in the darkness.

Sian sighs. 'I shouldn't. It's getting too complicated.'

'Please, Sian. You know it's good,' he wheedles. My blood turns to ice water. What are they talking about?

'It is,' she replies. 'But that doesn't make me feel any better about it.' There's a silence, and I try to see what's happening through the pantry door, but the slats are at the wrong angle.

After a short while, Sian says, 'OK, you convinced me. But we should go. She could walk in and see. Then what would you say?'

Callum whispers something, and Sian laughs softly. They walk out of the kitchen.

What the fuck? I definitely wasn't meant to hear *that*. What the hell is going on? The 'she' in the conversation was undoubtedly me. And what did Callum mean by 'You know it's good'? It must be innocent, surely. But whichever way I look at it, there's no other way I can construe his meaning.

And there's the fact that Sian's feeling bad about it. Then Callum whispering and her laughing—it was intimate. I just know without a shred of doubt what their conversation adds up to—they've been having sex behind my back.

My legs start shaking so badly I have to sit down on the floor. I close my eyes in the darkness. Oh God. Oh God. This is worse than my worst imaginings. Thinking Callum was having an affair with Aisla was bad enough. But Sian? This a whole new level of fucked up. She's one of my best friends . . .

I can't even . . .

I sink sideways until I'm lying on the pantry floor. With my head propped on a bag of flour, I curl up in a tight ball of shock.

After what feels like hours, but is probably in reality only five minutes, I realise I can't stay in the pantry all night. Someone's eventually going to find me. Feeling like I'm in a dream, I open the door and stumble back out to the lounge and stare around dazedly. No one's there. Huh? Is the party over?

I discover everyone congregated in Nathan's room, except Callum and Sian. Julie and Nathan are sitting on the bed with the black leather journal open, and the others are looking at some larger sheets of paper.

'Em! Where've you been? We're checking out Nathan's artwork. It's fantastic,' Julie says.

I meet Nathan's gaze. 'Another slight confession,' he

murmurs, looking embarrassed. Julie grabs my arm and pulls me down on the bed next to her.

'Where's Callum?' I ask. My voice sounds hollow to my ears.

'Oh, Sian had to leave, so he's waiting with her outside until her Uber arrives. Such a gentleman. She tried to find you to say goodbye. What's that in your hair? Dry shampoo?'

He's with her now. I have to physically restrain myself from rushing to the window and peering out.

'Uh, sure, yes.' I run a shaking hand slowly through my hair and a dusting of white flour falls onto Sian's black dress. I trace my finger through it. *Why* on earth has she been helping me dress up and buy sexy lingerie if she's having an affair with him? So I don't get suspicious? I shake my head uncomprehendingly and more flour sprinkles out.

Thank God Callum's not here right now. He'd know immediately something was wrong by the way I'm acting. I have to pull myself together and figure out how to play it. What I want to do, namely stand up, point my finger at him and yell 'Are you fucking Sian?', won't solve anything. He'll just twist it round and say I'm nuts.

Julie flips over the pages of Nathan's journal and I stare at the drawings numbly. There are intricate flowers, characterful people, detailed Edinburgh street scenes. He's definitely talented. I hold my breath, waiting to see if anything resembling me is in there, but I know it will be one of the larger sheets. Sure enough, there's a wolf whistle from

Alex.

'I think I might take up art myself if this is what's on offer.' He holds up the first drawing of me in the pose that doesn't show anything. It's so well executed it takes my breath away. Alex holds up the next one of me on my front. It's good, but I can tell he's disappointed nothing's on show.

'Now this is more like it, Cleopatra in all her glory,' he says, holding up the next one so everyone can see. I'm reclining on the daybed with my breasts exposed. God. Surely they can see it's me. But with the wig and Nathan's detailed depiction of the make-up, they don't make the connection.

Callum chooses that moment to stroll into the room and I stiffen apprehensively, but he doesn't look at me. His eyes are fixed on the drawing. He raises his eyebrows. 'I didn't know you were a life model, Julie?'

Everyone's eyes shift to her. I guess with the dark bob, it's an easy mistake to make.

'It's not me!' she protests. 'Tell him, Nathan.'

'It's not Julie,' Nathan confirms automatically.

I know what's coming, and my heart starts hammering. Alex holds up the final drawing, and there's a collective silence. I just stare at it in awe. I'm fully naked, but there's no vulnerability. The pose makes me look strong, confident, and in control. Completely the opposite of how I feel right now.

'That's fabulous! Whoever she was, she was brave to do it,' says Davita admiringly. 'I mean, I know I dance burlesque, but we do keep something on to protect our modesty.'

'Only a skank would take their clothes off for money,' remarks Callum, wrinkling his nose in disdain. 'And she probably only got a fiver for doing it. The whole thing's pretty squalid if you ask me.'

Little do you know, I think. *It was actually quite good pay.* It's obvious to me he's jealous because Nathan's such a good artist. Typical. He can't get over his own ego to let someone else shine.

'Steady on, mate,' says Nathan, frowning. 'You're making it sound seedy. She wasn't a skank.'

But I can see Callum isn't convinced. He looks at me, mouths 'skank', and grins conspiratorially. However, I've just noticed he has a smear of clear lip gloss on his cheek that looks suspiciously like the one Sian wears. My chest tightens as their betrayal hits me with full force. I can't be in the same room with him . . . I get up and run to the bathroom, where I'm violently ill. And I've only had one glass of red wine.

After that, the party pretty much winds up. Callum bustles around like a mother hen, bundling me into bed and getting me cups of lemon and ginger tea. I hear him explaining to the others in the hallway that it must've been something I ate, and I cringe for Nathan's sake. I need to get him out of the flat so I can think, but he's like a bad odour that won't go away.

'I'm fine. I don't want any more tea, Callum,' I say exasperatedly after the third cup. 'Maybe you should just go home. Is Julie still here?'

'Yeah, she and Nathan are in the lounge. For someone who's gay, he seems to be paying her an awful lot of attention.'

'He's not gay,' I mutter tiredly. He may as well know. Everything seems to be forcing its way into the open tonight.

'Why did you say he was? Now I look like a git,' says Callum in an annoyed voice.

'I didn't. I said he *might* be, and you latched on to it. I just didn't correct you.'

'So you lied to me?'

'Fine. Yes, I lied to you.' *You shit,* I think. I'm itching to have a go at him about Sian, but something holds me back. I guess I'm afraid that if I launch into full-scale attack mode, he's just going to deny it and say I mistook what they were saying. And then I'm going to doubt myself. But I know what I heard.

'You like him, don't you?' Callum asks suddenly.

'Well, yeah. I wouldn't have chosen him otherwise.'

'I mean you're attracted to him.'

Wow, he's got a nerve. He's fucking my friend behind my back, and he's accusing me of being attracted to Nathan (he is pretty much right, but still . . .).

I shake my head.

'It's a moot point anyway.' He takes off his jeans and polo shirt and gets into bed.

'What do you mean?'

'From what I saw in the lounge, he looked very much into Julie.'

That's it then, I think morosely. *He'll go to her place, sleep with her, and then they'll be a couple.* And I'll have to put up with it. To be honest, the thought of Nathan and Julie together is depressing me more than Callum and Sian.

The next morning, I wake up early after a night of tossing and turning. I feel like I've had a hard night on the tiles. Callum's sleeping peacefully beside me without a care in the world. How can he do that? He must've justified the affair in his head. That it's just sex and doesn't mean anything. From the conversation I heard, I assume they're getting together after the open home and using the bedroom or kitchen or whatever there. It would explain why he was so red-faced and sweaty after the one last week and why he didn't want me asking questions. I'm nauseous again just thinking about it.

Bleary-eyed, I put on my robe and drag myself out to the kitchen to get a cup of tea. I make some toast, smear it with butter and jam, and I'm half-heartedly nibbling it at the table when Nathan walks in.

'Mornin'.'

'Oh!' I'm so surprised to see him I almost drop my toast.

'You OK?'

'I thought you'd left to go to Julie's?'

'Nah. She offered, but it was getting late, and she lives in

Leith.'

'Right . . . So did she stay over instead?'

He pops two slices of bread in the toaster and leans against the counter looking at me. 'No, Mum, she didn't stay over.'

My relief is instantaneous. 'Why not?' I persist.

Nathan raises his eyebrows at me and I know I'm getting into 'none of your business' territory. He shrugs. 'She made it clear she wanted to. But I'd rather get to know her first, once bitten and all that. We're going out on a date.'

'Please don't sleep with her!' I blurt before I can stop myself.

Nathan's gaze intensifies and I shift uncomfortably.

'It's just a walk in the Meadows. But since we're on the subject, why shouldn't I?' he questions at last.

'I just don't think it's a good idea,' I mumble, looking down at my toast. He doesn't say anything, and I finally raise my eyes to meet his. The look that passes between us is so scorching I feel like I might be burned alive.

'Callum's probably awake by now,' Nathan says, not moving his eyes from mine. I know he's trying to keep me on track. To remind me I have a boyfriend. But all I want is for him to take me into his bedroom and shut the door so I can escape the nightmare I'm in.

Chapter 16

JACK AND LORNA

⁂

After that scene at the kitchen table, Nathan makes some toast and tea and has breakfast in his room. He doesn't say anything, but I sense he knows I've got the serious hots for him. The snapping electric current between us is now hovering just below the red 'danger' mark. But being the opposite of Callum, basically a decent person, I know he won't make a move. However much he might want to.

I don't particularly want him to think I'm a two-timing bitch either, but I can't say anything to him about Callum and Sian until I've seen it with my own eyes. Which is why I've decided to catch them in the act at the open home today. It's the only way that Callum's ever going to admit to it. Otherwise, it's going to be endless rounds of me accusing him and him placating me with dinners, jewellery, and lies dressed up as the truth until I'm back where he wants me—under his thumb. And what it all boils down to is plain and simple: I just don't trust him anymore.

The problem is, how am I going to do it? It's not like I can set up CCTV cameras in the bedrooms. The only way I can think of is to wear a disguise, hide in one of the wardrobes, then jump out with an 'Aha! Caught you!' and take a photo. I know, it's not ideal. Plus, I'm not sure if I can bear seeing them together. But what other choice do I have?

Since I'm doing another modelling session for the retirees beforehand, I can ask Lorna if she doesn't mind me borrowing one of her wigs. Then I can buy some clothes at one of the charity shops, wear sunglasses, and pretend to be a rich middle-aged American. I can do that accent pretty well.

To be honest, Callum's not stupid. There's a good chance he'll recognise me. But I have the element of surprise on my side. He's not expecting to be caught. There's also part of me that doesn't really believe that they are having an affair. That I've conjured it up because, deep down, I don't want to be with Callum anymore and it's a convenient way of letting myself off the hook. Otherwise, I'd have to break up with him, and I'll be the bad guy.

All this is going through my head as I'm doing the life modelling session. It's the same retirees as last time, minus Mrs Fraser, who has a cold, apparently. The poses aren't too nerve wracking either, just one that involves a full frontal. But after the Cleopatra session, I'm not bothered. I seem to have become desensitised to people staring at my body. In a weird way, it's starting to make me feel less self-conscious.

Lorna, of course, is effusive with praise and only too

happy to lend me a wig after the session.

'Yes, that's fine, as long as you bring it back next week, dear. Are you going to a fancy dress party?'

'Er . . . yes.' I think quickly. 'It's a US movie theme. I thought I might go as Meryl Streep from *The Devil Wears Prada*.'

'Oooh, what fun!' She looks through the chest and pulls out a short white-blonde wig. 'What about this one? I've got a pinstripe suit and a fur you can wear as well if you want. Have you got a white shirt?'

'Yes.' It occurs to me Lorna hasn't seen me in many clothes because I'm usually wearing a robe—or naked.

'Come and have a look in my wardrobe. We'll let the others have a cup of tea and chat with Jack.'

I don my leggings and sweatshirt and follow her along the hall to their bedroom. It, like the rest of the house, is stuffed to the brim with his antique purchases.

I can't help looking at the bed. It's king-sized. They definitely sleep together. Not in separate beds or rooms. Then I notice a massive framed painting hanging above the bed. It's of a naked blonde woman lying on a green chaise longue wearing just a gauzy scarf.

'Lorna!' I exclaim in astonishment. 'Is that you?' She looks gorgeous. I can see why Jack fell for her.

'Yes, dear,' she replies. 'It was about twenty years ago, when Jack still wanted to paint me. Now he just wants to paint pretty young things.' She laughs without a hint of jealousy. *Wow, she really trusts him,* I think. There's no way I'd leave Callum alone in a studio with a naked woman.

'How old were you in the painting?' I ask.

'It was a fiftieth birthday present.' So I was right—she's seventy.

I can't help it. I have to know. 'How did you and Jack get together, if it's not too personal a question?'

'It's a bit of a complicated story, dear. But I don't mind telling you if you want to hear it.'

I nod.

We sit on the bed, and Lorna takes a deep breath. 'So I first met Jack when I was in my late forties. He was a friend of my son, Niall. Jack was at art school and looking for life models. I was divorced from Niall's father and working as a secretary. I guess I was bored and wanted something more creative in my life. So I posed for Jack. The first time was nerve-racking, but he made me feel so comfortable and beautiful. I enjoyed his company too. We would chat as he worked. Have a laugh. Eventually, one thing led to another, and we fell in love.

'At first, I didn't tell Niall, but he found out and was very angry about it. Sadly, no matter how much we tried to talk him round, he couldn't accept that we were together. His friendship with Jack disintegrated, as well as his relationship with me. He didn't come to our wedding.' She looks down and plays with her wedding ring.

'So do you have any contact with him now?' I ask.

Lorna shakes her head. 'I'm hoping one day we will, but it doesn't look likely since it's been over twenty years. I've phoned, written letters, sent Christmas presents. He just ignores it all. He has a family of his own, two teenage girls. I haven't met them.'

I'm speechless. How awful. Poor Lorna. I thought her relationship with Jack might be controversial, but not to this extent. I don't know what to say, except 'I'm so sorry.'

'It's OK. I'm used to it by now. But it's still hard.'

'I'm sure it is. I can't believe he's that determined not to talk to you.'

Lorna smiles thinly. 'He gets it from his father. Graham was as stubborn as a mule. If he thought he was in the right, he wouldn't back down. Even if it killed him.'

I have to wonder if Jack was worth the angst.

'So even with the estrangement from your son, you have no regrets being with Jack?'

'No, I love him,' she declares staunchly. 'He's the best thing that ever happened to me.'

'And you trust him even though he's painting naked women and . . . er . . . naked men?'

'I know it sounds strange, but I do. He's incapable of telling a lie and getting away with it. If he was up to anything, it would be written all over his face. I'd know instantly.'

I wish Callum was that transparent. If he were, I wouldn't be contemplating dressing up as Meryl Streep.

'Anyway, enough about my messy life. What about you

and that boyfriend of yours? Does he know you're doing life modelling yet?' she asks.

'Things have gotten slightly more complex in that arena.' I take a shaky breath. 'I think he's having an affair with one of my friends.' Saying it out loud makes it all seem very real.

'Oh no, you must be devastated!'

I shrug. 'I'm OK. I'm dealing with it.'

Lorna looks doubtful. 'Are you though? How long have you been with him?'

'Two years.'

'I'm not sure you can be with someone for two years without feeling some kind of grief.'

'I was shocked but now I'm just angry that he's been carrying on behind my back and lying to my face. Maybe I'm not at the grief stage yet.'

'Obviously if you're going to a party tonight?'

'It's more of a disguise so I can catch them in the act.'

Lorna looks doubtful. 'Is that a good idea? Can't you just talk to him?'

'He'll deny it,' I state flatly. 'Unlike Jack, he's an excellent liar.'

Armed with the wig, a fox-fur coat, and a black-and-white pinstripe suit, I head back to the flat. Somehow, with this get-up, I have to convince Callum I'm a middle-aged American woman who's stinking rich. It's such a risky plan I'm tempted to forget the whole idea and just dump him by WhatsApp.

But the thought of catching him with his pants down is justice for the last two years of my life. I want to see the look on his face and hear how he's going to get out of it. A hot ball of fury is bouncing around my gut. Oh yeah, I'm definitely in the fucked off stage.

I've just opened the flat door and am in the hallway when Nathan comes out of his room. He eyes the pile of clothes in my arms. 'Been charity shopping? I thought you were trying to declutter?'

'Hah,' I say and awkwardly try to scuttle past him. But the fur coat is quite large, the hallway narrow, and Nathan's not a small guy. After a short scuffle and several instances of 'No, please, after you', I end up pressed up against the wall, laughing. He grapples with the coat as it slithers about in my arms.

'I hope this isn't real fur,' he teases. 'The animal activists will be after you.'

'I think it is actually. It's fox. Well, several foxes.'

He tsks and says, 'Poor foxes.' He strokes the coat and accidentally happens to brush my forearm with his warm hand. I immediately stiffen as a tingle of pleasure shoots right up to my shoulder. Nathan looks at me and doesn't say anything, then runs his finger lightly but purposefully down my forearm.

'You probably shouldn't do that,' I say breathlessly. But I want him to, so I quickly add, 'Or keep doing it. Whatever.' I try to sound nonchalant, but my heart clomps in my chest and my breath comes out in a shallow gasp as Nathan gently and deliberately strokes back up my arm. His light touch sends a shivery feeling through me and I stare at him wide-eyed and vulnerable, like a fox that's about to be made into a fur coat. He avoids my gaze but then I see him bite his lower lip in consternation. It's such a sexy expression that I almost pull him towards me and kiss him right then and there.

Fuck, I'm about to get completely out of control here. I press back hastily against the wall, a steady pulse of longing throbbing between my thighs. The fur coat slips over my arm effectively pushing his hand away, and Nathan immediately takes a step back. He leans against the opposite wall breathing heavily.

'Ah, sorry, that was . . .' he winces and rubs his hand over his face and then through his hair so the front part sticks straight up. He looks as guilty as hell so I know he was going to say was 'that was wrong of me'.

'Look, maybe we should have a talk,' he says abruptly, a slight frown marring his smooth forehead.

I let out a breath. Talking. Not kissing. Part of me is relieved; the other is mightily disappointed. But then—shit. Talk about *what* exactly? Is he thinking of moving out immediately because of what just happened?

'Ah . . .' I check my phone. It's getting on for 2 p.m. 'Can we do it later—I mean, talk later?' I ask, flushing. 'I have to go out.' He looks pained, and I know it sounds like an excuse to get away from him. 'What time's your date with Julie?' I question, trying to be practical.

'Three, but I really think we should—'

'We definitely will. Soon!' I respond, then grip the fur coat firmly and dart into my bedroom, out of the circle of temptation.

'Emma—' I hear Nathan say behind me, but I shut the door and lean against it, my chest heaving. It's a flimsy barrier between me and the superhot guy in the hallway. I'm flipping between unbridled joy and crippling angst: He likes me, oh my God, he likes me! I can't have him, oh my God, I can't have him!

Calm down, I tell myself sternly. *Technically, you're still with Callum, and you don't want to drag Nathan into that mess.* And what about his ex and daughter?

Besides, I can't think about all that now. I have to get dressed up like Meryl Streep and catch my boyfriend cheating. As you do.

Chapter 17

RAPUNZEL

✳

I have to admit, as I'm on the bus heading towards Dundas Street in the New Town, that not even my own mother would recognise me. I hardly recognise me. The suit fits perfectly. The fur coat looks elegant. And I'm wearing a leopard-print silk scarf, dangly (fake) diamond earrings, and Jackie O sunglasses—all courtesy of Lorna. I've also caked-on the foundation, gone heavy-handed with the blusher, and applied several layers of red lipstick. I'm earning a few stares, but I'm hoping it's because I look posh (or slightly like Meryl Streep), not because my wig's on crooked.

When I get to the address I looked up on Duncan Stratt's website, I'm buzzed in by a young female voice. It would have to be on the top floor, so I'm overheating in the fur by the time I make it up the gazillion stairs.

Standing outside the imposing dark-green door, breathing heavily, I try to compose myself and get my story straight before I make my entrance. I wish I'd brought a compact mirror along so I can check my make-up hasn't slid down my face. Hopefully it's still intact.

I press the doorbell, and the catch gives a click. Upon

entering, I see that there are three pairs of black brogues and a pair of nude heels lined up neatly by the door. This is good; it means I can blend in with the other millionaires who are viewing the property. However, it does mean I'm going to be without my power heels, something Meryl would frown upon, I'm sure.

Reluctantly, I take them off, stuff them in my handbag, and walk down the parquet hallway in my stockinged feet. It's brightly lit and lined with abstract artworks. I really need to get something up in my hallway. Maybe I could hang Nathan's drawings of me as Cleopatra. I give a small snort as I reach the kitchen, which attracts the attention of a blonde girl who's standing behind the counter. Callum isn't there. I gather he's showing the other people around. Perfect.

'Hello and welcome to the viewing,' she says. 'If I could just get you to fill in your details, that would be wonderful.' She hands me a clipboard and smiles beatifically.

I look at her properly, and my insides give a small hop. It's Aisla, from Camille's agency, dressed in a smart navy suit with a crisp white shirt underneath. Of course Camille has better things to do on a Sunday than sell properties, so she's sent her skivvy to help Callum.

'Why, thank ya, darlin',' I drawl. Aisla's eyebrows raise slightly when she hears the American accent. Her eyes travel over the fur coat and rest on my fake Prada handbag, then head up towards my face. I'm sweating profusely, so I hope to God my make-up is intact.

Quickly, I write my fake details in small neat capitals while she watches: *Diana Prendergast, Florida*. I jot down a fake mobile number and hand the clipboard back to her.

'Lovely.' She brightens when she sees where I'm from, and I can almost hear her thinking 'ka-ching'. 'Now if you come this way, I can give you a tour of the wee property, Ms Prendergast.'

I glance around. The open-plan kitchen is three times the size of mine, and the dining room has a mezzanine glass floor. There's nothing wee about this place at all.

'Oh, I don't wanna be any trouble,' I say, extending the word so it comes out as 'traaaubble'. I have no idea if this is a Florida accent at all. But Aisla seems to be swallowing it hook, line, and sinker.

'Och, it's no trouble,' she insists. 'I'd be happy to.'

Damn. This is working too well. But, at least it's her and not Callum showing me around. I might start giggling hysterically otherwise.

We're on the second floor, and Aisla's pointing out the features of the master bedroom (which has a walk-in wardrobe, an en suite with a Jacuzzi tub, and smart shades that can be raised or lowered using an iPhone app) when Callum strolls in. He's dressed impeccably in a dark-blue suit (the same shade as Aisla's) and a white shirt. They're like clones. The only difference is he's wearing a maroon silk tie with a gold tie clip. He looks slick, handsome, and ready to make a sale. My heart sinks. I can't do this. He's going to see right through me. I have to get out of here.

Aisla is prattling on about the Saxony carpet, and Callum waits patiently for her to finish. I can sense him checking me out.

'Callum, this is Diana Prendergast from Florida.' She turns to me. 'Ms Prendergast, Callum Stewart is the agent from Duncan Stratt handling the property.'

Callum gives me his bland realtor smile. 'Pleased to meet you,' he says formally without a glimmer of recognition. 'What are your impressions of the flat so far?'

'Oh my gaad,' I exclaim, trying to inject the correct amount of enthusiasm. 'It's totally amazing! Mervin—that's my husband—well, he's just going to die when he sees it.'

Callum nods. 'Yes, it's one of our premier properties. I'm not expecting it to be on the market very long. Has Aisla shown you the roof terrace?' She shakes her head. 'I'll do that now. You can go back downstairs, Aisla,' he says smoothly, relegating her to the ground floor to man the buzzer. 'If you'd like to come this way,' he adds to me.

Great. How am I going to give him the slip now? Callum leads me along the hallway to a door and a narrow set of stairs, which I've got no choice but to climb up ahead of him. They open out onto a sizeable wooden deck with a few potted plants, some folded-up deckchairs, and views overlooking the Royal Botanic Garden. I'm beginning to wish I was rich enough to afford this place. But it is freezing and blowing a howling gale, so I'm not sure how much time I'd spend sunbathing up here. I wrap the fur coat around me tightly. Even Callum's carefully gelled hair is starting to tremble in the strong gusts of wind.

After letting me exclaim about the views, he suggests we go back down to the kitchen. On the way, he takes the opportunity to tell me about the excellent eco-friendly central heating system. I 'Mmhmm' and 'You don't say, darlin'?' where appropriate. When we get back to the warmth of the kitchen, Aisla is there shuffling business cards and trying to look busy.

'So what brings you to Edinburgh?' Callum enquires. 'It can't be the tropical weather, surely.'

I proffer a tight-lipped smile and give him the spiel. 'Oh, Mervin often comes over for work. He does something in corporate finance.' I wave a hand airily as if it's all too boring for me to care about. 'We're looking for a base here. Our holiday home in France isn't practical for the commute.'

Callum raises his eyebrows slightly. 'Do you have children?' he asks. 'Just that there are five bedrooms—'

'We do,' I interject. 'But grown-up now, of course.'

'Really?' He pauses, scanning my face intently and I know he's trying to figure out my age without intending to insult me. The large sunglasses aren't helping him. 'Strange,' he comments, frowning. 'You look . . .' And for a sickening stomach-churning second, I think he's recognised me, but he just says, 'Hardly more than forty.'

I relax and force a merry little laugh. 'Why, thank ya, darlin'! That's very sweet of you. I do have a very good Botox aesthetician. As for the bedrooms, we need them for our overseas visitors.'

Callum's forehead smooths in relief, and without missing a beat, he trots out, 'Well, the property is ideally set up for guests since there are en-suite bathrooms in every bedroom.'

Nice, I think. He's ticking all Diana's boxes.

I'm just about to make up some waffle about where our guests hail from when the buzzer goes. Callum checks his Apple Watch, and I happen to see the time: 2.50 p.m. There's another ten minutes of the open home left. My stomach clenches nervously. Is it Sian arriving for their rendezvous?

A middle-aged couple appears in the kitchen in overcoats minus their shoes, and I relax. Not Sian. Not yet.

'Excuse me,' Callum says, then goes to greet the couple.

'I might just have another look in the master bedroom, darlin',' I say quickly to Aisla. 'To check the size of the walk-in wardrobe—I have an *obscene* number of shoes! I can let myself out.'

'Of course, do you want me to . . . ?'

'No, no. I can find my way.'

'OK, well, thank you for coming to the viewing, Ms Prendergast. Callum will be in touch,' she says with a business-like smile.

I smile back and nod, and she heads over to the couple, who are exclaiming about the glass mezzanine floor. No one notices as I leave the room and swiftly run upstairs. Earlier, I spotted a storage cupboard in the hallway that would make a perfect hiding spot.

The cupboard is roomy, but dusty and full of old Manila folders. I've had to stifle two sneezes already in the five minutes I've been in here. I don't have to wait too much longer before Callum comes by with the couple to show them the bedrooms. Luck is on my side as Aisla's with them, leaving downstairs unattended. There's a smaller spiral staircase off the mezzanine that leads to the kitchen and the main door, so I'm hoping they'll think I've gone down that and left.

It's well after 3 p.m. by the time the couple leaves, and I hear Aisla say to Callum in the hallway, 'I'll just do a quick check to make sure everything's in order.'

He says, 'OK, thanks. Is the American still here?'

'I don't think so. She must've left when we were with the last two. What did you think?' she asks.

'She's probably our best bet, but I'm picking it's the husband who holds the purse strings. I'll have to work on him.'

Huh? I think, bristling. *How do you know? Diana might have her own money independently of Mervin.*

Callum walks off, and the crack of light under the door disappears. I hear a few more switches being flicked. He seems to be turning off all the lights, which is odd. *Do they do it in the dark?* I wait for a bit longer, but I can't hear anything. If Sian arrives and they come upstairs to a bedroom, I'll definitely know about it. Unless they get it on downstairs. That's highly likely actually. Callum does have a thing for sex in the kitchen. I'm unsure what to do. After another five minutes of sweat pooling in my armpits, and an impending leg cramp, I cautiously edge open the cupboard door and poke my head out. It's pitch-black and quiet in the hallway. I listen, but I can't hear any voices.

I switch on my phone torch, creep along the hallway, and shine it into the master bedroom. Nothing. Perhaps they're in one of the smaller ones? No. They're all empty too. Downstairs in the kitchen, my toes curl on the cold black marble floor. It's quiet apart from the faint drone of traffic from the street below. Aisla and Callum have gone. There's only me standing here in the slowly fading afternoon light. Now I'm really confused.

Wasn't Sian meant to be coming over? Maybe he didn't mean the open home. Perhaps they're meeting somewhere else, like at his flat before I come round? Yes. It makes much more sense. I curse my lack of foresight.

I pad in my stockinged feet to the front door and turn the knob, but the door doesn't move. I yank at it, wondering why it's not opening, then realise in shock that Callum has double-locked the door. If I don't have the key, there's no way I can get out. Fuck.

After a few minutes of sheer, unadulterated panic, I tell myself to calm down. I'm not going to die here. All I need to do is think like Bear Grylls and take stock of my surroundings. There's water in the taps, and there may be food too. I stride to the fridge and pull it open. It's empty apart from a large bottle of sparkling mineral water. I fling open all the cupboards. Nada. Not even a box of crackers.

Well, OK. I've also got at my disposal a mobile phone charged at eighty percent. I can call someone to get me out. Hmm . . . The obvious choice is Callum since he has the key, but that's not happening. Camille? OK, I can't actually call anyone in relation to the flat since it will get back to Callum.

Maybe there's a fire escape. I poke my head out the lounge windows to find it's a sheer drop to the street below. *Too bad if there was a fire,* I think. I could feasibly call 999, but if firemen break the door down, then I'll have to pay for it. And answer to Callum.

A locksmith? It's late Sunday afternoon. No locksmith in his right mind will be working now. After a while of coming up with nothing but blanks, I'm starting to panic again. The open home is only on weekends. So unless someone makes an appointment to view it during the week, I could be here until next Saturday—without food. I'd have to ring Callum at some point, and the thought of that is excruciating.

There's only one person I can call who may know what to do. My finger hesitates over Nathan's number. It's bad form. He's on a date. But I have to ring him. He'll worry if I don't show up tonight.

'Hey, how's it?' he answers straightaway. I can't hear footsteps or leaves rustling, just a faint clinking.

'Hi. Sorry to disturb you on your walk.'

'It's OK. We've had it. We're in Söderberg. Julie's at the counter, ordering coffees.'

'Right. Uh . . . So I'm kind of locked in an apartment in New Town. I thought you should know. In case I don't show up for a few days . . . or a week.' A sob escapes before I can hold it in.

I hear a scrape of a chair and Nathan saying something in a muffled voice. Then he comes back on the line.

'I've gone outside. What's happening? Are you OK?' He sounds worried.

'I'm fine. I just did something dumb.'

'Tell me.'

I give him the shortened version of events, but I have to include the fact that I think Sian and Callum are having it off and I was trying to catch them at it. Otherwise, it doesn't make sense. He gives a grunt, which I'm not sure how to interpret.

'You'll have to ring him to let you out,' he says at last.

'I can't. I just really . . . I can't.'

'Fine. I'll come over. There might be a spare key under the doormat or something.'

'But you're busy.'

'Never mind that. What's the address?'

'I'll WhatsApp it to you.'

'OK, I'll be there in half an hour. I'll buzz you when I'm outside. You can let me into the building, eh?'

'Yes.'

I hang up and message him the address. I sink into the dining room couch, giddy with relief that Nathan knows. And yes, I'm also a teensy bit flattered that he's run out on his date with Julie to come to my rescue. Suddenly I'm Rapunzel in the tower, waiting for her handsome prince.

The apartment buzzer jolts me out of a low blood sugar doze. The entry system has a small camera that shows me an image of Nathan peering into the lens. 'Hi, come up. It's the top floor.'

He grins wryly. 'It would be, wouldn't it?'

I station myself by the door and wait for him to climb the stairs. I'm pretty sure there is a doormat, but I'm trying not to get my hopes up that there's a key under it. Eventually, there's a tap on the door and the sound of heavy breathing. 'Emma?' Nathan calls from the other side of the door. 'Can you hear me?'

'Yes. Any luck with the spare key?'

'I just looked. Nothing there.'

'Shit. Any other bright ideas?'

There's a silence. 'I could try and pick the lock.'

'Seriously?'

'Yep, I'll give it a go anyway.'

'Do you have any tools?' I query doubtfully.

'Yeah, I went back to the flat and grabbed some tools.'

He sounds like he knows what he's doing. Soon there's metallic clinking noises coming from the lock. Next Nathan drops something and swears. Then he calls out to me, 'Emma, can you try opening it now?'

With my heart in my mouth, I turn the knob. By this point, I'm praying to God, Buddha, and Allah.

It doesn't open. Arrgh! I kick the door in frustration but only succeed in stubbing my toe, which hurts like hell.

'Stink one,' Nathan calls out. 'We'll have to come up with something else.'

I'm not sure how he can sound so calm about it.

'Like what exactly? Look, you tried your best. Just leave me. I'll be fine. I'm sure there'll be another open home in a few days.'

'What are you going to do about food? Is there anything to eat?'

'No, but I could order a takeaway and tie some bed sheets together and haul it up through the window.'

Bear Grylls would totally do that!

Nathan snorts. 'Now there's a plan.'

'It wouldn't hurt me to lose a few kilos anyway,' I joke.

There's a silence, then a soft, 'Nah, then there would be less of you to like.'

My blood fizzes like a just-shaken Coke bottle at hearing that, and suddenly I'm very aware of his presence barely a metre away. I rest my flushed cheek against the door, and Nathan's voice reverberates next to my ear through the wood, like he's doing the same. 'Who's the owner?' he asks.

'Some guy from London. That's all I know.'

'Is there any paperwork lying around?'

'Possibly. I could look. Why?'

'I was thinking if you had his number, you could pretend to be another Duncan Stratt agent and ask him if there's a spare key.'

'Wouldn't he think that was really weird?'

'Just poke around and see if you can find anything. I'll have another go at the lock.'

After rootling around in the Manila folders in the dusty cupboard, I discover a bunch of old bills addressed to a 'Dean Redgrove' and some paperwork from a year ago to do with renting out the flat. There's a mobile number listed for him. So after coming up with something to say and taking a few deep breaths, I call it.

He answers on the second ring with a clipped 'Yes?'

This throws me a bit, but I launch in with 'Allo, iz thees Meester Reedgrove?'

For some reason, I've decided that putting on a French accent is an excellent tactic.

But just as he says 'Yes, this is he', there's a solid thunk. The door swings open, and I find myself looking up into Nathan's sweaty grinning face. He has a smudge of grease on his forehead. Oh my God, he did it!

'Hello?' Dean is still on the line, and I drag my attention back to him. Shit. Change of plan.

'Uh . . . Oui, thees iz Emilie. We 'ave your dry cleaning. Zere iz a veery large tomato keetchup stain on your shirt. Eet iz 'orrible.'

There's a beat of disbelief. 'You're calling me on Sunday night about a tomato ketchup stain?'

'Oui, eet iz veery urgent. Eet will cost extra to feex.'

'How much?' Dean queries.

Nathan is staring at me with an amused expression. 'Wrap it up!' he mouths.

'Ahhh, fifty pence, I theenk. Veery sorry, meester, I 'ave to go. Au revoir!'

Chapter 18

BIRTH OF VENUS

⁂

'Oh my God! Thank you, thank you!' I throw my arms around Nathan.

'No worries. Second time lucky.' He hugs me tightly. 'Learning how to break into West Auckland houses when I was a teenager has come in handy.'

'Oh!' I'm a bit shocked.

'I'm joking! I looked it up on YouTube once to unlock my own front door. It seems I'm out of practice, though.'

'You're full of surprises.'

'So are you.' He touches the wig, which I'm still wearing. For a moment, I think he's going to make the connection with Cleopatra. But he just says, 'Emilie.'

I give a half giggle and a half sob.

We walk to Princes Street in the gathering darkness. I've never been so glad to see traffic, lights, and people in all my life.

Nathan holds my hand on the bus going back like I'm a small child who needs supervising. I'm still wearing the fur coat, but I've taken off the wig and scrubbed at my face with a tissue. I can't help staring at him adoringly every few moments.

'Stop looking at me like that,' he says, embarrassed. 'It was nothing.'

'My hero! Is there any end to your proficiency?' I remark. 'I'm going to have to make it up to you somehow.'

He looks down at our joined hands, and I notice he doesn't twist my words into an innuendo.

'What did Julie say when you left?' I ask.

'Nothing. I told her it was an emergency, but she didn't look convinced. I'm in the doghouse there.'

I squeeze his hand. He hasn't asked me anything about Callum and Sian, and I haven't talked about it. I don't really want to.

We get off in Bruntsfield Place, and it's a short walk back to the flat, but he doesn't let go of my hand. I look up at him. 'I'm not going to run away.'

'You might,' he says in a teasing tone. 'I'm keeping hold of you until we get inside.'

I'm not going to argue. My small cold hand is enveloped in his large warm one, and it's incredibly comforting. I could walk the streets all night like this with him. But my energy boost is short-lived. As soon as we reach the flat, I flag with exhaustion.

'I'll make you something to eat,' Nathan offers. 'Why don't you hop into your jim-jams.'

I'd laugh if I weren't so knackered.

'Jim-jams, right. On it, sir.' I give a little salute and go to my bedroom. Then I curl up on my bed for a good five minutes with my eyes closed. I can't believe Nathan managed to get me out of the apartment. I'm catatonic with relief. My phone beeps, and without thinking, I reach a hand into my bag to check it.

Callum has left me a couple of messages. The usual: *Are you coming over tonight?* about half an hour ago, and another just now: *Are you ignoring me?*

I throw my phone back in my handbag. I can't deal with him right now.

There's a soft knock on the door. 'Do you want to come out or eat in your room?'

'I'll come out.'

I put on a clean pair of white cotton pyjamas and my bathrobe, tying it tightly.

The kitchen is almost too bright for my tired eyes. I squint at the table, which is laid for two. Nathan's made scrambled eggs, a stack of wholewheat toast dripping with butter, and cups of tea. Suddenly I'm starving hungry.

'Mmm . . . good,' I mumble between bites of toast and egg.

We munch away without looking at each other. Then Nathan finally pushes his plate to the side. 'Have you heard from Callum?'

I flinch at his name. 'Yes, he messaged, wanting to know if I was going over to his place tonight.'

'Did you reply?'

'No,' I answer grumpily.

'You're going to have to talk to him eventually.' His tone is gentle, but there's an edge of firmness.

I stab a corner of toast and scoot it round the plate to pick up smears of melted butter. Tears start stinging my eyes and overflowing down my cheeks. I wipe them away with my dressing gown sleeve, but more keep coming.

'It's probably not what you think.' Nathan is gazing at me with an expression I can't quite read.

'I know what I heard! It's obvious they've been carrying on behind my back.'

'Are we any better? What happened in the hallway—and just now, holding hands?'

'That's nothing. We're not . . . you know . . .' I trail off. I can't even say the words 'having sex' without wanting to tear his clothes off. There's no denying that it's a very big something.

He sighs. 'If you found out that it was all a mistake, would you still want to be with Callum? Or would you break up with him?'

It's a logical question. But I'm in no state of mind to answer it. 'Please don't ask me that.'

Nathan reaches over to collect my empty plate and drops it on his with a clatter, and I see with surprise that he's clenching his jaw.

'Maybe you should have a bath and go to bed? You're look stressed out to the max,' he says. *So do you,* I think watching him.

'OK, yes, that does sound nice actually.'

'Come on, I'll run it for you.'

I nod and make a detour to my bedroom for a hair tie while he heads to the bathroom. There's a metallic screech as he sweeps the *Birth of Venus* shower curtain to one side, and then I hear a gushing noise as he starts filling the bath.

Sweeping my hair up into a loose topknot, I enter just in time to see him pouring nearly the whole bottle of my Molton Brown Heavenly Gingerlily bubble bath, which I keep for special occasions, under the hot tap.

'Hey, steady on! A little of that stuff goes a long way!'

'Sorry, I thought you might like some bubbles.'

He lifts his hands helplessly as giant white peaks of foam start to form. 'Geez, it's so . . . frothy!'

I catch his eye, and we laugh, which eases the tension slightly. White steam fills the room, thick and hot. Suddenly, a deliciously naughty feeling runs through me. Nathan doesn't seem in any hurry to leave, and Callum's doing God knows what with Sian—surely I'm allowed a little leeway . . .

'Um, do you want to have a bath too?' I venture, half-jokingly, hardly expecting him to agree.

'Ah, I don't know,' Nathan replies uncertainly, eyeing the bubbles. Chunks are starting to break off and float up to the ceiling like airborne icebergs. 'It does look like fun. But it would be wrong on so many levels.'

I shrug, trying to look unconcerned, and kick the edge of the bath mat so it lies flush against the floor. 'Bathing with someone is very eco-friendly. They do it all the time in Scandinavia. It doesn't have to mean anything.'

'Isn't that what people usually say just before they end up in bed together?'

Oh, wise Nathan.

I turn off the taps smartly. 'Well, suit yourself. I'm getting in. Shut your eyes.'

Before he can protest, I hastily take off my robe and pyjamas. *Emma, you are such a tease,* I think. But Nathan hasn't run screaming from the room, so perhaps he's enjoying the show.

I step into the snowy froth and sit down, gritting my teeth as the hot water scorches my bum. I blow some bubbles at Nathan, who's standing there with a goofy grin on his face.

'Ouch! It's scalding, but it feels really good.' I smile at him invitingly. 'Are you coming in?'

His eyes are glued to mine, and I can see some kind of internal conflict taking place.

Go on, urges broad-minded, *do it. You only live once.*

He must come to some kind of decision because he mutters, 'Fuck it', and pulls his T-shirt over his head. Then he unzips his jeans and eases them down over his slim hips. It's like my own personal strip show. I'm ogling him unabashedly, but I wouldn't look away if you paid me. He has such a great body—lean, tanned, with muscles in all the right places, and a decent amount of manly chest hair. Callum waxes his off, and the regrowth is always so prickly.

Nathan hooks his thumbs into his black boxer briefs and shoots a warning glance at me. 'You might want to shut your eyes for this next part.'

Fat chance of that, I think. 'OK,' I say but cross my fingers under the water.

'Hmm . . . Why don't I believe you?'

'There are so many bubbles I can hardly see anything anyway. Fine. If you're shy, I'll put something over my eyes.' I grab a clean flannel from the shelf behind me and drape it over my face. 'There.'

'OK, bunch up. I'm coming in.'

Water goes careening over the side of the bath with a large slosh as he sits down at the opposite end. 'Whoops,' he says.

I take the flannel off and see Nathan's legs stretched on either side of me, with his feet up near my ears. I'm not exactly sure how to sit.

'Maybe lie back and put your feet up on my shoulders,' he suggests.

I hold on to his calves and ease my legs up, trying not to kick anything I shouldn't in the process. He grabs hold of my ankles to help.

Eventually, we're both lying full length, and I sink back into the mound of bubbles with a sigh as the heat of the water works its magic on my tense muscles.

'Feeling more relaxed?' Nathan asks.

'Yeah, this was definitely a good idea.'

'I have plenty more.'

'Oh really? Like?'

'Like—'

Nathan starts massaging the arch of my left foot, kneading his thumb right in the sore place I get from wearing high heels. I groan softly.

He watches me with half-lidded eyes through the steam. 'Does that feel good?'

'Mmhmm, but it's not something a flatmate would do.'

'Should I stop?'

I shake my head slightly and lay my hand very casually, as if by accident, on the top of his thigh.

Nathan arches an eyebrow. 'I think your hand is starting to wander, and that's not appropriate flatmate behaviour.'

I snigger. 'Sorry, but you have very nice thighs.'

'Thank you. I'd return the compliment, but I haven't seen your thighs.'

'Oh, so you did shut your eyes?'

'Sure.'

He's grinning, so I don't really believe him. I think he kept his eyes open the whole time.

'Right.' I start scooping bubbles aside near his groin.

'Hey!'

'Fair's fair.'

Just as I'm about to launch into full-scale bubble attack, there's a knock—knock on the front door.

I freeze and look at Nathan.

'Expecting someone?' I ask nervously.

He shakes his head. 'Nup.'

There's a louder knock—knock, this time accompanied by Callum's muffled shout: 'Emma! Are you there? Open up!'

Oh no. I shrink down into the bubbles as if they can hide me. Hopefully, if I don't answer, he'll leave. God knows what the neighbours will think about all the racket he's making.

Then I hear the distant sound of a key turning in the lock and the front door opening. I feel all the blood drain from my face despite the heat and steam. Callum has a key! How the hell does he have a key? I rack my brain and vaguely remember him saying he had a spare in case there was an emergency.

'Emma?' His voice sounds closer, he's inside the flat. Nathan and I are stone-like in the water. All I can hear is the drip, drip from the tap and Callum's purposeful tread as he checks my bedroom and then moves down the hallway towards the bathroom. Fuck!

I have to say something. Otherwise, he's going to come in.

'I'm in the bath, Callum!' I call out. 'What are you doing here?' I make myself sound pissed off, which actually isn't too hard to do. If I sound the slightest bit guilty, he'll sniff it out like a bloodhound.

His footsteps stop outside the bathroom door. 'Oh, you are here,' he says. 'Are you OK? I didn't get a reply from you, and I got worried. I thought you might have collapsed or something since you were ill last night.'

'That's thoughtful of you, but I'm fine. Sorry I didn't message you back. I was having a nap.'

'Can I come in?'

'Ah . . .'

I watch in horror as the bathroom door handle starts turning downwards.

'Fuck,' I mouth at Nathan, my eyes wild with panic.

He shakes his head slightly. 'I locked it,' he mouths, and I roll my eyes at him in relief.

Thank God for Nathan's foresight. That's the second time he's saved my bacon today.

Callum presses his shoulder against the door, and sure enough it doesn't open.

'It's locked,' I say, trying to sound helpful.

'Can you unlock it? I want to talk to you properly.' Callum sounds agitated.

'Callum.' I sigh, letting him know he's well and truly disturbing my peace and quiet. 'I'm soaking wet.' I make a few sloshing noises with my hands. 'I've just put a face mask on, and I'm having a glass of wine. I'll come over tomorrow night.'

'Where's Nathan?' he asks suddenly.

I stare at Nathan, whose eyes go wide.

'He's out,' I reply quickly and add, 'With Julie. They've gone to dinner—on a date.' I'm pretty sure Callum doesn't know the date was for three o'clock this afternoon.

'Oh,' he says. 'So you're definitely OK?'

'Yes! Thanks for checking up. I appreciate it. But honestly, I'm fine. Just having some me time.'

'Are you sure you don't want me to come in? I could wash your back . . .'

I gulp. 'I'm all good. I'll just go straight to bed afterwards,' I say airily.

Callum says immediately, 'I can wait until you get out.'

Shit. 'You know me and baths.' I force myself to laugh. 'I could be in here for hours.'

'That's true.'

'It's probably best if you just go home. I'll see you tomorrow night.'

A hard knot forms in my stomach at the thought of the conversation we'll be having. But right now, I just wish he'd go. *Please leave!* I plead silently.

'Well, OK, sorry for disturbing you,' he states apologetically.

'OK, bye!' I call cheerily. 'I'll message you before I go to bed.'

I make a few kissing sounds, and he says, 'Bye.'

The front door bangs shut. I rub my sweaty face with my hand in relief then realise the bubbles are starting to disappear. Yikes. If Nathan gets a good look at my boobs, he may recognise me as Cleopatra. Swiftly, I cover my chest with my arm and give him a shaky smile. 'That was close. I can't believe Callum came into the flat like that!'

'He did sound genuinely worried about you,' Nathan points out. His playful flirting tone has vanished. Great, is he on Callum's side now?

'He's probably feeling guilty after having an afternoon of kinky sex with Sian,' I say edgily.

'I think I might get out,' he says abruptly. 'Leave you to your me time.'

'Fine.' I drape the flannel over my face, burning with the injustice of it all.

There's a small tidal wave as Nathan gets out of the bathtub.

'I've got a towel on. You can take it off.'

He's standing there, wet and glistening, muscles taut. But all I can focus on is his mouth set in a grim line.

'You're pissed off, aren't you?'

'Yeah, at myself. I like you, but—'

'I like you too,' I interject before he can say anything else.

He takes a deep breath. 'You need to talk to Callum about Sian.' Then he unlocks the bathroom door, leaving me alone in the lukewarm water.

Chapter 19

PANIC IN THE NIGHT

❊

So we end up in our separate rooms platonically after all. It's for the best. Just because Callum is going behind my back with Sian doesn't mean I should start messing around with Nathan behind his. *Two wrongs don't make a right.* This is what I tell myself as I lie in bed, restlessly tossing from one side to the other, unable to sleep. Is Nathan doing the same?

Eventually, I drift off and dream I'm in the bath, but it's Callum sitting opposite me. He's smoking a cigar and drinking red wine with a supercilious expression. I really don't want to be in there with him, so I start getting out. But he lunges at me, forcing my head under the water and holding it there. I wake up gasping for breath in a pitch-black room. Terrified he might come into the flat again, I stumble out of bed to check the front door is double-locked, then lean against the wall in the hallway, my lungs on fire, taking deep, wheezing breaths.

Nathan must hear me as he pokes his head out of his room and asks in a sleepy voice, 'Are you OK?'

I shake my head.

'Did you have a bad dream?'

I nod, and he holds the door wider.

'Do you want to come in for a bit?'

So I do end up in bed with him, but it's just because he's comforting me. I lie on my side and he rubs my back and makes soothing noises, which helps to calm me down. It's not sexual at all. It's purely for medical purposes. Well, OK, when he slides his hand under my pyjama top to better access my back, that does turn me on slightly.

'Was the dream about Callum?' he asks eventually when I'm in a pleasantly sleepy, semi-aroused state.

'Mmm, yeah. More of a nightmare though.'

'Want to tell me about it?'

'Just the usual—being choked to death,' I say shakily.

'Usual?'

'I've had one before. Not like this, though.' I tell him about the bath and Callum trying to drown me. My chest tightens again.

'Shhh, you're all right now,' Nathan whispers in my ear. 'It's just because he came round unexpectedly. It's completely my fault. I shouldn't have got in the bath with you.' He shifts closer.

'Uh, speaking of compromising situations, did you put pyjamas on after the bath?'

'Nah. I usually sleep commando,' he says.

'Oh. Maybe . . .'

He sighs. 'You're right, I should put some clothes on.

Unless you're going? I'm not kicking you out,' he adds. 'You can stay if you need to . . . if you want to.'

You should leave! exclaims Prude immediately. *Are you kidding?* Broad-minded is incredulous at the suggestion.

'I'll stay.' My alter ego is incredibly bossy at times.

Nathan gets out of bed and rustles around. Then he jumps in again making the mattress judder.

'What are you wearing now?' I ask sleepily.

'T-shirt and shorts.'

I yawn. 'Very decorous.'

'Do you think you can sleep?'

'I can try.'

When I wake up, I have no idea where I am. Then I see my bookcase, and it starts coming back to me. The panic attack. Lying in Nathan's bed. Nathan rubbing my back. Slowly I turn over to face him. It's barely light, but I can make out his eyes; he's looking right at me. It seems like he's been awake for a while.

'Morning,' I whisper.

'Mornin',' he returns.

'Did you sleep at all?'

'Yeah, a bit. This bed isn't exactly big enough for the both of us.' He shifts position, his elbow bumping my hip, and my heart starts beating faster. The semi-aroused state from last night hasn't abated at all.

'Mine's bigger,' I suggest flirtatiously before I can help myself.

'Don't tempt me. I feel guilty enough as it is after last night.' He rolls onto his back, away from me.

'You don't need to feel guilty. Nothing happened.'

'Hmm . . . I'm not sure Callum would approve of me taking a bath with his girlfriend.'

'He's the one who's in the wrong, not us.'

'You don't know that.'

'I know what I heard. I've been paranoid about him having an affair for a while. It seems I was right.'

'So why didn't you break up with him before?'

'I don't know. He has a way of twisting things round. He makes me feel like I'm the one with the problem.'

'And because he's good in bed probably,' Nathan states flatly, staring up at the ceiling. 'That's always why women stay with guys like him.'

'I'm not that shallow! Besides, I wouldn't call four minutes good in bed.'

He turns his head to look at me. 'You're joking?'

I give a bitter laugh. 'I'm not. I timed it once. I even bought BDSM lingerie . . . to tempt him.' God, it's all coming out now. And I'm breaking Callum's cardinal rule of not telling Nathan about our sex life. But stuff it. 'He doesn't really want me unless I'm wearing it. Otherwise, we have "pipe maintenance" sex, as he calls it. A few thrusts, and that's it.

Is that normal?'

Nathan frowns, shifting into psychologist mode. 'He could have some kind of premature ejaculation problem. But if it's not consistent, I don't know . . . It's possible he might have something on the side. You really need to talk to him and find out what the story is.'

That's what I'm afraid of. Last time I accused him of having an affair, we ended up going out for another twelve months.

After Nathan gets up to have his Weet-Bix, I go back to my room and climb into bed. I can't face work today. Not with Sian completely unaware that I know what's going on. She'll want to do lunch or chat in the stacks, and I'm not sure if I can act normal. Besides, I haven't even examined her part in all this properly. Every time I think about it the pain becomes too overwhelming. She's my friend. How could she do this to me? It's inconceivable. No. I need to talk to Callum first before I deal with Sian.

Nathan pops his head in to say goodbye and nods when I say I'm pulling a sickie. 'I'll talk to you tonight after you've seen Callum then.'

'OK.'

'Good luck.' He flashes me a 'you can do it' smile.

I leave a message on Blaire's voicemail, telling her I'm ill. Then I go back to sleep until lunchtime. After all the drama and emotion of yesterday, I'm exhausted. The day passes slowly, and I move distractedly from one room to another in my pyjamas and robe, not doing anything productive. In the afternoon, I end up back in Nathan's room, lying on his bed. I imagine his arms around me to try and gain some inner strength for the coming discussion. It's strange. I find it so much easier to talk to him about emotional stuff. With Callum, it's difficult to get below the surface.

I fall asleep on Nathan's bed for an hour, then reluctantly message Callum at 5 p.m. to let him know I'm heading to his flat. I don't bother dressing up for the occasion or even putting on much make-up. I'm only going there to extract a confession from him. I don't know what's going to happen when I accuse him of having an affair with Sian, but Callum is clever. If he can find a way of being the one in the right, he will. But I really can't see how he's going to get out of it. The conversation I heard from the pantry was pretty damning.

On the bus, a message from Callum arrives: *Great! Looking forward to it x*

It throws me. The fact that I'm seeing him on a Monday night is also disconcerting. We've had the Tuesday and Thursday rule in place for so long that it's become a well-worn groove in my life.

So I'm out of sorts and completely unprepared when Callum throws open the door and kisses me long and hard on the mouth. He takes my hand and immediately starts leading me to the bedroom. Whoa, this can't happen. I tug my hand out of his and say firmly, 'Callum, we need to talk.'

'We can talk afterwards. I've missed you.' There's a wheedling tone in his voice, the same one that he used on Sian. I harden my resolve and fold my arms.

'I mean it.'

He stares at me for a long moment to see if he can weaken me, but I look back at him stonily. 'Fine. Let's go to the lounge,' he says at last. He strides off, and I trail along behind.

When we get there, he loosens his tie from around his neck and tosses it on the sideboard. I can tell he's grumpy that I said no to sex. Oh well, he's about to get even grumpier.

'So what do you want to talk about? You've been acting really weird lately.'

I ignore the barbed comment and take a deep breath. 'Cut the attitude. I know, OK?'

He moves half a step back. 'Know what?'

'About you and Sian.'

Something in his eyes flickers. 'What about me and Sian?'

God, do I have to spell it out? 'I heard you talking in the kitchen on Saturday night, just before she left. It sounded very much to me like you're fucking her behind my back.'

Callum winces as though he has delicate sensibilities. But I know he doesn't.

'So?' I persist. 'Are you?'

His mouth turns downwards as though he's disgusted at the thought. 'No,' he says defensively.

'Really? So what were you talking about then?'

'I'm not exactly sure what we said. You'll have to jog my memory.'

'You were trying to get her to do something, and she was saying she shouldn't, that it was getting too complicated. Then you said it was good, and she agreed, but that she felt guilty about it. Then you were doing something to convince her, and there was whispering and laughing about what you would say if I happened to walk in.'

Callum doesn't react at all to this except to ask, 'Where exactly were you when you heard this conversation?'

'In the pantry.'

'Right. Well, the conversation you heard—or, should I say, eavesdropped on—was us talking about the flat in Stockbridge that Sian and her partner are thinking of buying. It's the same one that Davita has made an offer on, and Sian is feeling guilty about competing with her for it and was about to pull out. I was trying to get her to have another viewing. I showed it to her on my phone to convince her that it was a good buy. We were talking about Davita walking in, not you.'

I'm shocked. 'Sian's buying a flat? She has a partner?'

'Yes.' He smirks, and suddenly, I'm not at all confident

that I'm in the right. Fuck.

'Why don't I know about this?'

'The reason you don't know about it is because . . .' Callum pauses for dramatic effect. 'Her partner is your boss.'

'My boss? Who . . .? Not Blaire?'

He nods. What the hell? My head swims in disbelief. Is this for real? It can't be! Sian would've said something. But realisations keep hitting me from the left and right like punches from a heavyweight boxer. Sian's sexy outfits at work, her pay rise, her edginess around me lately . . . I feel dismayed. Not because Sian's a lesbian (I kind of guessed that anyway) or that she's with Blaire (which is even more out of left field), but because I've completely misread the situation and accused Callum of a big fat nothing.

'So as you can see,' he says smugly, 'I'm not having an affair with her. She's a dyke, for Christ's sake! Don't you trust me at all?'

His smugness riles me up. 'Honestly? No! If it's not Sian, then who?'

Suddenly I notice Callum's forehead is sweating, and my spidey senses kick up a notch. I've never grilled him like this before and he's starting to crack. I was right, there's definitely something going on. Aisla? Hmm, I don't think so, their conversation sounded too businesslike.

'How many times do I have to tell you?' he retaliates, 'I'm not having an affair! Your paranoia is getting boring.'

'For God's sake, just be honest, Callum!'

'Be honest? That's a fucking joke!' he snaps, his ice-blue eyes boring into mine. 'What about you and Nathan? Lying about him being gay!'

I roll my eyes. 'Old news.'

'It's obvious he has the hots for you. And you know it, don't you?'

'Leave Nathan out of it. He's just a flatmate. And stop trying to change the subject!'

We glare at each other. Callum is scowling, and I'm red-faced and starting to feel like I'm banging my head against a brick wall. He's never going to admit to it.

Then his face softens, and he sighs. 'Emma, this is senseless. I don't want to fight with you. What will it take to get you to believe me?'

He suddenly drops down on one knee. Oh dear God. Surely he's not . . .

'Callum, get up!' I hiss frantically. 'Don't be daft.'

But his expression is determined, and when he gets that look, nothing can dissuade him.

'Emma McTavish, I love you,' he intones solemnly. 'Will you do me the honour of becoming my wife?'

I'm completely put on the spot. Never in a million years did I think Callum would propose. But here he is, looking up at me with an angelic expression. Yet instead of being happy, I feel sad. If he'd asked me a few months ago, I may have agreed. Now there's not a chance in hell that I will. However, in saying that, a proposal is a proposal. So I hesitate before I shoot him down in flames—only very slightly. But he sees it and immediately pounces. 'Say yes, Emma. I'm not getting up until you do.'

'I can't marry you, Callum.'

'Of course you can. Just say yes. I haven't got a ring, but we'll go shopping for one on the weekend. You can have anything you like.'

There's a long silence while I wrestle with the desire to be married and the thought of it being to him.

'I . . . I'll think about it,' I say at last.

It seems that's good enough as a 'yes' for Callum because he leaps up and hugs me.

'I haven't agreed to it!' I say sharply.

'Well, at least it's not a "no",' he replies, looking happy.

He probably thinks he can 'work on me' like he was going to with Diana's fictitious husband, Mervin, and get me to say yes at some point down the track.

Callum puts his arm around my shoulders. 'I know I let my job get in the way of our relationship sometimes. But all that will change. I promise I'll be more attentive to your needs, starting now.'

He gently caresses the back of my neck, and I stiffen. This is exactly what happened the last time. He showered me with attention until I felt so loved and secure that I didn't mind the odd night of 'pipe maintenance' sex. Then he started increasing it. What makes me think just because we're married, it will be any different? I can see myself in five years' time having the exact same conversation with him.

I pull back slightly so I'm out of range of his caressing hand.

'So we can give up this "pipe maintenance" sex business? You'll want me au naturel, even if I'm not wearing kinky lingerie?'

His eyes get that weird flicker again; then it's gone, and he smiles at me.

'Yes,' he says, looking at me affectionately. 'No more "pipe maintenance" sex. From now on, since we'll be engaged, things are going to be much more intimate. And for that to happen, I think we should get our own flat. I'm sure Nathan won't want to be around a loved-up couple.'

It suddenly dawns on me what's really going on. Callum has realised he can kill two birds with one stone. By proposing, he can make me feel more secure in our relationship and, at the same time, get me away from Nathan, who's become a real threat to breaking us up.

I've got to hand it to him. No wonder Camille is always after him to sell her million-pound properties. He's a great real estate agent.

Chapter 20

THROUGH THE LOOKING GLASS

⁂

It would be so easy to give in to Callum's offer. To turn a blind eye to my gut feeling that he's messing around. But I'm not in the mood to give in.

'There's something you need to know, something you're not going to like,' I say.

He smiles confidently. 'You can tell me anything. We shouldn't have secrets from each other.'

I look at him steadily. 'I've been doing life modelling, on the side.'

His smile slips slightly, but then it's fixed back in place.

'Oh? Well, that's not too bad. You probably wear some kind of robe or something, don't you?'

'No, it's life modelling, Callum. I'm completely naked.'

'Completely?' He looks astounded.

I nod. 'Completely. I do wear a robe at the end of each pose, though.'

'How . . . how long have you been doing it?' He's breathing erratically.

'I've only done a few sessions, but the money is quite good.'

'Money,' he repeats slowly. 'You get paid for it?'

'Of course,' I answer. 'I wouldn't do it for free!'

'Of course,' Callum echoes faintly.

'But there's something else. It's quite funny actually.'

He looks like he doesn't want to hear it, but he's going to. 'What?'

'Well, one of the sessions was an art history group, and I noticed Nathan amongst them. It was a bit embarrassing, but I was wearing a wig and make-up, so he didn't know it was me.'

I watch as Callum puts two and two together. His face drains of colour. 'The Cleopatra drawing of Nathan's—that was you?'

'Yeah, that was me—I'm the skank.'

Callum gulps. I can see his mind working overtime. Is he thinking he should retract his offer before he's married to a woman who takes her clothes off for money?

'Well, I wouldn't have said that if I'd known it was you. Thanks for telling me,' he says with a sarcastic edge. He draws himself up to his full height. 'You're going to stop all that once we're engaged.'

'I don't want to stop. Now Nathan's paying me rent, and I don't have to do it solely for the money. I'm quite enjoying it. It's very liberating.'

'Emma, seriously?' His voice is laced with annoyance. 'It's not you.'

'It *is* me. Who else is it?'

'I don't want people looking at my fiancée starkers! It's

bad enough that Nathan's seen you. Jesus! Besides, who knows where those drawings will end up? Hanging on some pervert's wall?'

'Well, funny you should say that. Jack Sutton—he's the husband of the woman who runs the art classes—is quite a well-known artist. There's a painting of his in the gallery in Morningside at the moment. He thinks I have promise and wants to do a one-on-one session with me. So yes, it's highly likely I could end up hanging on someone's wall.'

Callum looks like he's going to pass out. 'There's no fucking way I'm agreeing to that!'

'Yeah, I'm not sure about posing for him, even if his wife trusts him implicitly,' I say. 'But I do want to continue life modelling for the groups.'

He grunts.

'Does that mean you'll think about it?' I ask. 'Like I'm thinking about your proposal? It has to be a two-way street, Callum.'

'I guess.' He looks extremely peeved.

'Thank you.'

After that, there doesn't seem to be anything else to say. We both have a lot to think about, so he suggests we meet up on Thursday night as per usual to talk further. His proposal hangs in the air, next to my life modelling admission. He doesn't kiss me goodnight when I leave, just gives me a frosty 'bye'.

Back at my flat, I discover Nathan in the last stages of cooking a stir-fry. The rangehood roars at full power, ineffectively sucking up billows of spice-scented steam.

'Hi!' I yell above the noise.

He clocks me over his shoulder. 'Gidday! I didn't expect you back for dinner.'

Feathers of dark hair are damply plastered to the back of his neck and the black T-shirt he's wearing clings to his torso. His frayed denim cut-offs show off long, tanned, muscular legs, and bare feet. He shakes the wok, and the muscles in his smooth bicep ripple. Jesus. It's like walking into a raunchy *Hell's Kitchen* episode.

I groan weakly as a surge of lust races through me and I flop down at the kitchen table. Never mind Callum, what the hell am I going to do about the unbearably sexy chef? His presence is driving me crazy.

Nathan eyes me curiously. I'm sure he's dying to know what happened, but he just says, 'There's enough for two if you want some.'

'Yes, please.'

He flicks off the rangehood and dishes up two heaped plates of a spicy noodle, chicken, and vegetable concoction. We tuck in. It's so good to eat a meal cooked by someone else. Marrying Callum would mean continually ordering takeaways. That's a negative on my 'Callum: pros and cons list' I've just started.

'You always seem to be feeding me lately,' I tell him

between mouthfuls.

'I thought my cooking skills were why you chose me to be your flatmate,' he teases.

'That, amongst other things.'

'What else?'

I smile at him. 'Leaving the toilet seat down was a definite plus.'

Usually, he'd come back with a witty rejoinder, but he looks down at his half-finished plate and asks quietly, 'So what happened with Callum?'

Here we go. I lower my fork and launch into it.

'It seems I got it all wrong. Sian was actually buying a flat, and Callum was helping her. I haven't talked to her yet to confirm it, but from the other things he told me, it's probably the truth.'

I hesitate about telling him the full story; it's Sian's business about being with Blaire.

'Oh, so he's off the hook then?' Nathan frowns and stabs at a piece of carrot with his fork.

'Not entirely. I said I didn't trust him.'

'And then what happened?'

'Things took a rather interesting turn—he proposed.'

'He *what*?' Nathan looks incredulous.

'I know! It totally took me by surprise. He went down on one knee and everything.'

'Uh, what did you say?' His eyes flick to my bare left hand.

'I said I'd think about it.'

'So you're considering it?' I'm not sure whether it's the spicy stir-fry or Callum proposing, but Nathan suddenly looks extremely flushed and his face is beaded with sweat.

'I think I owe him that much.'

He reaches for a nearby blue-and-white-checked tea towel and mops his face slowly. 'This is really—unexpected,' he says at last.

'Yeah, I still can't believe it. We're going to talk more about it on Thursday night,' I continue blithely.

Nathan rubs his temple as if it pains him and frowns. 'What's with the whole Tuesday, Thursday business?'

When he first moved in, I mentioned that I saw Callum on those two nights every week. I'm surprised he's remembered it.

'Oh. It was something Callum devised so we get to see each other regularly.'

He screws up his nose. 'Sorry, but I smell a rat. What does he do on Monday and Wednesday nights?'

I shrug. 'I don't know. Work? Gym?'

'I think you need to find out what he does.' He grabs my empty plate and puts it underneath his half-finished one.

'I'll definitely put it on my long list of things to think about before agreeing to marry Callum,' I say. 'I'm not just going to say yes without careful consideration.'

Nathan nods and avoids my eyes. Callum's right; I think he'd move out if we got engaged. I don't blame him. He's probably sick to death of us.

'It's none of my business. I shouldn't get involved,' he mutters.

Surely you are *involved?* I think. But Callum proposing seems to have relegated Nathan back into flatmate mode. It's like taking a bath and sleeping next to him last night never happened.

'It's OK. You've got enough to worry about,' I say, picking up the plates and heading over to the sink. 'There's your ex and daughter.'

'Yeah, it looks like we're going to sell the flat we owned and split the proceeds. The situation with Katie is more difficult. I'm probably going to have to go down to London shortly and discuss things with Naomi.'

I squirt a jet of green dishwashing liquid aggressively into the sink. 'See, lots going on!'

Nathan comes over to the counter and stands next to me. 'Emma, I've been trying not to think of you as more than a flatmate because you're with Callum. But I don't know if I can keep doing that. It's getting difficult . . . Maybe I should move out.'

OK, maybe he does have some feelings for me. But moving out? That's his solution? Scrubbing the plates in the sink, I'm annoyed despite myself. But what do I want? Nathan to fight Callum in a duel at dawn or something? That's so medieval.

'Fine, whatever,' I mutter. Yet something is building, a feeling that I need to tell him something more intimate before he walks out of my life forever. But it needs to be done in a low-key manner so he doesn't get freaked. I rack my brain. *What to say?*

Nathan starts to head out of the kitchen. In desperation, I grab the sopping wet dish sponge, throw it at his back, and shout, 'You drew me naked!' Classy, Emma, classy.

Unsurprisingly, he's completely confused. 'What the hell?' He plucks at his wet T-shirt and frowns uncomprehendingly at me. Then he suddenly narrows his eyes, and I freeze. 'The life modelling class, Cleopatra—that was you?'

I nod meekly. 'I thought you should know.'

'Why didn't you say something before?'

'I was too embarrassed.'

'Jesus! Does Callum know?'

'Yeah, I told him tonight. He wasn't happy about it.'

Nathan groans and facepalms. 'He probably thinks I'm some kind of pervert stalking you.'

'No, I told him it was a complete coincidence that you were in the class and that it was quite funny. But he didn't think so.'

He chuckles. 'I can imagine.'

Apart from the initial shock, Nathan seems pretty cool about the fact that I was life modelling at all. He's looking at me with genuine respect.

'So you don't mind that I did that?'

'Why would I mind? You were a great model. You saw the finished product. I couldn't have drawn you half as well as I did if you weren't able to hold a pose properly.'

'So you wouldn't care if I kept doing it?'

'Of course not. It's up to you.'

'I mean, even if we happened to . . . if there was a chance that we . . .' I take a deep breath. 'Got together?'

Nathan smiles at me readily. 'Even if we were together.'

On my mental clipboard, I flip the page for a new pros and cons list. At the top, I write: *Life modelling: Callum* ✕ *Nathan* ✓

It feels like it's a good start.

On Wednesday afternoon, I'm sipping coffee and nibbling on a blueberry muffin in the cafe across from Callum's office in Hanover Street. This is the entirety of my undercover act. There's no wig, fur coat, or sunglasses. As I told Nathan this morning, I'm just going to follow him after work. The chance of discovering anything is pretty low. But it's the best idea I can come up with at short notice. I've taken another couple of sick days off work, and it's prompted Sian to start sending me messages, each sounding more and more worried when I don't reply. I know I have to send her something. Otherwise, she's going to turn up at the flat in a state.

I've just finished typing: *I'm OK, thanks for checking. Just something I ate. Am on the mend . . .* when I see Callum exit his office and walk jauntily down the street. Hastily, I send the message, leave a half-finished cup of coffee, and race out the door in an effort not to lose him. I nearly collide with a couple of elderly ladies who are about to enter the cafe. Outside, the cold air makes me flinch, and I pause to wind my scarf around my neck. But by the time I've finished, Callum's nowhere in sight.

Scampering across the street, I peer around the corner and catch a glimpse of his dark hair and blue coat going down the stairs to a basement flat. My heart is pumping wildly. A gym or a bar with colleagues would be OK; a basement flat is suspicious. Loitering around at the top is preferable to discovering what's going on below, but my feet are freezing. I screw up my courage and head down the steps before I can change my mind.

The door has glass panels, but it doesn't give any indication of the interior because it's covered over with black paper. The door handle opens easily, and inside is a lair. Well, it feels like a lair. There's a rosy glow emanating from a bare red light bulb in the middle of the ceiling. A brown leather couch is along one wall; in front of it is a coffee table strewn with magazines—BDSM ones, by the looks of the covers.

A tall, slim girl wearing a red bustier top, black PVC leather hot pants, fishnet stockings and black stilettos enters from a door at the back of the room. She has short, spiky blonde hair and the longest fake eyelashes I've ever seen. 'Can I help you?'

'Are there any jobs going here?' I query, taking a stab in the dark that it's some kind of brothel.

'What experience do you have?' she asks, looking me up

and down.

'What kind of experience do I need?'

The girl sighs as if she gets asked this a lot. 'We offer a full range of BDSM services. It depends on the customer's preference. But you have to be willing to do oral, anal, and penetrative. Some want one or two. Others want the full works. We have a lot of regulars.'

'Right.' I gulp. 'So, say, the guy who just came in—is he a regular?'

'I can't tell you. We have an excellent customer privacy policy. It's like watertight, unbreakable, carved in stone . . .'

'I can make it worth your while.' I nod at my handbag.

She sighs again and rolls her eyes. 'Go on then. Give me a twenty.'

She looks both ways and whispers behind her hand, 'He's a regular, and he always gets the full works.' My heart sinks. Of course Callum *would* get the full works.

'Is there any way I can see into the room? You know, so I can see if it's the kind of thing I've done before?'

She hums and haws. 'Well, I suppose I can let you have a ten-minute peep. But you'll have to give me another twenty.'

She's not stupid, this girl.

'Fine.'

I follow her through the interior door and down a dimly lit hallway. 'He's in this one.' The girl points to a closed door. 'Here, use this. You can ask me any questions. Don't worry. The rooms are soundproof, so they can't hear us.'

She hands me a small telescope lens, and motions for me to put it to the peephole. With a shaking hand I do so. My stomach is clenched tight. *What on earth am I going to see?*

The scene before me makes me gasp softly. If it wasn't right there in front of my own eyes, I never would've believed it. Callum is naked and strapped to a black chair by a leather belt around his waist. His arms and legs are tethered to the chair with smaller belts. I notice with shock that he's also got a clamp attached to each nipple and they're connected by a thin silver chain. A woman decked out in a black PVC leather catsuit and stilettos stalks around him saying something with a sneering expression. She's wearing a fetish eye mask with studs and has a long chestnut ponytail that cascades down her back. She's taller and thinner than me, but apart from that, it actually could be me!

My legs start trembling so much I can barely stand up, but I can't take my eye away from the peephole. It's like watching a car crash.

'Is it the same woman every time?' I whisper to the girl, not taking my eye off the lens. I sorely wish I could photograph this to use as evidence.

'It depends on the customer's preference. But this guy books Mistress Rhapsody in advance. Apparently, she gives really good oral.'

Sure enough, the woman drops to her knees between Callum's thighs. I want to look away, but I force myself to watch her head bobbing up and down. I can tell by the way his eyes are closed and the smile playing around his lips that he's enjoying it. She rises after a moment and picks up a bottle of amber liquid stationed near the chair and spurts it all over his chest so it drips down to his crotch. Then she starts licking it off while tugging on the nipple clamp chain. I can't hear anything, but judging by his expression, Callum is in ecstasy.

'What's the stuff she's pouring on him?' I remove my eye from the lens and look at the girl, slightly perplexed.

'Oh, he has a food fetish, so she's incorporated liquid honey into the routine. Clients can choose from a number of foodstuffs on the checklist. We can cater to anyone who's gluten-free or vegan too.' The girl shifts position against the wall and inspects her blood-red gel nails.

I return to the scene. The honey licking has ended with more bobbing of the domme's head between his legs, but she's not down there for as long this time. Then she stands up and rips away the PVC part of her costume to reveal a black cage bra and a pair of crotchless knickers with metal spikes all over them. It's a pretty hot outfit, I have to admit. Something that I imagine he'd like me to wear. I watch as she stalks around some more with a disdainful expression. For his benefit, I'm guessing, so he can see her body. Then she stands in front of him and leans slightly forward. I can't see what's happening as her back is to me, but I'm assuming she's letting him suck her nipples. Then she gets on top of him and starts gyrating around. Wow, OK, the blow job was bad enough. But now she's having full-on sex with him! Heat rushes to my face. He's so totally over the line it's not funny.

'Is there kissing?' I ask the girl.

'Very rarely,' she replies. 'Only if the customer wants it. I guess most of them feel it's too intimate.'

I watch numbly as Callum and the woman start kissing passionately. I guess he doesn't have any qualms about it being too intimate. It occurs to me right about now that I should be feeling anguish. But instead, all I'm experiencing is inner paralysis.

'Right, that's your ten minutes up,' the girl tells me.

That was only ten minutes? How much more is there? The word 'anal' comes to mind. I'm so glad I don't have to see that.

'How long is a session?' I question hollowly.

'It depends. Some of them just want whatever they can get in fifteen minutes. But for the full works, we recommend at least an hour.'

Jesus, an hour.

'How . . . how do the customers last that long?' I ask as we walk back down the hallway. The girl seems very chatty now that she knows she's about to get forty pounds.

'A good domme can keep her subject in a state of arousal right until the end of the session until they're begging to come. It's quite difficult, but Mistress Rhapsody is an expert at it.'

'I bet she is,' I mutter. My sex life with Callum is starting to make a lot more sense. No wonder he's so quick with me.

I don't tease him for an hour until he's begging me for an orgasm.

'So what did you think? Are you interested in working here?' The girl is waiting for my reply and looking expectant.

I open my purse and take out forty pounds. 'You've been extremely helpful,' I say, handing it over. 'But I think I'll pass for the time being.' Her face brightens when she sees the money, and I feel slightly sorry for her.

She nods understandingly. 'It was the honey that put you off, wasn't it? It's a bit much, I know.'

Chapter 21

SHOWDOWN AND SOBERING UP

⁂

When I'm back out on the street, images of what I've just seen march across my brain, each eliciting a fresh wave of disbelief. My vision starts blurring and I feel like I'm going to faint. With an effort I try and ward it off by breathing slowly and deeply. *Just keep walking*! I tell myself sternly.

But by the time I reach the cafe, my stomach is on shaky ground, and the coffee and muffin I purchased earlier make an unexpected appearance in the gutter right outside.

The two elderly ladies I elbowed out of the way are sitting in the window, drinking tea, so they have a clear view of proceedings. Groggily, I wipe my mouth on the back of my hand and happen to look up as one of them shakes her head and mouths 'Day drinking' to the other, who screws up her face in disgust.

I'm actually quite pleased in a dazed kind of way that I'm finally reacting in a humanlike manner to what I've just experienced—namely, seeing my boyfriend having a variety of BDSM sex with a dominatrix. I defy anyone in my position to *not* puke into the gutter. At least it shows I have some sort of turmoil going on inside me, even if I am emotionally defunct.

Facing Callum is not something I particularly want to do right now, but I know I have to. Otherwise, I'll lose my nerve. Maybe if I walk to his flat, I'll come up with a suitable speech that states eloquently how hell would have to freeze over before I ever marry him.

So I keep walking to the West End, only pausing briefly to visit a convenience store and buy a bottle of water to rinse out my mouth and remove a splash of vomit from my left trainer.

While I'm in Randolph Crescent, Sian replies with: *Glad you're alive if not 100%. I was getting worried! We need to talk about something. Are you at work tomorrow? Sx*

I frown and stop walking. All the messages she's been sending suddenly make sense. Callum's obviously told Sian I know about her and Blaire, so she's in damage control.

I'm relieved they weren't having an affair but I'm still mightily ticked off that she told Callum about Blaire and not me. Buying a flat with someone suggests a proper committed relationship. Hardly a fling. If that's the case, surely, as a good friend, shouldn't I be in the know?

But that's another hard conversation it looks like I'm going to be having in the near future. These things come in threes. Who's next? Nathan probably. He's making noises about moving out and feeling guilty about liking me when I'm with Callum. We seem to have formed a fledgling relationship that's starting to encroach on my current one.

But that's not going to be a problem for much longer. I'm about to chuck my scumbag boyfriend once and for all.

I'm sitting on the stoop, planning my speech, when Callum comes barrelling up the path, sweaty and red-faced. His hair is mussed and his tie is crooked. This time, I know for sure he hasn't run to get here. He's been doing a different kind of exercise.

He pulls up short in confusion. 'Huh? I thought we were seeing each other tomorrow night?'

I stand up, fold my arms, and launch right into it. 'I saw you, Callum. At the brothel. With the domme.'

His lips press together in a firm line. 'Don't be ridiculous.'

'I followed you.'

'I don't know what you're on about.'

He moves to go past me, and I grab his shirt and rip it open to the waist. Buttons go flying. His chest glistens with the remnants of a sticky substance.

'Behold exhibit A: the accused, covered in honey!' I crow. I can't help adding sarcastically, 'Wasn't a wet wipe included in the price?'

Callum's face turns white, then goes a deep shade of red. 'That was extremely private,' he chokes out.

I shrug. 'Apparently not if you have enough spare twenties in your purse.'

'Fuck. I'm going to kill that receptionist!' I've never seen him look so livid.

'You and me? It's . . . so . . . over,' I say slowly and carefully so he doesn't misunderstand.

He grabs at my hand. 'It doesn't mean anything, Em! It's just a kind of . . . hobby.'

I grimace and pull my hand away. 'Playing with trains is a hobby. Getting the full works from a dominatrix most definitely is *not*!'

'Christ, did you see all of it?' he whispers. He looks like he's about to keel over.

'No, thankfully! I saw enough, though. How long has it been going on for?'

Callum closes his eyes and sighs. 'About three months.'

'*Three months*!'

He has the grace to look suitably ashamed.

'Em, I'm so sorry. I'll stop. As of right now.'

'I don't think so. You looked pretty enamoured with Mistress Rhapsody. You couldn't get enough of her *oral skills*.'

He sucks in his breath. 'Christ. Look, I don't care about her! I don't even know her real name.'

'Whatever! I'm just glad I found out before I said yes to marrying you. What a fucking disaster that would've been!'

I stride purposefully down the steps and head to the nearest bus stop. Callum follows me, hastily buttoning up his coat to hide his sticky chest. 'Please come back to the flat, Em! We can talk about it.' His voice takes on that wheedling tone that I'm starting to loathe.

'I'm not setting foot inside your stupid flat ever again.'

'I just want you to understand why.'

He's trotting beside me in the street now and peering around at my face to see if I'm listening. I speed up to get away from him.

'Sometimes men have special . . . needs,' he explains. 'Think of it as the equivalent of a woman getting a facial.'

What he's saying is so ludicrous that I almost laugh out loud. 'If you equate what you were doing with getting a facial, you're severely deluded!'

'OK, that was a bad example. But I'm trying to explain it so you'll understand.'

'Nothing you say will make any difference!'

The bus arrives as I reach the stop. I get on, turn around, and look him straight in the eye. 'Fuck off, Callum, you cheating bastard!' I proclaim loudly and clearly so everyone on the bus can hear.

There's a hushed silence, and Callum looks like he wants the ground to swallow him whole. It's perhaps the most satisfying moment I think I've had since I was born.

After enduring curious looks on the bus from the locals and getting a fist pump and a 'Way to go, honey!' from an American woman, there's only one thing I want to do when I reach Bruntsfield: hit the nearest pub and drink myself silly. Luckily, in Edinburgh, you don't have to walk too far before you get to a pub. Drowning one's sorrows is a national pastime, after all.

The place I go to is one of those old gentleman pubs, the type nice young ladies shouldn't set foot in. It has that smell about it: stale beer, smoke, and unwashed armpits. Too bad. They'll have to put up with a woman. The barman is incredibly young and looks like he's still in high school. He's tall and lanky with a buzz cut, pale translucent skin, and no trace of any facial hair. He's wearing a black T-shirt with some rock band's logo and has a couple of silver piercings, one in his nose and one in his eyebrow. Perhaps he's the owner's son.

'What can I get you?' he asks as I approach the bar.

'Scotch on the rocks. Make it a double,' I say, levering myself up onto a bar stool.

'Glenlivet OK?' He takes down a half-full bottle of whisky from the shelf behind him. 'Or I've got Macallan?'

'Glenlivet's fine.'

At this point, I'm not fussed about what I drink as long as it has an extremely high alcohol content.

The barman adds ice to a glass tumbler with tongs and pours over the amber liquid. The ice crick-cracks. He slides it over, and I take a decent slug. The effect is instant—fire in my throat, burning in my stomach, a warming in my ears. Thank God for whisky. I sigh out loud in relief.

The barman leans against the counter and watches me drink. 'Hard day at the salt mines?'

'You have no idea,' I say and tip back the glass to finish

it. 'Another double, please.'

He chortles. 'Whoa, steady on, lass! You'll be dancing on the tabletops soon if you keep drinking like that.' He pours another double shot of whisky into my glass, adds more ice, and gives me a slow wink as he hands it over. 'Not that I'd mind.'

God, is the pubescent barman flirting with me? I look him over. He's kind of cute, but *way* too young to even contemplate a one-night stand with. Not that I would—I do have some standards.

'How old are you?' I enquire before I can help myself. Well, there's no harm in asking, is there?

'Twenty,' he says and flexes his bicep, which I have to admit is quite muscled for someone so slim.

'Bollocks! You look about fourteen.'

'Trust me. I'm old enough to drink, drive, pay taxes—and anything else you may want to do.' He leers at me.

'I think I'll just stick to the whisky. But thanks for the offer,' I say dryly.

'Pity. You look like you're a bit stressed. I could help you relax, if you get my drift.'

I almost choke on my whisky. He's so unbelievably blatant it's kind of funny.

'Do you come on to all your female customers like this? Or don't you get many in here?'

He grins. 'We don't usually get pretty ones who drink Scotch like it's going out of fashion.'

'Wow, you've got a mouth on you.'

He sticks out his tongue to show me another piercing, then leans closer and whispers, 'And it's at your service.'

I look around to see if anyone is overhearing what this brass-necked guy is saying. Surely his father is about to storm in and tell him off for being so explicit? I stare at him, completely at a loss as to how I should respond. The frosted glass of whisky is poised in my hand, and droplets of ice water are trickling down the inside of my arm. Time seems to stand still. All I can think is *I've broken up with Callum. Who knows when I'll next get sex? Maybe it's not a bad idea . . .* Dear God, I'm actually considering fooling around with a twenty-year-old barman! I must have whisky goggles on. I have to leave. Now. Before I do something I'll regret.

I knock back the rest of the whisky, get down off the bar stool, and reach for my handbag.

'Aw, you're not going?' He obviously thought he had me in his clutches.

'Yes, I am,' I say, trying to think clearly and focus on what I need to do: (a) give him money and (b) get out of the pub. I've had to resort to slow, deliberate movements so I can extract my purse from my handbag without dropping all the junk I've got stashed in there on the floor.

I hand him a ten-pound note, and he pouts sulkily. 'Go if you must then.'

'Thanks for the whisky and the chat. You're very—nice.'

He looks marginally placated. Am I now trying to soothe

his bruised ego? This is getting very weird. I need to go home.

I make it back to the flat without further incident, though I have a little trouble putting the key in the lock. It takes me about three tries. I still can't believe I almost succumbed to the barman's offer. God, what a lightweight! A few drams of whisky and I'm anyone's. It must be because I'm distressed about Callum. I'm not in my right mind.

I know Nathan's home because the light in the lounge is on. I breathe a sigh of relief. Just what I need. His calm, solid presence to soothe my frazzled nerves. 'Hi,' I say as I enter the lounge. Then stop in my tracks. Nathan's sitting on the window seat, reading *The Undomestic Goddess,* with his long, jean-clad legs stretched out in front of him. It's hot in the room, and he's taken off his T-shirt rather than turn down the heating. I just stand there and gawp. He always looks fantastic, but my whisky goggles have elevated him to a whole new level of hotness.

'Hi!' he returns, reaching for his T-shirt and hastily pulling it back on. But it's too late. What with the flirty conversation with the barman, the whisky, and now the sight of Nathan's finely muscled half-naked body, my hormones have started clamouring.

I dump my handbag on the nearest chair, lean against it and smile at him tipsily. 'Phew, it's roasting in here. You should probably turn the heating down.' I enunciate slowly and clearly so he thinks I'm sober.

'Probably.'

He doesn't get up to turn it down. *Fine*, I think, *two can play at that game*. I take off my coat and then my jumper and my trainers and dump them on top of my handbag. Now I'm just in a lavender silk camisole and tight black jeans. I sway slightly. *Oh God, I'm so smashed.*

Nathan has gone back to his book, but from the glances he keeps flicking my way, I can tell he's not reading at all.

'What bit are you up to?'

'She's just got together with the gardener. There was a mutual striptease in the glasshouse . . .' He trails off, looking at me. In my befuddled state I take it as encouragement to keep going. Wordlessly, I take off my camisole, then unzip my jeans and pull them down. I step out of them unsteadily and kick them to one side.

'Kind of like this?' I ask.

Nathan's eyes widen in surprise. Ha! I've shocked him. Good.

'Um . . . yeah, like that.' His gaze travels over my body. For a heart-stopping moment, I think I'm wearing the beige lingerie ensemble. But amazingly, I'm not. I remember I put on my sexy black lace bra and knickers this morning. It's a good moment.

I insert a finger into the edge of my knickers like I'm about to pull them down.

'Uh . . .' he says worriedly, and I giggle drunkenly.

'You've seen it all before!' Is it just me, or is the room tilting?

Nathan frowns. 'You look a bit out of it.'

'I'm perfectly fine.'

'Walk over to me then, in a straight line.'

With quite a lot of wobbling, I manage to walk over and kind of fall into his arms accidentally on purpose, but he doesn't seem to mind. It's pretty obvious he wanted that to happen.

He buries his nose in my hair. 'You smell like a distillery.'

'Eau de whisky,' I mumble against his neck, which smells slightly familiar. I take a deep heady sniff of him. 'Mmm, nice. What is that?'

'Just soap.'

'An unlikely story.'

'OK, I confess, I borrowed your body wash after work.'

'Ah, good old Jamaican Delight.'

'Yep.'

'You can keep it. I've got another one.'

'OK, ta.'

Nathan hugs me, and we stay like that for a while, unspeaking. Then I slowly pull his T-shirt up and slide my body against his, and he doesn't stop me. His chest and abs are scorching hot on my cooler flesh. Since his hands are roaming over my bum, I take one and thrust it down the back of my knickers to get the party started. He squeezes my bare butt cheek, and I close my eyes. 'Mmm.'

'We should stop,' he says in my ear. 'Callum.'

But I don't want to stop. I'm caught up in heady whisky-fuelled desire and too busy enjoying the feel of his skin on mine.

'Fuck him,' I reply distractedly, planting kisses along his collarbone. 'He's a cheating scumbag.'

'Emma . . .' Nathan removes his hand from my knickers and grasps my shoulders so I have to look at him.

For a moment, I'm confused, then I get his meaning. 'Yes, sure, bedroom,' I say breathlessly.

'I need to know what's happening with Callum.'

'Oh.' Scenes from the brothel start flooding my mind, and I'm suddenly as sober as a judge. 'I guess I should get some clothes on then if I'm going to spill my guts about that.'

'Meet you in the kitchen in ten? I'll put the kettle on.'

'Fine.' I sigh.

Nathan gives me a quick hug, and my dented ego is somewhat appeased. I know he's right to stop, but dammit, he's got way better self-control than I have.

Chapter 22

NATHAN AND NAOMI

*

In between sips of tea and bites of peanut butter on toast, I tell Nathan what I discovered Callum doing. Then the showdown I had with him at his flat. I spare no detail. Apart from what happened with the barman afterwards, which is inconsequential.

Nathan doesn't say much throughout the telling of it, but he does interject with 'Jesus!' at the part where Callum had sex with the domme and a disbelieving 'No way!' about him equating it with a facial. Sharing it with him makes me feel slightly better, even if the whole sordid tale starts my stomach churning again. When I'm finished, he covers my hand with his. 'Are you all right?'

'I threw up in the street.'

'Oh no!'

'Och, I'm OK now.'

'I feel a bit sick myself, and I'm not the one who saw it. You must be gutted.'

'I don't really feel anything. I think I'm numb.'

'It's probably shock.'

He opens his mouth to ask me something, then closes it

again.

'What?'

'So silly question, but would you say it's definitely over then?'

'Definitely! There's no way I'm ever getting back with him again. I told him that.'

He sighs. 'I think that's a very good decision.'

'Thanks for listening. I'm sorry about before, in the lounge. The whisky made me do it,' I say, trying to lighten the mood.

Nathan squeezes my hand lightly. 'No worries. I get it.'

'I know things are messed up right now,' I continue. 'But maybe after things calm down . . .'

He nods, and I finish drinking my tea. We don't say anything for a bit. Then he clears his throat. 'Ah, so remember I told you I have to go down to London? I booked a train ticket.'

I lean back in my chair. I'm not numb enough to avoid the pain of hearing that. 'When?'

'Tomorrow. Early.'

'Tomorrow!'

'I know, it's not great timing. I want to be here for you. But I really need to sort out stuff with Naomi. You're lucky you don't have a house and a kid at least.'

Suddenly, I realise I know next to nothing about Nathan's past relationship. I've been so focused on Callum and he's been so good at focusing on it with me that it's slipped through the cracks.

'Since we're comparing sob stories, are you going to tell me the rest of yours? Why did you and Naomi break up?'

'I thought I did?'

'No, you didn't. You said you quitting architecture was part of the reason. So what's the other part?'

His face instantly contorts like he's eaten something nasty. 'It's long and complicated. You don't want to hear it.'

'I do, Nathan. Tell me, please.'

He shakes his head. I'm starting to get worried. How bad can it be? Surely not 'strapped to a chair and honey dripped on you' bad?

'If you don't tell me, I'm going to start making things up to fill in the gaps. And after what I've just witnessed Callum doing, I'm warning you, things could get blown way out of proportion.'

'I know. It's just difficult to talk about.'

Hmm, the light in the kitchen is kind of glaring. Not exactly conducive to him revealing his deepest, darkest secrets. Maybe we need a different setting. I get up and hold out my hand. 'Come with me.'

'Where are we going?'

'A safe place.'

Nathan looks sceptical. 'Not the bath again?'

'No, not the bath. My bedroom.'

'I hardly think your bed is going to be safe.'

'Not the bed either. Just trust me.'

When we get to my bedroom, I take a couple of pillows off my bed and arrange them on the floor. Then I grab my fluffy purple throw off the end of the bed and light a few candles on the nightstand. One is a Jo Malone Lilac Lavender & Lovage candle; my mum gave it to me for my birthday, and it's supposed to be good for relaxing. I'm not sure if it is because I've never lit it before.

'Are we having a seance?' Nathan asks, bemused. With the dark night pressing against the windows and the wind shaking the tree branches outside, I have to admit it does look slightly spooky.

'It's supposed to be a soothing, calm atmosphere. Just sit down and focus on your breathing.'

Dutifully he does as he's told and leans against the side of the bed stretching out his long legs. I plonk down on a pillow next to him and cover us with the throw. He takes a few deep breaths and coughs. 'What is that smell? Lavender?'

'Shhh. It's to help you relax. Shut your eyes.'

'OK, OK, I'm shutting them. I'm growing sleepy . . .'

'I'm not hypnotising you! Just start from the beginning. You're in London. You're living with Naomi and Katie.'

'Yes, we're all living together in the flat in Belsize Park. I'm working as an architect at a firm in Tottenham Court Road. Naomi's given up her job at an accounting practice and is looking after Katie. But she's job-hunting for part-time work so I don't have to do overtime to pay the mortgage. We're going to put Katie into the local day care. I'm looking forward to having my evenings and weekends back.'

It's strange hearing Nathan talk about his London life like this. But it's good; he's opening up at least.

'Is Belsize Park a nice area?'

'Yeah, it's quite posh. It's a fifteen-minute walk to Hampstead Heath, and it's only five stops on the Northern line to my work. We've got a three-bedroom flat, and there are trees lining our street.'

I'm jealous despite myself. 'It sounds idyllic.'

'It is. It was.'

'What happened?'

The candle is throwing shadows over his face, and I can see his eyes are scrunched up and his mouth is twisted.

'Take a deep breath,' I say quickly.

Nathan breathes in slowly and then out and relaxes slightly beside me.

'There, that's it.'

'We . . . we went out to a restaurant. It was an ex-colleague of Naomi's. Some woman's birthday. I forget who. There was a big group of people, at least fifteen or twenty. I didn't really know anyone there apart from Naomi.'

'What kind of restaurant?'

'Indian, I think. It was in King's Cross.'

'Did something happen at the restaurant?'

'Yes.'

My heart starts thumping, and my palms are clammy. The suspense is killing me. 'What?' I whisper.

Nathan rests his head back on the edge of the bed, still with his eyes closed, and keeps talking. 'It was weird. We'd all just ordered our mains, which took forever, and I happened to glance up the table. I saw this dude staring at Naomi. Just for a second. It was so quick, like a flash. The only reason I noticed him was because he had these intense light-blue eyes that really stood out because he was so tanned. I can still see them now, in my head. It was like I was meant to notice his eyes.'

I'm a little confused by this, but I try to keep him talking.

'So you saw this guy at the restaurant. Did you ask Naomi about him?'

'I did later, at home. She said his name was Nicholas and she'd worked with him briefly on some auditing project.'

'What happened then?'

He takes a deep, shuddering breath. 'I privately went to pieces.'

Am I missing something?

'I don't get it.'

Nathan digs his phone out of his pocket and flicks through the camera roll. He brings up a photo and holds out his phone to me. It's of a child looking up into the camera with a wide-eyed stare and an adorable grin. She's about three years old and has a mop of tangled dark hair, olive skin, and the most beautiful light-blue eyes I've ever seen.

'Please don't make me spell it out,' he says.

Realisation hits me. 'Oh no!' I grab his hand and hold on to it tightly. 'Are you sure?'

'I wasn't at first. I just sat on it and chewed it over in my head. But the more I kept thinking about it, the more I just kind of *knew*. It was instinctive. Besides, every time I looked at Katie, I just kept seeing him, Nicholas. It was driving me crazy. So eventually, I sat Naomi down and told her my suspicions. She got angry and said I was being stupid and that of course Katie was mine. And how hurt she was that I could even think that about her. She cried and carried on, but something in me didn't believe her. I told her I wanted a paternity test.'

'Did you get one?'

'Yes.'

'And?'

'It confirmed Katie isn't mine.'

I don't know what to say except a choked 'Oh God, I'm so sorry.' My eyes start watering.

Nathan blinks rapidly and looks away. 'Don't cry,' he tells me gruffly. 'You'll set me off.'

I wipe my eyes on the sleeve of my sweatshirt and try and hold it in. Breathe. 'But why did she do it?'

He shrugs. 'She wanted a baby, and I was working too much. Simple.'

'But to pass her off as yours! What was she thinking?'

'I'm still trying to understand it myself.'

'So who is this guy to her?'

'It all came out after the test, and that's the weirdest part. It wasn't even an affair or anything—just a quick screw in the supply closet a couple of times when they were working late. Then they barely spoke afterwards. It was like she was using him as a sperm donor or something.'

'Does he know?'

'Apparently not, and she wants to keep it that way. She wants me to keep being Katie's father.'

'There are a lot of "she wants" in that sentence. What do you want?'

'I don't know.' He rubs a hand over his face. 'To be with someone I can trust, someone who doesn't sleep with other guys behind my back and lie to me.'

'It's a basic human right,' I say softly. 'Everyone deserves that. You deserve that.'

'But I still love Katie.'

'I'm sure you do.'

'Anyway, I moved out, and it was just meant to be for a few weeks. But it kind of ended up being months. I was paying rent and the mortgage, which was hellish. Then I quit my job and came up here for a break. I wasn't sure what I was doing. I just had to get out of London before I went crazy. Naomi freaked out when I quit. She thought that meant they'd be living on the streets. I organised a boarder to move in to help out with the mortgage. Naomi wasn't happy about it.'

'Quick thinking on your part.'

Nathan shrugs. 'It was desperation more than anything. But she's getting used to it, and it's better now that she's gone back to work full time. The woman who's boarding is happy to pick Katie up from day care and look after her too. So Naomi doesn't have to rush back from work.'

'Is she . . . Is Naomi with someone?' I ask tentatively.

He shrugs. 'I'm not sure. She could be seeing Nicholas or someone else, for all I know. We're not in each other's lives like that anymore. We've both moved on emotionally. I'm sure if it was serious, she'd tell me, and vice versa.'

My head is spinning from trying to process all the information. It's a lot to take in, especially after the day I've just had.

Nathan peers at me in the candlelight since I've gone very quiet all of a sudden. 'Maybe we should call it a night. You must be feeling wrecked after what happened with Callum.'

'Yeah.'

I'm just about to hand him his phone back, which I suddenly notice I'm still holding, when a text pops up on the screen: *Hey Nathan, hope you sorted out that emergency. Do you want to meet up again this weekend? Julie ☺*

'Looks like you're out of the doghouse,' I say lightly. Shit, I'd forgotten all about Julie having the hots for Nathan.

'Huh?' I give him the phone, and he reads the text. 'Ah. I'll tell her I'm not interested.'

'Are you sure?'

'Yeah, I'm sure.'

He keeps staring at his phone but leans towards me ever so slightly until our shoulders touch. His meaning is unmistakable and a small explosion of fireworks goes off in my solar plexus.

I gulp. 'Right.'

I'm relieved but also wincing inwardly. Julie's always getting the short stick with guys she likes, and even ones she doesn't. Now she's going to get rejected again because I selfishly wanted to live with Nathan even though I already had a boyfriend. OK, Callum wasn't the best boyfriend, but it was still a relationship. I'm being greedy. I should back off and let her have a turn. But I can't. Not with Nathan—he's special. If he got together with Julie now, I think I'd throw myself off a cliff in despair.

'Don't worry, I'll be gentle,' he tells me, reading my mind.

I close my eyes and listen to him typing a text to her, feeling like the worst friend in the world. I say an urgent prayer to the dating gods to please find Julie someone really nice. A sexy Latino guy with muscles on muscles who'll take her salsa dancing and make love to her all night long.

'Cool. That's done.'

I look over guiltily. Nathan's sent her the text and really doesn't look too cut up about it. Well, I can't force him to go out with someone he's not interested in, can I?

I lie on my back, looking up at the ceiling rose. It's barely light outside, and I've been awake for a while, pondering if I should have another day off. But I know I have to go back to work today. It's time to face Sian and hear about her relationship with Blaire and their love nest. Ugh. Does this mean I have to like her now? I pull a face and make a silent groaning noise so I don't disturb Nathan.

Yes, he's in bed next to me and fast asleep. Before you jump to any conclusions, he's fully clothed, and nothing happened. We were just tired and emotionally drained after talking, and since we were right next to the bed, we climbed in and went to sleep. There may have been a little hand holding, but definitely no kissing or anything else. Otherwise, I'd be lying here dreamily remembering what it was like to—

The alarm on Nathan's phone suddenly shrills, making me start in fright and disturbing a full-blown erotic fantasy.

He fumbles with his phone on the nightstand and rolls over sleepily to face me, his dark hair sticking up in all directions. He always looks so cute when he wakes up, like a groggy kitten.

'Mornin'.'

'Morning. What's with the alarm?' I enquire. 'Do you have to be somewhere?'

'Yeah, London. Remember?'

'Oh.' So it wasn't just a bad dream. He's definitely going today.

'I'll be back as soon as I can.'

'That's what they all say.' I stare up at the ceiling rose again.

'Hey.' Nathan turns my face to his. 'You trust me, don't you?'

'Yeah—' But now his lips are dangerously close to mine, and it's seriously distracting. I move slightly closer, but he pulls back.

'If we start kissing, I'm going to want to take it further,' he says softly. Blood rushes to my head and I feel slightly dizzy. Maybe my erotic fantasy is about to become reality.

'Is that such a bad thing?' I ask, breathing a little faster.

'Nah, but I've got a train to catch, and you have to go to work. And I want to do things . . . properly.'

I'm not exactly sure what he means by that. Wait until we've both cleaned our teeth?

'Properly?'

'You know, cook you a nice dinner, ply you with expensive wine, and then seduce you.'

I let out a snigger, then realise he's being serious. 'Ah, well, that sounds very nice. I look forward to being seduced,' I say politely.

Acute disappointment washes through me and Nathan must sense it. Because the next thing I know his hand is caressing my cheek and his lips are pressing against mine. The kiss is brief, we barely open our mouths, so it's not exactly the French kissing snog fest I've been fantasising about. But it's still fairly arousing. I want more. A whole lot more. I twine my arms around his neck for another go but his snooze alarm goes off. Nathan groans and twists round to the nightstand, putting a stop to any further shenanigans. He checks the time. 'Sorry, I want to. But I really have to shower and pack.'

I try not to mind. 'What time's your train?'

'Seven thirty. I should rattle my dags.'

'Huh?'

'Kiwispeak for "get a move on".'

'Weird. What are dags?'

He starts to explain. 'It's to do with sheep . . .' Then thinking better of it, he says hastily, 'Never mind!'

Chapter 23

HULA CAFE AND A MAKEOVER

⁂

I trudge to work through the Meadows, trying not to brood about Nathan and London. But it's all I can think about. He said he'd be down there for a week at least, but it could be longer. He sent a message from the train saying that he missed me already. But I haven't replied yet because I don't want to seem too eager, especially after the kiss that went nowhere. Besides, I have no idea what's going to happen when he comes back. Do we just start having a relationship as if I've never been with Callum? How is that going to work? The whole thing makes me uneasy, like it's doomed to failure.

It starts raining, a misty spray that falls in relentless sheets over the park and cause me to shiver despite being bundled up in a hat, scarf, and thick winter coat. This cold and dreary day is matching my disgruntled mood. Maybe I need to go away too. Somewhere warm, where I can sip cocktails by a pool and get some vitamin D.

Then it suddenly hits me: I'm a free woman. I can do anything I like! For the first time in two years, I don't have to run it past Callum to approve or disapprove. God, it's been like having another boss. I've lost count of the number of times I asked him about going on an all-inclusive holiday to Spain. He always screwed up his nose and said cheap package deals were tacky. He said he'd take me somewhere classier, like the Maldives. But he never did. Promises, promises.

I wait for some kind of nostalgia, despair, or heartache to wash over me. But strangely, I still can't dredge up anything except a faint sense of relief. Maybe I've had an emotional lobotomy where he's concerned?

Anyway, now that I have a plan of sorts, I brighten up and start walking faster to work. Thoughts are tumbling around in my brain like clothes on an easy-care wash cycle. I'll book a meeting with Blaire to see about taking some leave for the next couple of weeks. Even if Nathan comes back when I'm away, what of it? It'll show him I'm not hanging around gagging for it. That I have a life. Perhaps I'll also ask Julie if she wants to come for a girls' trip, as long as she doesn't start asking questions about Nathan. That could be awkward . . . OK, maybe it's not a good idea to invite Julie.

I've managed to think enough happy thoughts that by the time I get to work, I'm almost approachable by members of the public. But then I catch sight of Sian walking towards the poetry aisle, and my pleasant smile droops.

Her blonde hair is tied back neatly in a bun. She's wearing a brown tweed skirt, a salmon-pink cashmere jumper, a string of pearls, and, horror of horrors, brown lace-up brogues. She's actually starting to look like a librarian—and not in a hot way. It must be Blaire's influence. God, next she'll be sporting a pudding-basin haircut.

I've been trying not to think about it too much. But seeing her now looking like that, it makes the whole thing more concrete—Sian and Blaire are a couple. A couple that's bought a flat together. Is Sian nuts? She could do so much better. I take a deep breath. Open-minded and non-judgemental, that's what I need to be. I follow her into the aisle and say, 'Hey, Sian.'

'Hey, Em! Welcome back. How are you?' She looks me over critically. 'You're really pale. What the hell did you eat?'

'I think it was a prawn salad from Tesco.'

'Yuck.' She wrinkles her nose. 'You should ring their customer complaints.'

'Are you free for lunch today? I thought we could have a catch-up.'

Sian avoids my eyes. 'Sure, if you think you're up to it?'

'I should be fine. Hula Cafe?'

'OK, great.'

So that gives me exactly four hours to practice arranging my face into a pleasant expression when she tells me all about Blaire. Lucky for me, I studied drama. In the meantime, I've got a few days' work to catch up on. It feels good to have a legitimate distraction right now. It's mid-morning by the time I start to feel on top of my workload.

Then I get an email from callum@duncanstratt.co.uk, with the subject line 'Us':

> *Em, I know you're angry and you have a right to be, but I don't want us to be over. Please let's talk about this. We can work through it. – Love C*

A shiver of dread goes through me. I know what he's trying to do. He thinks he can 'work on me' like he does with his clients. Well, it's not going to happen. I delete the email and keep replying to the others in my inbox.

Just before I'm about to go to lunch with Sian, I get another email from callum@duncanstratt.co.uk with no subject line:

> *Emma, I know you've read my email. If you don't respond by COB, I'm coming to yours tonight. – C*

Dammit, he must have a read receipt notification on his emails. The tone of this one is slightly threatening, which worries me a little. But I'm determined not to be afraid of him. I'll double-lock the door and tell him to fuck off if he shows up and causes a scene. Part of me is glad Nathan's not here to get tangled up in this, but the other part is wishing he was here to provide some muscle.

Maybe I'd better reply to Callum to manage the situation so it doesn't get out of control. I'm not exactly sure what to say, so I leave it and go to meet Sian in the foyer.

At Hula, I order avocado on toast and a Popeye juice to fortify myself. Sian has a latte and a poke bowl. She eyes my green juice approvingly. 'That'll give you some vitamins. Has Nathan been looking after you?'

I cough and avoid looking at her. 'Yes, he's been very attentive.'

Sian puts down her fork. 'What's going on?'

'Nothing!' I hasten to assure her. 'Now what did you want to talk about?'

It's her turn to look uncomfortable. 'I don't know how much Callum's told you. But . . .' She takes a deep breath and laughs shakily. 'This is harder than I thought it would be.'

I can see she's really nervous, and I soften.

'You and Blaire are a couple, and you've bought a flat,' I state, putting her out of her misery.

She looks bemused. 'Ah, OK. He told you everything. He just sent me a vague text saying I should talk to you about Blaire asap. So I assumed something had happened.'

'Yeah, it did,' I say.

'You seem OK about it. Did you freak out?'

'Erm, there was other stuff going on at the time, so probably not as much as I should've.'

'What other stuff?'

I take a long sip of my Popeye. 'Callum asked me to marry him.'

Sian's hazel eyes widen. 'He didn't!' She glances at my left hand, which is devoid of a ring. 'So did you say yes or no?'

This is conveniently getting off the subject of her and Blaire. I need to steer the conversation back on track. But she should probably know.

'We broke up yesterday.'

She looks astonished. 'No wonder you haven't been at work. I'm sorry to hear that.'

I nod. 'Anyway, enough about my love life. Tell me about you and . . . ah . . . Blaire. How did that start?'

She seems reluctant to move the conversation away from my drama but obliges. It all comes out that Blaire had the hots for her and kept finding excuses to have meetings with her after work for inane reasons, like doing a stocktake of the stationery cupboard together. Then she would turn up on weekends when Sian was working and talk to her while she was reshelving.

'I got suspicious one Saturday when I was up the ladder. When I looked down, I caught her trying to peer up my skirt. I kind of got the hint then. I was curious to see what she'd do if I tried to make a move on her. So the next time she called me in for a meeting after work, I brought a bottle of wine with me and suggested we have a drink. Then I offered to give her a neck massage.'

Out of politeness, I ask, 'What happened after that?'

Sian looks a bit embarrassed. 'We had sex on the couch in her office.'

I gulp. 'Oh . . .'

'Yeah, it all kind of started from there.'

'How long have you been going out?'

'About six months. I'm sorry, I couldn't say anything. She didn't want people knowing since we work together. She swore me to secrecy. Besides, I didn't know if it would last. She's quite a lot older than me.'

'But you've bought a flat with her! That's kind of serious, isn't it?'

'Technically, it's more Blaire's flat than mine. She's the one with the deposit. I'm just going to help her pay the mortgage.'

'So how did Callum get involved?'

'She'd been wanting to move for ages and finally found a flat she liked. It just happened to be one of Callum's. So I had to tell him what was going on since I was viewing it with her. Then he mentioned Davita wanted the flat too, and it was all getting complicated. I was going to get Blaire to pull out, but he convinced me she should stick with it and said he'd put in a good word for her with the owner. Thanks to him, her offer was accepted. I feel crap about Davita, though.'

Good old Callum, he always makes sure he gets his commission one way or another.

'I did know about the flat in a roundabout fashion,' I say. 'I overheard you and Callum talking at the house-warming party. I was just . . . having a quiet moment in the pantry while you two were in the kitchen. From what I heard . . . I thought you were having an affair with him.'

'Oh, Em, I wouldn't do that to you.' She looks offended

at my insinuation.

'I know that now! But I was paranoid that he was mucking around behind my back. At the time, what I heard all made perfect sense. Or I wanted it to.'

Sian looks pointedly at my left hand again. 'I take it things came to a head?'

I hesitate. Callum is their real estate agent now so I'm reluctant to go into the details. Maybe I'll tell her the whole story one day. 'Yeah, we're definitely over. But I'm happy for you.'

'Thanks. Blaire's been terrified about how you'll react. She confessed last night that she was jealous of you.'

'Really? I can't imagine why.'

'Because she thought I liked you.'

I laugh nervously. 'That's daft.'

Sian grins at me and takes a forkful of salad. 'Yeah, you're not hot at all.'

'Ha ha.'

Just what my self-esteem needs to hear now that I'm newly single. Speaking of hot, I wonder what Nathan's up to. He must have arrived in London by now, but there's been no message. Where is he staying? He didn't mention a hotel or anything. I guess he must be kipping down at their house. But he said it was a three-bedroom. So if the boarder's in one room and Katie's in the other, is he going to be in with Naomi? Great. I seem to have transferred my paranoia about one guy onto another!

'Are you sure there's nothing else going on?' Sian watches me as I nibble on my avocado toast absent-mindedly. 'You look really spaced out.'

'No, nothing else.' I straighten up and smile, firmly pushing thoughts of Naomi and Nathan in bed together out of my mind. 'So there's one thing I'm dying to know.'

'Shoot.'

'I can understand why Blaire is into you. But why are *you* into *her*?'

To my relief, Sian laughs. 'I know she seems kind of uptight. But trust me, there's multiple levels going on beneath that haughty exterior. She has a crazy sense of humour, for one.'

I screw up my nose in disbelief. Blaire has a sense of humour? I don't think I've even seen her smile, let alone crack a joke. 'I'll take your word for it.'

'And she's very kind.'

Nope, another attribute I don't think I'd ever associate with Blaire. Maybe you have to get into her knickers before all these wonderful qualities start showing themselves.

'Well, that's great,' I remark, trying to be positive. 'I was actually thinking of asking her if I could book some time off. I know it's not ideal as I've just taken a bunch of sick leave.'

'I can't see why she wouldn't approve it. Just don't mention you've broken up with Callum. She thinks the sun shines out of his arse since he got her the flat. Say you're run-down and need a holiday. She'll understand.'

'Right.'

Back at work, Sian's comment about Callum is still ringing in my ears. He always seems to come out smelling of roses. I should take out a full-page ad in the *Scottish Times* to let people know the truth. What if he does the same thing to someone else? Surely I have a responsibility to warn unsuspecting women? But knowing Callum, he'd probably sue me for defamation and win thousands of pounds. And I'd end up looking like a bitter, twisted ex-girlfriend who's out for revenge. I think the best thing I can do is count my lucky stars I didn't marry him and move on with my life.

However, judging from the emails he's sending, getting him to move on might be more difficult. He seems to be having trouble accepting it. I guess if I have to see him, it's better to do so in a public place.

Keeping my reply brief, I reiterate what I said yesterday so he knows I'm sticking to my guns:

Callum, I'm not sure what we have to discuss? But fine, if you want me to tell you again that we're over I'll meet you at the cafe by my flat, on Saturday, 11am. – Emma

Hopefully, by Saturday, I'll have my head slightly more together. I don't think there's any danger that I'll fall for his promises, not this time. But he's going to try every trick in the book to get me to forgive him.

The rest of the afternoon passes slowly, but I do manage to pin Blaire down to a meeting at 4 p.m. As I trudge upstairs, my neck muscles tighten in apprehension. This is going to be interesting.

I haven't seen her for a while, so I'm totally unprepared when I walk into her office. I actually do a double take.

'Hello, Emma. Take a seat,' she says and gives me a passable imitation of a smile. My legs buckle, and I sit down forcibly on the chair and stare at her, astonished. Fuck me.

The glasses are gone (she's gotten contacts, I presume), and so is the pudding-basin haircut. She's sporting a shorter bob with highlights and layers that feather around her cheekbones. I peer closer. Good God, she's wearing make-up too! Foundation, blusher, mascara, and eyeliner—all expertly applied—and a generous slick of rose-pink lipstick. And her clothes! She has on a sexy black scoop-necked silk top with a chunky rose gold chain necklace. I can't see the bottom half as she's ensconced behind her desk, but I'm sensing a skirt and heels. This is obviously Sian's influence, and she's given her one hell of a makeover. Blaire honestly looks about twenty years younger. If I saw her in the street, I wouldn't recognise her.

Before I can help myself, I blurt out, 'Wow, you look fantastic!'

Blaire colours and immediately starts shuffling bits of paper around on her desk, but I can tell she's pleased.

'Thank you. It's certainly a different look for me. I'm not used to thinking about my appearance, but I'm quite enjoying it.'

She gives me a coquettish grin, and I almost fall off my chair. She's definitely got a touch of mystique or allure going on. I kind of get why Sian is with her now. Multiple levels indeed! I glance at the navy corduroy couch against the opposite wall—where the said sex took place. Yikes!

'Now, Emma, what did you want to see me about?'

I drag my attention back to Blaire and try to focus.

'Ah, would it be OK if I booked some annual leave—just a couple of weeks, for a holiday?'

'Ah, yes, I know you've been unwell the last few days. Perhaps a holiday is just what you need.'

Her tone is kind, and all of a sudden, I want to tell her exactly what's been going on. How I'm now terrified Callum is going to make things extremely difficult for me. How I'm even more terrified of what's going to happen with Nathan. I'm worried that things are going to implode between us because I might start accusing him of things he's not even guilty of. I'm going to drive him away and end up alone—a sad, pathetic loser who can't trust anyone.

But even though Blaire is a new and improved version of herself and is with one of my best friends, she's not a counsellor—she's my boss.

So I smile vaguely. 'Yeah, I'm feeling a bit run-down, and this weather isn't helping,' I tell her, gesturing at the lattice window which outlines a gloomy patch of sky.

Blaire glances at it. 'Yes, the weather this time of year can be quite mentally draining. That's fine, Emma. Just let me know your dates when you're ready, and I'll block it out on the staff calendar.'

'Great, thank you. That would be wonderful.' I breathe a sigh of relief. Leaving the country means I can avoid the Callum situation at least.

'When you come back,' she continues, 'I thought we could talk about you moving into a senior librarian role with a salary to match. I've had a good think about it, and you're right. Retaining quality staff is important, and I wouldn't like to think of you having to change jobs because you can't get ahead here.'

Seriously? That's a bit of a turnaround. I don't know what to say except 'Uh, thank you. I'd really appreciate that.'

'It's also been brought to my attention that you didn't receive the five percent pay rise that some of the other staff members did. I'll rectify that as of your next pay. I want you to know that I do value your work here, Emma.'

Dumbfounded, I nod automatically and say, 'Thank you.' But what I really feel like saying is 'Gosh, having a friend that's sleeping with the boss is definitely working in my favour.'

All the generosity that's overflowing from her is slightly overwhelming. I know it's because of Sian, that she's pleaded my case. So it doesn't feel like a victory on my own merits, but if Blaire's finally offering me a promotion and a pay rise, I'd be stupid to turn it down. Ironically, if she'd agreed to promote me at the last meeting we'd had, I probably wouldn't have done the life modelling gig or needed Nathan to move in. And I'd still be none the wiser about Callum. But I guess everything happens for a reason, and it's better that everything's now out in the open.

When I get back to my desk, Sian is hanging around nearby, waiting to see if everything went OK. I give her a thumbs up, and she looks relieved. Callum hasn't sent through any more emails, but there's a Google invite in my inbox. He's set up an official meeting for Saturday. God, he's so pedantic.

Chapter 24

MR UNARTISTIC

⁂

The flat feels empty without Nathan when I get home after work. It's also weird that I'm not going round to Callum's since it's Thursday night. As I've just been given a pay rise and a promotion, I feel like I should be celebrating, but there's no one to celebrate with. I make a cup of tea and hold it up to toast the empty kitchen. 'Yay me!' I say out loud and instantly feel ridiculous.

I wander into the lounge. Nathan has left *The Undomestic Goddess* on the window seat with an orange Post-it Note marking his place. Sure enough, he's just finished reading the lovemaking scene. He must've read that particular bit a few times because there are smudged fingerprints, which I'm sure aren't mine, all down the margin. That's funny, kind of sweet too. And it makes me start wishing he were here. I grab my phone from my handbag and quickly type: *I miss you too. How's London?*

I figure there's no point playing hard to get. He knows I like him. Thirty seconds later, my phone rings as if Nathan's been sitting there watching for a message. My heart expands. 'Hey!'

'Gidday.' His gravelly voice resounds in my ear, triggering a warm glow. 'I got your message,' he says.

I laugh. 'I know, I just sent it.'

'Well, yes. You did. I got it.' He seems to be having difficulty forming sentences of more than two words.

'So, how's London?' I ask.

'Yeah, sweet. Busy, crowded. A bit of a culture shock after Edinburgh actually. What about you, how was work?'

'Better than expected,' I reply. 'I got a pay rise, and it looks like I'm going to be promoted!'

'Aw, that's great, Emma!' Nathan sounds chuffed for me, and I wish he were here so we could celebrate together.

Then I hear a woman's voice in the background saying something to him.

'Is that Naomi?' I ask.

'Yeah, hang on.' He covers the mouthpiece, and I hear muffled talking. Then he says, 'She wants to chat with you.'

I'm a little disconcerted. 'She does? Ah, sure.'

There's a slight kerfuffle as his phone is handed over. 'Hi, Emma. Nathan's been telling me all about Edinburgh and your awesome apartment. I hope he's being a good flattie?'

She's got a softer New Zealand accent than he does; she almost sounds British. And wow, she's really friendly. For some reason, I pictured her as a cold bitch. From her voice, she sounds pretty too. Pretty women always have nice voices.

'Och, yes, he's been a perfect flatmate,' I say politely. *Apart from having a bath with me, and the kiss in bed this morning. But he's only human. He's allowed a few slip-ups.*

Naomi gives a genuine chuckle. 'I love hearing your accent. Scottish people are the best. I've only been to Edinburgh once, but we had a fun weekend staying with Nathan's aunt in Stockbridge.'

'Oh? I haven't met her.'

I can hear Nathan asking to have his phone back. 'Anyway, I just wanted to say hi, and you're welcome to visit any time you're in London.'

'Oh, thanks. That's nice of you.'

'No worries! Here's Nathan again.'

Nathan's back on the line. 'Sorry about that. Naomi can talk the hind leg off a donkey once she gets started—ow! You can!' She's evidently whacked him on the arm.

In my head, I picture them in a light-filled white lounge with a high ceiling. It has polished dark wood floorboards covered with a Moroccan area rug, leafy green houseplants, a tasteful leather couch they chose together, and Katie's toys—building blocks, a Barbie, a dollhouse—are strewn around. His London family life.

My stomach twists. I need to ask him the question that's bothering me: *So where are you sleeping?* I thought I'd just casually drop it into the conversation. But now it seems too petty-minded to ask it after Naomi's proven to be so nice.

'I should go. You sound busy,' I say instead.

'Yeah, I've been relegated to cook dinner.'

I force a cheerful tone. 'Ah, I see your cooking skills are

just as much in demand in London as they are here.'

'Hmm, yeah. We're definitely getting takeaways tomorrow night,' he grumbles good-naturedly.

I get the feeling Nathan hasn't said anything to Naomi about me, except in a flatmate sense. And that's what I'm worried about. What if he gets back together with her and plays happy families? It's starting to make me feel really stressed . . .

'Hello?'

I realise I've spaced out, and Nathan's been waiting for me to say something.

'Yes, sorry, I'm here. It's been a long day.'

'You sound tired. Callum hasn't been harassing you, has he?'

'A little. He wants to meet up to talk, so I said I would on Saturday at the cafe by the flat. I don't particularly want to, but it's better than him banging the door down because I won't answer his emails.'

'He's going to try and get you back.' Nathan's voice has a warning tone.

'Yes, I'm aware of that. But it's not going to happen, no matter how much he wants it to.'

'Sorry I'm not there to provide moral support. Just ring me if you want to talk, OK? If I don't pick up, leave a voicemail, and I'll ring you back.'

I breathe a sigh of relief. He still cares. 'OK, thanks. I appreciate that. And likewise—if you ever want to talk, I'm here.' I pause and then add, 'I really miss you.'

'Me too,' Nathan says in a low voice. From the echoey tone, it sounds like he's gone into another room, so he's out of Naomi's hearing. Then all my fears dissipate like morning mist with his next words: 'I can't wait to see you again.'

On Friday night, I'm cooking up a storm in the kitchen. Nathan had been hogging the hob lately, so I'm enjoying having it to myself for once. I'm just putting the finishing touches on a Thai green curry when my phone beeps on the counter. After wiping the sweat from my forehead with the back of my hand, I check it. Damn, it's a text from Lorna asking if I can do a session tomorrow morning at 11 a.m. She says she's sorry about the short notice, but the model has just texted her, pleading illness.

It would have to be the exact same time I'm supposed to meet Callum, wouldn't it? I'll just tell him I'll meet him later instead. I reply to Lorna saying I can do it, then bring up Callum's Google invite and propose a new time of 2 p.m. He's probably going to flip out since he's such a control freak, but too bad. What can he do?

The next morning, I put on my usual leggings and sweatshirt (no underwear), shrug into my coat, and head out into the frosty air to catch the bus to Morningside. Callum hasn't accepted my update to our meeting or sent any protest email either. Maybe he hasn't received it yet? Too busy having drinks with Camille, engaging in sex with the domme, or toning his abs—who knows, who cares.

When I get to Lorna's, I can see from her face she's relieved I've turned up. She quickly ushers me inside. 'Thank you so much for doing this, Emma. You're a lifesaver! Sophie is usually reliable, but she's got some stomach bug that's going around, perhaps that's why you felt ill the other day? Anyway, it's quite a large group this morning. I'm going to have to add more easels.'

'How many?' I ask nervously, following her upstairs.

'Oh, ten, maybe twelve,' she throws back over her shoulder.

My first big group of artists—that's a little daunting! When we get to the top of the stairs, Lorna sees my dubious expression. 'You'll be fine, Emma. Honestly, you're a pro now. Just relax and let it all hang out.'

I giggle a bit at that, and she laughs too. 'Probably not the sort of thing I should say to a life model!'

She busies herself getting some more easels and chairs from a storage cupboard, and I head into the anteroom to get changed into a cotton robe. After that, I check my phone and see Callum has messaged me: *Where are you? I'm in your flat.*

For God's sake, what's he doing in my flat? I type rapidly: *I've got an appointment. I sent you a new time last night for 2pm. Check your email!*

I have to go as people will be arriving soon, so I chuck my

phone in my bag. I can feel my blood pressure rising. He gets me so riled up. Deep breaths. Think serene thoughts: fluffy clouds, sunlit meadows, trickling streams . . . Hmm, I need to use the bathroom before I start the session.

Everything's going well, and I'm in the middle of my third pose, a standing-up one. I've managed to overcome my nerves of having such a large number of people studying my naked body intently. The trick is to look at a spot on the wall beyond their heads, not directly at individual faces. Otherwise, I'll start reading into their expressions: 'He's staring at my tits with a smirk. Does he think they're too big, too small?' or 'She's frowning at my thighs. Does she think they're fat?' Honestly, it can drive you mental if you start going down that path.

I'm zoning out, wondering if I'll get to talk to Nathan this weekend and what I should make for dinner tonight, when I become aware of a commotion outside the studio door. I can hear Jack protesting to someone, 'You can't go in! There's a session on.'

Is it an artist who's running late? I wonder.

Lorna looks at me and raises her eyebrows. She heads across to the door. But just before she gets there, it bursts open, and to my utter horror, Callum comes barrelling into the room, with Jack on his heels. Jack grabs hold of Callum's arm, but he yanks it out of his grasp. 'Get your hands off me!'

he roars.

All the artists' heads swivel towards him as one, but Callum ignores them. His gaze falls on me, standing there starkers with my mouth open in shock. I know I shouldn't be embarrassed or ashamed, but the expression on his face is one of pure disgust and I shrivel.

'For fuck's sake, get your clothes on, Emma!' he barks.

There's a titter from the group of artists at the little scene unfolding. Most of them seem amused by Callum's theatrics, but Jack's not impressed.

Judging from his agitated manner, I can see Callum isn't about to go away quietly, so I put on my robe and walk with as much dignity as I can muster to the anteroom. Everyone's whispering and staring. The class is pretty much over, and I'm sure there's no way Lorna's going to charge them for an incomplete session and such a rude disruption.

'What the *fuck* do you think you're doing?' I hiss at Callum, who's followed me into the room. 'You just cost me two hundred pounds!'

'That's all you care about, isn't it? The money!' he throws back at me. 'You're prostituting yourself!'

I shrug off my robe and reach for my sweatshirt and leggings. 'Don't be so bloody dramatic! There's no sex involved!'

'Emma? Are you all right?' Lorna pokes her head in.

I pick up my handbag, and Callum grabs my arm. 'She's leaving. Now.'

He steers me out the door, and Lorna has to step back hastily to avoid getting whacked in the face.

'Emma, what's going on?' Jack is scowling, his lips pursed in annoyance.

'I'm really sorry. This is Callum, my ex. We've just broken up. He's obviously a bit upset,' I say apologetically.

'Don't tell him that!' Callum raps out immediately. 'It's none of his business!'

'It is my business when you come barging into my house without being invited and start ordering people around. Who the *hell* do you think you are?' Jack retorts.

'Callum, let's just leave,' I urge quickly, seeing his fist clench. 'You've done enough.'

'Good idea,' adds Jack. 'We don't really want your type here.'

'My type? What exactly is *my* type?' Callum sneers.

Jack looks him up and down and says witheringly, 'Unartistic.'

Callum snorts derisively and pushes me out the door in front of him. Eyeballing Jack, he says loudly so the whole class can hear, 'At least I don't go round painting naked schoolboys with big cocks!'

Then he slams the door loudly behind us. I groan. Oh God, kill me now!

'Let's go!' he says briskly in my ear. 'These people are a bunch of degenerates.'

'No, they're not!'

Furiously, I march down the stairs and out of the house with Callum following me. When we're on the street, he tries to talk to me, but I walk off without listening. I can't bear to be anywhere near him.

'Hey!' he calls out. 'Don't storm off like that!'

Angry tears are blinding my vision, so I can hardly see. I wipe them away and yell back to him, 'Fuck off! You've just humiliated me in front of a roomful of people!'

'I think you'll find you humiliated yourself, Emma!' he replies smugly when he's caught up to me in a few strides.

'Just leave me alone!'

If this is his revenge for me finding out about him and the domme, then he's made his point. We reach the main road, and he's still sauntering alongside me. I get to the bus stop and try to calm down, but I'm having trouble managing my anger. 'How did you find me anyway?' I growl.

'It wasn't hard,' he says, sounding pleased with himself. 'I just went to the gallery and asked the owner where Jack Sutton lived. I said I wanted to meet the famous artist in person. He was only too happy to oblige. That painting of his is dire, by the way. You should be glad I've saved you from being the laughing stock of Morningside.'

'Saved me? Is that what you're trying to do? I'm perfectly capable of making my own decisions! Besides, you're a fine one to talk. You're hardly a fucking saint!'

To my chagrin, Callum just smiles and states, 'Well, maybe we're more alike than you think.'

'What do you mean?'

'I mean, you're just as bad.'

For two years, I've put up with his sanctimonious shit, and he's still trying to ram it down my throat—even after cheating on me. It's unbelievable. I stare at his self-righteous expression, and something inside me snaps. 'What you did to me is nothing like life modelling!' I scream at him, 'NOTHING!'

All the screaming I'm doing is making passers-by stop and gawk at us. An attractive couple having a domestic in Morningside Road is a rare-enough occurrence that it's bound to draw attention. Someone starts filming us with their phone, and Callum sees them. He instantly turns his back on the filmer to hide his face. Of course, if it gets posted on Facebook and shared around, then his reputation will be in tatters.

But I start yelling, 'This is Callum Stewart, everyone! He's a real estate agent for Duncan Stratt! He's a cheater! He's been having it off with a—'

Callum tries to cover my mouth with his hand to shut me up, and I shove him off me, hard. He staggers into the street—right into the path of an oncoming dark-blue Toyota Prius, which slams on its brakes. He flies up over the bonnet, hits his head on the windscreen, and slithers down into the road to lie there like a limp rag doll. Someone gives a blood-curdling scream, and then the reality of it hits home: *Fuck! I think I've just killed Callum.*

It turns out that Callum isn't dead; he just got knocked out for a bit. A large group of MAMILs (middle-aged men in Lycra) who are out for a Saturday jog happen to be going past and immediately take charge of directing the traffic. One of them puts his tracksuit top over Callum and then crouches down to ask him questions to keep him awake. Perhaps he has some kind of first aid or medical training?

Now there's a crowd of curious onlookers surrounding us, and they form a barrier that pedestrians are having to push past. A middle-aged woman with a Waitrose shopping bag says that she's called an ambulance and it's on its way. She puts her free arm around me, and I lean against her gratefully. Everyone's being very kind and helpful now that there's an injured party in their midst.

The driver of the Prius, a guy in his forties with thinning brown hair, has pulled up onto the kerb and is talking to a couple of the MAMILs. He keeps throwing distraught glances at Callum as if he's going to cark it. Callum has his eyes closed and is very pale. He also has a big purple lump on his forehead, so I'm not surprised the driver is worried.

'Should we put him into the recovery position?' I wonder aloud to the woman. That's the only thing I can recall that you should do in these situations, but she shakes her head and says something about not moving him in case there's a 'spinal injury'. An image of pushing Callum around in a wheelchair while he sullenly rebukes me for causing him to be disabled flashes through my brain. Great, my life as I know it is officially over.

The wailing of an ambulance is heard in the distance and gets louder until it's blaring and flashing its lights right next to us. Then a police car pulls up too. After that, everything happens quickly. The police start talking to the driver of the Prius, and a couple of ambulance guys jump out the back and take over looking after Callum from the MAMILs, who decide to continue on with their jog now that they have nothing to do.

'He'll be all right, love,' says the MAMIL who was crouching next to him. 'He'll just have a bit of a sore head for a while.'

One of the ambulance guys notices the exchange and comes over. 'Are you with Callum?' he asks me.

I nod, deciding not to explain the nature of our relationship. I'm not sure how he's found out his name. Callum must've told him. To my relief, the guy doesn't ask what happened; and if he knows, he doesn't appear judgemental.

'His vitals are good, and there's no spinal injury that we can determine.' I send a silent prayer of thanks to God for that. 'But he's likely concussed. They'll probably keep him overnight in hospital to run some checks. Do you want to come in the ambulance with us?'

'I . . . I guess. Do I have to talk to the police, though?' The police have finished speaking to the driver and don't seem to want anything from me. Maybe no one said anything about what I did?

Callum has already been loaded into the ambulance on a stretcher, and one of the guys lends me a hand to pull me up the short ladder on the side. I shuffle over and see that Callum's eyes are open. They've put a neck brace on him.

'Hi,' I say. 'How are you feeling?'

He mumbles something, so I lean closer to catch it. He says in a low, but clear voice, 'Stay away from me, you crazy bitch.'

I jerk back in alarm. Suddenly, being locked in the back of an ambulance with Callum is the last place I want to be, especially if he blames me for putting him in there.

'I've changed my mind,' I declare hastily to the ambulance guy and clamber out before they close the doors. 'I'll visit him later at the hospital.'

'Right, suit yourself.' He gives me a curious glance, and I know I'm coming across as an unfeeling cow.

The ambulance drives off with its lights flashing, and I immediately burst into tears. The guy in the Prius, who turns out to be an Uber driver called Martin, kindly offers to give me a lift to Bruntsfield for free. But as soon as I get in the car, he promptly starts talking about how guilty he feels. I reassure him that it was an accident and that if it's anyone's fault, it's mine. We keep batting the blame ball backwards and forwards over the tennis net until we reach my flat. I almost ask him in for a cup of tea so we can continue, but it's not really helping anything. So I just say, 'Thanks for the lift.' I manage to get in one last 'It's not your fault—it's mine' before I shut the car door on his protesting face.

I can hardly climb the stairs. I'm so drained. All I want to do is curl up in bed, go to sleep, and forget this day ever happened. When I finally get to the top floor, the door is slightly ajar. Oh no, don't tell me I've been burgled as well! Then I remember Callum messaged me from here, before he figured out that my 'appointment' meant I was doing a life modelling session. He must've left in a hurry and forgotten to close the door.

In the hallway, there's a scrap of white paper with a charcoal mark on it lying on the carpet. Weird. Then as I look up the hallway, I notice a whole series of white paper scraps with charcoal marks leading like a trail of breadcrumbs to Nathan's room. With a feeling of dread, I push open the door and see his sketchbook lying spread-eagled on the bed but there's just the cover and a few jagged remnants of pages. Bits of paper are everywhere, all over the bed and the floor, like someone's stood there and deliberately torn the pages into tiny pieces, then strewn them like confetti around the room.

My eye is drawn to the other side of the bed, where there's a larger mound of torn paper. It's Nathan's life modelling drawings—every one of them ripped to shreds. I slump onto the bed in stunned disbelief. This is spiteful, even for Callum. But then again, he's a stickler for having the last word.

Chapter 25

DRINKS WITH JULIE

⁂

'He did *what*? The fuckwit!'

Understandably, Nathan is fuming. I'm not exactly sure what to say to make him feel better. I put it off for as long as I could—slowly drinking a cup of tea, having a long shower—but eventually I had to ring and tell him the whole story. He listened without saying anything until the part where I came home and found his room covered in confetti.

'I'm so sorry. If it's any consolation, he's probably feeling incredibly guilty right now and, since he's in hospital with a sore head, quite a bit of pain too.'

Nathan snorts. 'Nah, I doubt he's even feeling a twinge of guilt. God! I put so much time and effort into those drawings, especially the ones of you. That was *some of my best work*!'

I blanch at his irate tone. 'I know, they were brilliant. You're so talented. But you can do more.'

He grunts. 'Somehow I doubt you're going to be posing as Cleopatra again.'

I don't say anything. Apart from a text from Lorna to check that I was all right, things have been stonily silent. Callum bursting in unannounced may have ruined that for me too.

Nathan sighs in exasperation. 'Look, Emma, I have to run. Thanks for telling me at least. Take care.' He hangs up.

I feel an inward clutch of unease. OK, that was abrupt and kind of hurtful. If he's got doubts about getting involved with me (and I'm sure he does), a jealous ex-boyfriend who's out for revenge may have just tipped him over the edge.

I feel so bad for him. But what can I do about it? Give him some space to process the loss, I guess?

My phone rings, and I sigh in relief. That was quick; apparently, he's processed the loss already.

'Hi,' I say eagerly.

'Hi, Emma? It's Davita.'

'Oh, hey!' I try to inject enthusiasm into my voice.

'Hey. So I'm at the hospital visiting my granny, who's recovering from a bad flu, and guess who's in the room two doors down from her? Callum!' she announces dramatically.

'I know he's there,' I say dejectedly.

'What happened?'

'He got hit by a car.'

'Oh my God! Is he OK?'

'I think so.'

There's a confused silence. 'But why aren't you here by his bedside?'

'Davita, it's a long story,' I tell her, unwilling to go into it. Then I think, *Fuck it.* 'I broke up with him a few days ago. We had an argument on the street today, in Morningside. He was upset and stepped out in front of a car and hit his head on the windscreen. He's probably got a concussion, so they'll keep him in overnight.'

'You've broken up?' Davita is breathing heavily. She hasn't registered anything else I've said except that fact.

'Yes.'

There's a loaded silence, and I immediately picture her with a hand over her mouth, stifling a cry of joy. She's been waiting for this moment for a very long time. Davita's so into Callum that I think she'd go for it even if she had to push him around in a wheelchair complaining his head off.

I venture, 'If it's not too much trouble, would you mind—'

'Of course I'll visit him! I'd be glad to,' she interrupts. 'Granny May will be fine for a bit. Won't you, granny?' There's a croaking reply, and I get the feeling Granny May might have to fend for herself, even if she's on death's door.

'I'll ring you later, Emma.'

'Thanks, Davita. Please tell Callum I said—'

But she's hung up on me. I have to laugh. I'd love to see Callum's expression when she comes careening into the room high on the knowledge that he's now single.

The next few days slip by uneventfully. It's midweek by the time Davita calls me back and says that Callum's been discharged from hospital. Apparently, the concussion was quite bad, and he told the police he was having trouble remembering how he got hit by the car. But judging from his comment to me in the ambulance, he knew exactly what happened, so that's odd. It could be that he doesn't want the police asking too many questions about his private life. I doubt he's trying to protect me—protecting his own arse, more like.

Anyway, Davita tells me he's taken a few weeks off to recuperate. She also mentions she's been food shopping and cooking meals for him. I raise my eyebrows at that. She makes it sound perfectly innocent, as if she is doing her Christian duty by cooking him a casserole. But Davita's no nun. If Callum gives her the slightest sign that he's interested, then she'll be in like Flynn. But I think it's highly unlikely he will, especially once he comes to his senses. She's a burlesque dancer, after all. Surely it would make him a bit of a hypocrite to get involved with her? Besides, there's a good chance I'll warn her about his 'hobby' that involves black PVC leather and liquid honey.

So far, I've kept my mouth shut about all that and haven't told anyone apart from Nathan, who's still in London and who's gone very quiet on the messaging and calling front. *He's processing,* I keep telling myself. But his silence is starting to worry me.

In an effort to stop thinking about it, I've started researching Spanish towns where the weather's still reasonably warm in October. Lloret de Mar in Costa Brava, set against a backdrop of craggy green hills, is the top contender. It has a bunch of three-star hotels with pools, all within walking distance of a long curving strip of golden sand beach. Now I just have to choose one of them and tell Blaire my dates. For the first time in two years, I'm going on holiday as a singleton. The thought of it is making me balk.

On Thursday night, after doing an online cardio workout, I'm in the kitchen sniffing a kale and wheatgrass smoothie purchased from the cafe downstairs. It's all part of my new 'get healthy' routine. After one foul-tasting tentative gulp, which has me wondering if I should alternate sips with squares of dark chocolate, a WhatsApp message from Julie appears: *Just heard about you and Callum from Davita, r u ok???! Want to go for a drink (or four) tomorrow night?*

So much for health and fitness. The green gloop gets dumped in the sink. It tastes like shit anyway.

My phone, which has been as quiet as the grave for the last few days, now starts beeping madly with messages of condolence from friends and acquaintances who've heard about the break-up. Apparently, Davita has decided to tell a few people and the news has spread like wildfire. It feels like the final nail in the coffin of my relationship with Callum. There's no going back now. We're officially over. Our lives are about to head in different directions. We're never going to have a chicken curry takeaway or watch Netflix together ever again. I'm never going to stand in his swanky kitchen and drink my cup of Earl Grey tea while he reads the *Financial Times*. And he's never going to look at me *that way* and run his sexy manicured fingers down his blue silk tie, the one that matches his eyes.

A nostalgic ache starts up somewhere deep down in my chest and keeps getting stronger. I hastily head to the lounge, flip open my laptop, and begin another cardio workout. The best thing to do is exercise to the point of exhaustion so I fall sound asleep, then I won't have to feel anything. Well, that's the plan anyway.

Julie and I meet at our usual pub in the West End after work the next day. It's quite close to Callum's flat, which makes me nervous. But it's not like he's taken out a restraining order on me or anything. I almost suggested she come to the pub in Bruntsfield, but I don't think I can cope with that outrageously flirtatious barman.

When I walk in, Julie's already there, nursing a glass of red and scrolling on her phone. I slide into the booth opposite her.

'Hey, Em.' She peers at me, then hands me the glass. 'You take this. I'll go and grab some more.'

I take a long swallow of wine, then another. Stuff cardio workouts for getting over a break-up. Alcohol is needed—and lots of it. Julie is back with two bottles of red and another glass.

'Are you trying to get me drunk?' I ask, eyeing the bottles. 'Because that's just what the doctor ordered.'

'You look like you need it. God, Em, what's been going on? Davita said Callum was hit by a car and that you'd broken up.'

'Yeah,' I confirm, taking a sip of wine. 'But it was the other way round. We'd broken up *before* the car hit him.'

'Tell me exactly what happened.'

Where do I even begin?

'So I found out Callum was seeing a dominatrix behind my back.' Julie's mouth drops open. 'Please don't ask me the details,' I say hurriedly. 'Believe me, you don't want to hear them. Anyway, I broke up with him on Wednesday last week. He wouldn't accept it and wanted to meet up to talk. I told him Saturday morning, but then I got a life modelling session for the same time.'

'Life modelling!' Her eyebrows shoot up under her fringe. 'How long have you been doing that? Hang on . . . It was you, wasn't it? You were Cleopatra, in Nathan's drawing.'

Oh shit, I didn't expect her to remember that.

'Well, yes, but he didn't know it was me at the time. I was in disguise.'

'At the time? So he knows about it now?'

Yikes, this is getting awkward. 'Yes, I told him.'

She purses her lips and folds her arms. 'Go on.'

I slosh some more wine into my now empty glass with a

shaking hand.

'So, ah, I was doing the session in Morningside, and Callum figured out where it was and came bursting into the studio. He yelled at me to put my clothes on in front of everyone. It was mortifying.'

Julie doesn't say anything. I clear my throat. 'So then we left, and he followed me to the bus stop. He said we were both as bad as each other, and I was angry and kind of . . . pushed him, and he stumbled into the street and got hit by an Uber driver. I thought I'd killed him, but I guess I'll have to try harder next time,' I finish weakly, attempting to make a joke.

'Jesus, Emma!' Julie stares at me, aghast. 'In Morningside, no less.'

'I know, it sounds like something out of a soap opera. But it gets worse . . .'

'Worse?'

'I got back to the flat, and Callum had torn up Nathan's artwork and scattered it all over the room. There's nothing left. Now Nathan won't talk to me. He's in London, by the way, sorting out house stuff with his ex.'

'Is something going on with you and Nathan?' she asks immediately.

'No!' I protest vehemently. Maybe too much so.

Julie looks at me in disbelief. 'But why would Callum do that then?'

'Because he'd asked me to marry him, and I came clean

about the life modelling and that it was me Nathan had drawn. And he really didn't like it. I guess he was jealous.'

She sits back and shakes her head. 'Gosh, your life is so much more exciting than mine.'

And I haven't even told her about Blaire and Sian!

'I wouldn't say it was particularly exciting. Stressful, more like.' I'm relieved she hasn't asked any more questions about Nathan.

'You have to admit, Callum has a point,' she says.

'Huh?'

'Well, both of you are living double lives. Keeping secrets because you think the other person won't be happy if they know the truth.'

'Uh, yeah, though my secret is a little less damaging than his. I wasn't having sex with someone!'

Julie narrows her eyes. 'And you and Nathan haven't . . . I mean, you do live together.' *Uh oh.*

'No, we haven't.'

'Just that he sent me a text last week that made me wonder.'

I look at her questioningly.

'Oh, you can see it if you want. I don't mind.' She finds the text and hands her phone to me.

Basically, he's let her down gently with a 'it's not you, it's me' stance. He thinks she's great, but he's not sure it would work because he's emotionally involved with someone. And that he hopes they can be friends. It's actually really well worded. I think even I'd feel OK if I received it.

'I assumed he was talking about his ex,' says Julie, holding out her hand for her phone. 'But now I'm not so sure. He's talking about you, isn't he?'

There's no point trying to deny it. 'OK, I admit it. There was a mutual attraction there when he first saw the flat. It was dumb to choose him, but I couldn't help it. Callum was being—well, Callum, and I just wanted . . . I don't know.'

'A tasty treat,' Julie finishes for me. Then she licks her lips, which makes me giggle.

'More of a "look but don't touch" treat. I honestly didn't plan on anything happening. But we've bonded, I guess. And he's been really supportive about Callum.'

'He's a nice guy, and it definitely sounds like he's got feelings for you.'

She's taking this really well. They didn't really spend that much time together, so perhaps that's why she's not too heartbroken.

I shrug. 'Yeah, well, that was before Callum ripped up his drawings. Now my name is mud.'

'Och, he'll get over it. So . . . ?'

'So what?'

'You and Nathan?'

'I don't know.'

'You're not thinking about getting back together with Callum, surely?'

'No! Definitely not. We're done. At least I think we're

done.'

Julie frowns. 'God, Em, don't go running back to Callum because you're afraid of being alone.'

'I *am* afraid of being alone.'

She rolls her eyes. 'I've been alone for the past three years, and it hasn't killed me yet. Besides, why not Nathan?'

I take a deep breath. 'I don't know if it will work. I think I have trust issues.'

'What makes you think he can't be trusted?'

I shrug. 'Just a gut feeling.'

Julie clicks her tongue. 'Gut, schmut, that's not the way to approach it. What are the pros and cons? Make a list. You must know him well enough by now.'

'I did start doing that! I'm not completely clueless.'

She clicks her tongue, opens the notepad app on her phone, and types 'Nathan - Pros'.

We look at each other, and she automatically types 'Sexy as hell'. Well, it goes without saying. 'Next.'

'He's easy to talk to.' She types 'Good listener'.

'He makes me laugh.' She types 'GSOH'.

'He's arty.' She types 'Creative'.

'He likes reading.' She types 'Intelligent'.

'He's kind.' She types 'Caring'.

'He cooks . . . Oh, and he cleans too.' Julie laughs and types 'OMG!' But then she deletes that and replaces it with 'House-trained'.

'He's also fine about my life modelling. You should

probably add that,' I say. She dutifully types 'Open-minded'.

She contemplates the list and then asks, 'What are the cons?'

I shrug. 'I don't think he has any.'

Julie stares at me. 'Oh my Lord, you've got it so bad for him that even his cons are pros!'

'Don't be silly. I'm sure he has loads of cons. He's just been on his best behaviour. No one's that perfect. There has to be a catch.'

'Emma . . .'

'I'm sick of discussing men,' I state hurriedly. 'Let's talk about something else.' I finish what's left of my wine and reach for the half-empty second bottle. 'Sooo, I'm just about to book a long-overdue two-week holiday to Costa Brava. Do you want to come with me? It's going to be a girls' trip.'

Chapter 26

THE STOCKBRIDGE FLAT

⁂

The next morning, I'm fighting off a hangover and in the middle of a bikini-body workout in the lounge when I finally get a message from Nathan: *Hey! I'm back, just staying in Stockbridge for a bit to help my aunt out with a few things.*

I instantly pause the workout so the girl with the toned abs is suspended mid-sit-up. I'm relieved that Nathan's back and speaking to me, but the message is vague enough that it makes me suspicious. How long is he staying there? A few days? A few weeks? Is he using his mysterious aunt as an excuse? Does she even exist? What if he's got a secret girlfriend tucked away in Stockbridge?

OK, I realise that last one is a bit far-fetched. But you do hear about these things happening, so it pays not to be too naive. Testing the water, I type back: *Hey! I'm not doing anything this weekend, I don't mind helping out too?*

Instantly, he replies: *Nah, all good. But thanks.*

OK, so he definitely doesn't want me poking my nose in. This calls for thinking outside the box.

I message Sian: *Hey S, can you give me Nathan's aunt's address in Stockbridge? I'm meeting him there to go for a coffee.*

I wait for half an hour. Nothing. So I decide to ring her. Eventually, she picks up.

'Hi, Em.' She sounds wary.

'Hi,' I say breezily. 'I just messaged you, but you may not have got it. Can you give me Nathan's aunt's address? He's there at the minute, and he invited me for a coffee.'

'Why did he not give it to you?'

I think quickly. 'He forgot. I messaged him back to get it, but he's helping her with something. He's not answering his phone, and I have to catch the bus shortly.'

'Well, if he invited you . . . It's 19 St Bernard's Crescent. Ground-floor flat,' she reveals grudgingly.

This is getting weirder and weirder. What's the big deal about giving me her address?

'Thanks, Sian.'

'So he's told you then?'

Told me what?

'Yes,' I say confidently, 'I know all about it.'

'And you're fine with it?'

'Of course!'

'It wasn't his idea.'

OK, now I'm really curious.

'Whose idea was it then?'

'Well, mine mostly, but . . .' Suddenly, she hesitates as if sensing a trap. 'Are you *sure* he's told you?'

'He hasn't told me a damn thing,' I state pleasantly. 'Why

don't *you* tell me?'

She swears under her breath. 'Look, maybe you should talk to him about it.'

'I knew it,' I say bleakly. 'He's got a girlfriend stashed down there, hasn't he? And you've been helping him keep it a secret from me.'

'Emma, that's not what—'

'Bye, Sian.'

I hang up on her. She rings me back immediately, but I don't answer. I'm too busy looking in my wardrobe. What should I wear to spring Nathan?

The bus down to Stockbridge can't move fast enough. I'm an extremely agitated woman on a mission. My instincts were right. I knew he was too good to be true. The secret girlfriend is the one he's emotionally involved with, *not me.* I'm uncovering male deceptions all over the place. I should start my own bloody detective agency! Tears begin rising and threaten to overflow, but I press my hands hard against my eyes because I'm *not* going to feel sorry for myself (and because I don't have a tissue).

The bus stops in Kerr Street, and I walk across the stone bridge that leads into Stockbridge. It's a beautiful morning—cold, but sunny. The intense blue sky is streaked with fluffy white clouds. There are lots of dog walkers, shoppers, and tourists out enjoying the day. I wish for a moment that I actually was meeting Nathan for a coffee. *That would be nice,* I think wistfully. We could get an intimate corner table in a warm cafe, shrug off our coats, and share a chocolate muffin (or maybe he can have that, and I'd watch him eat it as I'd still be on my new healthy routine). But no, this is reality, where the Nathan of my dreams doesn't exist.

Determinedly, I turn left before the main street and march towards St Bernard's Crescent. It's a curved double-storey Georgian terrace with wrought-iron railings and fluted columns. Number 19 is right in the middle of the poshest part, where the columns are taller and grander than the rest of the street. It has a black door. Now that I'm right outside, my courage is starting to ebb. I don't really want to find out about Nathan's other woman. I want him to be single.

My phone rings in my coat pocket, and I pull it out. Sian again. I decline the call. I can't deal with her at the moment.

Right, here we go. No point mucking around. Just rip off the Band-Aid and get the pain over with. I take a few deep breaths to psych myself up. With a shaking hand, I press the buzzer for the main door flat, which doesn't have a name. My heart rate is going through the roof. There's a click, and I hear Nathan's voice. 'Yep?'

Thankfully, I do have a plan for this, so I say in an Irish accent, 'Amazon delivery.' Thank God for acting classes; my degree is really starting to earn its keep. The buzzer goes, and I push open the door to find myself standing in a black-and-white-tiled entrance foyer. Before I can collect my thoughts, the blue door with a gold knocker directly on my left suddenly opens and Nathan strolls out, but stops mid-stride, his eyes widening in shock when he sees me.

Then I hear a woman's voice behind him. 'Are those the extra boxes and masking tape, Nathan?' Then she comes out of the flat. My mouth drops open when I see her feathered bob haircut. It's Blaire. *Blaire is Nathan's aunt.* For a few seconds, we all stand there staring at each other; no one knows what to say.

Then I find my voice. 'What the *fuck*?' I exclaim loudly, and they both jump guiltily.

'Come inside, Emma,' says Nathan, glancing at the stairwell. But I don't care if the neighbours hear me. At this point, Blaire kind of melts away back into the flat, leaving us together. A wise move; she can see I'm annoyed.

I frown at him and fold my arms. 'No, thanks, I prefer to be out here. So why the big conspiracy? Why didn't you just tell me Blaire was your aunt at the interview?'

He runs his hand through his hair and avoids my accusing stare. 'Ah, I don't know. I was going to at some point. It's complicated.'

'Oh, for fuck's sake! I know, all right? They're lesbians who work together! So what?'

'Shhh! Keep your voice down. OK, obviously there's been some shit going down while I was in London. I haven't had a chance to talk to her yet. But yes, that's the upshot of it. Blaire didn't want you knowing about her and Sian because you all work together. She asked me not to say anything.'

'Right.'

So I was well and truly kept out of the loop. Who do they think I am, some kind of petty gossipmonger? I take a step away from him towards the main door, then another.

'Don't leave. Please, just come inside, and we can talk about it some more.' I can tell by his tone he really wants to smooth things over, but a fissure of hurt is splitting inside me. Nathan *knew* Sian and Callum weren't having an affair and he didn't say anything!

'You could've told me the truth about Sian and Callum after I went to the open home,' I say stiffly. 'But you didn't. You sat there at the kitchen table and watched me suffer instead. Because that's your philosophy on life, isn't it? Do nothing and it will all work out.'

Tears swim and my vision blurs, damn, I'm not going to cry in front of him! Blindly I push at the door, and stumble outside taking deep breaths of cold air. Despite everything Callum's done, I feel a sudden yearning to see him. But I know it's a bad idea—he'll take advantage of the situation and he might try and get me into bed. We could end up back together. Even though I know it's stupid, it's all I can picture. Me sobbing on his shoulder and him saying soothingly, 'Fuck him, Em. He's from the colonies, what did you expect?'

I start walking but my legs feel weak and wobbly. My chest is tight. I lean over a nearby railing, gasping for breath, while cold sweat trickles down my back. Great, now I'm having a full-on panic attack in Stockbridge. Then I hear thudding footsteps and feel Nathan's arms wrap around me from behind.

'I've got you. It's OK. Just take some deep breaths.' But I struggle feebly against his chest.

'No, I want Callum.'

'He's gone, Emma.'

'I need to see him,' I gasp.

'Have you forgotten what he did to you?'

In his calm psychologist voice, Nathan starts reminding me about Callum. His controlling behaviour, the cheating—even his subtle put-downs that I hadn't picked up on. There's so much of it I can't bear to hear any more.

'Stop it!' I cry.

'You deserve better, Emma.'

I don't say anything, because I'm distracted by the way he's nuzzling his face against my hair. It feels really nice and his arms are solid and comforting. My hurt lessens a little and I lean back into him. He threads a hand inside my coat holding me close. 'I want you so much,' he breathes in my ear. Suddenly he's no longer psychologist Nathan, he's extremely sexy Nathan.

My resolve weakens into desire. Oh God, I want him too. If I turn my head slightly I could . . .

Yes! Kiss him now, urges Broad-minded, *before he changes his mind!*

No! You need to think, cautions Prude. *This is how you*

ended up with Callum!

I wrench out of Nathan's arms, breathing heavily, and manage to get some distance between us. I clutch the railing for support. My legs don't seem to want to hold me up. But at least now I'm thinking more coherently.

'Don't say that,' I pant. 'You're just like Callum. Telling me exactly what I want to hear.'

Nathan grunts sarcastically. 'Um, yeah, sure. I'm just like him. Whatever. I'm not the one screwing a dominatrix.'

'How do I know that?'

He swears under his breath. 'Emma, come on. You know me. You can't seriously think I'd do that to you.'

'You've demonstrated you're a competent liar. How can I believe anything you say?'

'I wasn't lying. I just couldn't break my aunt's confidence. There's a difference. Jesus, don't let one small thing ruin what we could have together!'

Nathan shivers and wraps his arms around his body for warmth. He has bare feet and is wearing only a khaki T-shirt and thin black tracksuit bottoms. 'Please, just come inside. It's bloody freezing out here.'

I'm torn. I want to go inside with him but some kind of weird self-preservation won't let me. I trusted Callum, and look where that got me.

'It's not a small thing,' I insist stubbornly.

Nathan frowns in annoyance and purses his lips.

Uh oh, I think. I may have just pushed him too far.

'That's rich! You let Callum treat you like *dog shit*. But I try respect my aunt's privacy, and suddenly, *I'm* the bad guy? I think you're royally screwed up, Emma. You need some serious counselling.'

Wow, OK. I just stand there and look at him, agog. Maybe he doesn't mean it. He's just saying that because he's cold and frustrated, but I can see from his stern expression he means every word. He thinks I'm a fucking psycho.

Suddenly, I feel very alone. I take a deep shuddering breath. 'Tell Blaire that I'm taking my two-week leave effective *immediately*. We'll discuss our living arrangements when I get back,' I declare frostily.

Nathan raises his eyebrows in alarm and takes a step towards me. 'Hey, wait a minute!'

But I ignore him and march off down the street. As soon as I turn the corner out of sight, I break into violent racking sobs. The kind of ugly crying that you should really only do in private. It's not a good look on the streets of Stockbridge.

After a miserable bus ride back to my flat, wiping snot onto my coat sleeve, I pull myself together. I don't need to listen to anything Nathan says. He's not the boss of me. And we're definitely not going to be flatmates anymore, let alone anything else. What a stupid idea! I was *so* right not to kiss him just now. At least I kept my dignity and waited until I was around the corner to start noisy crying.

I blow my nose, wipe my eyes, and take action. There's a

flight leaving for Barcelona late this afternoon, so I pull the trigger on that, then book a room in an airport hotel. Lloret de Mar is an hour and a half up the coast, so I'll catch a bus there tomorrow morning. Then I book a twin room in a three-star hotel for the next two weeks. I don't even bother checking reviews. I just choose the one with the nicest-looking pool that's reasonably close to the beach. From our conversation the other night, Julie's pretty much on board but just needs to confirm dates. So I'll email her the details, and she can join me when she's sorted.

I grab my suitcase out of the wardrobe and start packing. I don't even mix and match, just throw in anything that's not winter clothing—T-shirts, shorts, swimsuits, a cover-up. The buzzer for the main door suddenly goes at the same time as my phone beeps. It's Sian: *I'm outside, can I come in? We need to talk.*

I sigh and buzz her in. Might as well get this over with. I nudge the flat door ajar, then go back to my bedroom and keep packing. She comes in five minutes later and leans against the doorjamb, watching me. 'What are you doing?'

'I'm going on holiday, as of right now. Didn't Blaire tell you?'

'I've been at work. Nathan messaged me about what happened. He sounded worried, so I came straight here.'

'Worried I might kick him out of the flat, no doubt.'

'He's not like that. He cares about you.'

I make a harrumphing sound.

'Blaire was adamant she didn't want anyone knowing. What was he supposed to do? If you want to blame someone, blame me. It was my idea for you to include him in your flat interviews.'

'He still went along with it. He might've known I'd find out eventually.' I chuck a pile of underwear from my dresser drawer into the suitcase.

'Look, I'll set the scene. Nathan turns up out of the blue and asks if he can doss on Blaire's couch as he had, in his words, 'shit going down' in London.'

'I know about that,' I say.

'So you know he wasn't in a good space?'

I lift a shoulder sulkily in acknowledgement.

'He was surprised, to say the least, to find out that me and Blaire were together. Him staying on the couch was . . . slightly inconvenient for us. So he started looking for a job and a flat straightaway. He managed to get a construction contract quite easily, but the flat was harder going. There was a lot of demand, and he kept getting passed over in favour of girls because they're cleaner and tidier than guys apparently. No amount of him insisting he could cook and clean was doing it.

'You told me you were looking for a flatmate, and I knew Nathan was desperate. After the interview he really liked you and wanted to move in. I helped matters along by encouraging you to go for it.'

'By lying. You said her name was Anna!'

'Blaire's middle name is Anna, so I wasn't technically lying . . . Anyway,' Sian continues hastily, seeing me roll my eyes, 'Nathan was between a rock and a hard place because Blaire's so uptight about anyone finding out, and especially because we work together. It's not easy for a woman her age and in her position to suddenly come out of the closet. It wasn't a personal attack against you that we kept it quiet.'

'It all sounds very convoluted,' I say distractedly. *Do I need more T-shirts?* I toss in a couple extra for good measure. 'So I take it you'd already met Nathan before the party?'

'Yeah, I'm sorry. I thought it was better that way so you didn't ask questions about "Anna".'

'Well, you guys certainly had me fooled. Good job! Here I was, thinking my life was complicated. You had your own little double act going on.'

I give her a slow clap and walk into the en suite, where I grab my toiletry bag and sweep everything on the counter, including my toothbrush, into it. I dump it in the suitcase and try to zip the lid, but it's bulging. Damn, I may have slightly overpacked. Puffing, I manage to do up the zip and look around for my handbag and coat. I feel like I'm forgetting something. Ah, passport! I take it out of the nightstand drawer and stuff it into my handbag.

Sian's been watching me flit around the room like a hyperactive squirrel, and I see her frowning.

'What?'

'You seem kind of distant. Are you really angry? I . . . I

thought that if you knew the whole story, that everything would be OK.'

I double-check to make sure I've got my e-ticket.

'Sian, I really need to get going. My flight leaves at five thirty. Tell Nathan he can stay here for the time being if he wants. I'll be away, so it doesn't make any difference to me, and he may as well keep paying rent.'

'You're not going to kick him out when you get back, are you?'

'I don't know. I've just broken up with Callum, and now I've found out a couple of other people who I thought were good friends have been lying to me. So forgive me if I'm a bit "distant". It's a lot to take in.'

'I understand that. Just try to see it from—' She starts protesting, but I interrupt her in exasperation.

'I don't want talk about it anymore!'

Sian bites her lip, and at the sight of her distraught face I soften a little, aware that I'm acting like a proper bitch.

'We'll talk when I get back, OK? I promise. I just need a bit of space. We're still friends.'

She nods and manages a half-smile. 'OK.'

I heave my suitcase off the bed and lug it into the hallway. 'Uh, I might need some help with my luggage,' I gasp.

Sian takes the handle and tries to lift it. 'Jesus, what did you pack in here?'

'Just clothes and a little light reading,' I reply, puffing. 'But I think I'll order an Uber rather than try and deal with the bus.'

Her mouth twitches. 'Good idea.'

Chapter 27

COSTA BRAVA

⁂

Julie's laughter makes me glance up from my copy of *Pride and Prejudice*. I'm on a sunlounger by the pool, wearing a black bikini and a wide-brimmed sun hat, and she's on the other side of the pool in her red one-piece, talking animatedly to two guys in their thirties. As I watch, she gestures to me, and they look over. I shrink down behind my book and peep cautiously over the top. God, what is she telling them? I can't make out any features, but they have longish light-brown hair and great tans.

Eventually, Julie swims back over and gets out of the pool. She flops down on the lounger next to me, and I move my book to the other side so she doesn't splash the pages. 'Who were they?'

'Hmm? Oh, two brothers from a town in Yorkshire. I forget which one. They're a bit of a laugh.'

'Are they twins? They both look the same.'

She laughs. 'No, they're different close up. The slightly taller one is Dex. He's the eldest. Adrian is his younger brother. They're single apparently.'

'So they're on the pull?'

'Highly likely. Dex did ask if we wanted to have dinner tonight and go for a drink after. I said I'd run it by you.'

'I thought we said no men?'

Julie stretches out on her lounger, presenting her fake tanned legs to the afternoon sun. '*You* said no men, Em. I'm going to take any opportunity that arises.'

She has her mouth set in a determined line, so I don't press my luck. 'OK, which one do you like?'

She considers. 'Dex, I guess. He's got really nice teeth.'

'Right. Good teeth are important in a husband.'

'I don't want to marry him!'

'What do you want to do with him then, Julie Campbell?' I ask, narrowing my eyes at her.

'Just talk, of course,' she says innocently, tilting her face to the sun. 'I'll be like Elizabeth Bennet bewitching Mr Darcy with my scintillating wit.'

'Talk, my arse,' I mutter, turning over the page, and she giggles.

It's Wednesday, and I've been at Hotel Samba since Sunday night. Julie arrived yesterday evening after she managed to persuade her boss into letting her have a week and a half of leave. Today was brilliant. We went to the beach in the morning, and now we're hanging out at the pool, slathering ourselves in SPF 30 and soaking up the gorgeous sun. I haven't thought about Nathan at all.

OK, that's a slight fib. The whole thing keeps playing over in my mind. I hate the fact that I got so hysterical. I should've just gone into the flat and talked with him and Blaire in a calm and rational manner. Instead, typical me, I end up being all melodramatic on the street outside, like I'm acting in one of Alana's plays.

Anyway, I've calmed down and can see that I may have overreacted slightly, especially hearing from Sian about how it all panned out. Actually, I can totally see why Blaire didn't want him saying anything to me. I think I'm probably the last person she would've wanted knowing something like that since we didn't exactly get along. I like her better now, but my previous antagonistic behaviour makes me feel a bit ashamed. I wish Nathan could've just told me but I get why he couldn't. So I've gone from hating him to forgiving him and wanting to talk to him. But I'm too chicken to ring. At first, I typed a WhatsApp message but it sounded trite. Now, I think it's best not to try and make up with him over WhatsApp. Things can get lost in translation. So I've been typing a short snappy speech on my notepad app to refer to when I see him next. But the current version may need editing. It's got around twenty paragraphs.

Being in a different country is also giving me much needed space from Callum and time to process our break-up. The yearning to see him has definitely gone; it must've just been post-break-up angst or something. I made Julie promise not to tell me anything Davita says about him, just in case.

There's a possibility that she'll manage to get Callum on the rebound, so I have to be OK with that. To be honest, I've started thinking of them as a couple already; that's how much I care about what he does with his life now. I'm just not sure if I should mention his after-work activities to her. She is still kind of a friend even if she is muscling in on my ex-boyfriend.

In the late afternoon, when the sun's lost its heat, we traipse back to our minimalist (but newly renovated) room with its fake wood flooring, crisp white duvets, and square orange bed cushions. It's time to get ready to meet the brothers. Oh joy. After I get out of the shower, I'm surprised to see Julie's all dolled up in a backless tropical-print minidress, no bra, and high-heeled silver sandals. I don't want to give Adrian any encouragement, so I put on a basic white T-shirt, a demure knee-length black pencil skirt, and unsexy black ballet pumps.

Julie peers at me over her mascara wand. 'Are you sure you don't want to wear something dressier? You may as well take advantage of being single.'

'I'm not going to hook up with some random guy I don't even know. Not that I'm judging you or anything,' I say, sitting on the nearest bed and primly crossing my legs. 'In some circumstances, it's perfectly fine. I mean, if I'd been single for six months, then I'd probably throw myself at him. But I'm just coming out of a difficult break-up. I'm understandably a little cautious where men are concerned.'

She just raises her eyebrows and grins knowingly.

'What?'

'You've got it bad for Nathan.'

'I don't! Fine. If it makes you happy, I'll borrow some of your red lippy.'

She smirks and hands me a gold tube from her make-up bag. 'That's my girl.'

The hotel has an attached restaurant and bar, which is good because Julie's heels are causing her to swerve into the potted palms lining the foyer. I clutch her arm. 'For God's sake, don't break an ankle. A cast with a moon boot is not a sexy look!'

The brothers are waiting for us in the foyer. They're wearing slightly creased blue jeans and short-sleeved cotton shirts that seem like they've been dug out from the bottom of their suitcases. I grudgingly admit Adrian isn't bad-looking, but Dex is definitely the handsomer of the two. I sense an unspoken agreement that Julie's with him. And by the way he's checking her out, he seems to appreciate the effort she's gone to. I say a silent prayer to the dating gods that she'll get lucky.

After my second cocktail (some fruity number with so much rum it's got a kick like a donkey), I realise that I'm actually having a good time. We're sharing a delicious assortment of tapas, and the brothers have an endless supply of funny anecdotes to entertain us. Plus they seem really interested in what we have to say. They love that I'm a librarian who does life modelling on the side. In fact, Adrian choked on his beer so hard that Dex had to pound him on the back. But apart from mentioning that, I'm trying not to draw attention to myself and to let Julie do most of the talking.

We finish the latest round of tapas, and I take a breather to check out the al fresco restaurant. The place is full of twenty- and thirty-somethings, either in couples or small groups like ours. The drinks are flowing, there's upbeat Spanish dance music playing, and everyone's having a blast. I sigh and feel myself relaxing for the first time in months. Then Adrian starts stroking my thigh under the table.

Julie and Dex are having an intense conversation about their favourite movies, so Adrian's taken the opportunity to make a move on me.

'You're brave taking your kit off in front of people. Not sure I'd be able to do that—unless it was in a private setting.' He grins, white teeth flashing against his tan, and squeezes my knee. Damn, I knew I shouldn't have mentioned the life modelling.

'Oh, it's not too scary. It's mainly retired people that can't see very well.'

I gently lever his hand off my knee and clear my throat, trying to catch Julie's eye. But she's looking the other way and giggling as Dex whispers something in her ear. I cough loudly, and she looks around, startled.

'I'm going to the ladies. Do you want to come?'

'No, I don't need . . .' she begins, but I widen my eyes at her meaningfully. 'Ah, yes, perhaps I do.'

In the ladies, she checks under her eyes for mascara smudges while I lean against the edge of a toilet stall. 'How exactly is this going to work?'

'What do you mean?'

'I mean, if Dex asks you to go back to his room, where is Adrian going to go?'

'I thought he could sleep in my bed.'

'Seriously? He's starting to get gropey.'

'Just explain to him that you're damaged goods and you're not interested.'

'He's still going to try it on.'

'Please, Em, I really like Dex.'

'Fine, I'll manage Adrian somehow,' I say reluctantly.

'Thank you! Thank you!' Julie throws her arms around me in a bear hug and nearly knocks me into the toilet stall.

'This is meant to be a girls' getaway, you know,' I remind her, laughing and extricating myself.

'Yes, but life works in mysterious ways.'

'True.'

How can I deny her this when I'm the one who's been praying for it to happen?

Sure enough, Dex asks Julie back to his room after we've had another couple of drinks in the bar. So Adrian and I are lumped together. We perch on the single beds in my room and look at each other nervously. To my relief, he appears to have lost his bravado from dinner now that we're actually in a private setting.

I kick off my shoes and desperately flick through endless Spanish TV channels, trying to find something in English we can watch, while he lounges awkwardly on Julie's bed and scrolls on his phone. The brothers' room is two floors up from ours, so at least we don't have to listen to the headboard banging against the wall. That would be truly awkward.

Eventually, Adrian tries to make conversation.

'So, have you got a boyfriend?' he asks.

'Not currently.' Flick, flick.

'How long ago did you have one?'

'Exactly two weeks today.' Flick, flick, flick.

'Oh! A recent break-up then.'

'Yup.'

'So why did you break up?'

I sigh and lower the remote. 'I caught him cheating with a dominatrix.'

His mouth drops open. No matter how many times I say it, I'm always surprised that it shocks people so much. And their reaction puts me right back in that basement hallway, looking through the peephole at Callum naked and strapped to a chair. Maybe I should just get a T-shirt printed. Then people can read it at their leisure so I don't have to say the words ever again.

'That's wild!'

'Yeah, we were on the rocks before that. But still . . . it wasn't pleasant.'

Adrian shakes his head. 'Life modelling and BDSM—fun times in Edinburgh. Nothing like that ever happens in our village. Not that I know of anyway. Maybe I should move up there.'

'You'd move to Edinburgh just from meeting a couple of random girls on holiday?'

He shrugs. 'Why not? I've exhausted Tinder. There's a severe lack of single women under forty in Haworth.'

I stare at him. 'Did you just say "Haworth"?'

Adrian nods. Oh my God, he's from where the Brontës lived! Why did he not mention that before? He sees my rapt expression and laughs. 'Are you fangirling over the Brontës right now?'

'Possibly.' (I am, I am!)

'So what's your favourite book? You look like a *Wuthering Heights* rather than a *Jane Eyre*.'

'Aha, wrong! I'm a *Tenant of Wildfell Hall* actually.'

'Right, the one where she ran away from an abusive relationship,' he counters jokingly, but it hits a bit too close to the bone.

I clear my throat. 'Yeah, that's the one. So, did you read them?'

'Only for school. I preferred Thomas Hardy, to be

honest.'

'I can't believe you live there. That's so cool.'

'I get a bit sick of the tourists. It's totally overrun with middle-aged women doing Brontë pilgrimages in the summer.'

'Maybe you could stride around on the moors like Heathcliff to attract someone?'

'Nah, the only striding I do is down to the pub. Then I sit on my arse and talk shite with my mates.'

I snort. Suddenly, Adrian is looking much more attractive. Or maybe I've just got Brontë goggles on . . .

I've been sitting on the edge of the tub, gnawing my fingernails for what seems like forever, when there's a soft knock on the bathroom door and then a whisper. 'Emma?'

In the early morning light, I'm relieved to see Julie, albeit a little rough around the edges with mussed-up hair and panda eyes. She comes in carrying her sandals and shuts the door.

'What are you doing here?' I ask sotto voce. 'Dex didn't kick you out, did he?'

'No, no. Nothing like that. I just didn't want to do the walk of shame when everyone's going for breakfast. I'll see him later on.'

'So how was it?'

She grins at me. 'It was fantastic!'

I breathe a sigh of relief. Thank you, dating gods!

Julie leans against the door with a blissful look on her face. 'I think I'm in love.'

'What?'

'I mean it—he's amazing! And we've got so much in common.'

'Whoa, steady on. One orgasm and you're about to walk down the aisle?'

She sniggers softly. 'It was more than one actually.'

'Julie!'

'Shh, you'll wake Adrian.'

'Oh, is he . . .?'

'Still in my bed asleep.'

'Ah.' I chew on a ragged hangnail.

'Are you OK?' she asks.

'I think I've made a really big mistake.'

Her eyebrows rise. 'You slept with him!' she exclaims, forgetting to keep her voice down.

'Shhh! No!' I reply quickly. 'It didn't get to that. We had a nice chat and were getting on well. And then we just . . . kissed a little.'

'Oh. That's OK, isn't it?'

'No, I feel terrible about it.'

'Of course, because of Callum. It was too soon.'

'No, not him. Nathan!'

'Oh, because you've kissed Nathan too?'

'Er, yes, a little.'

'I knew it! You dirty stop-out!' Julie comes over and sits on the edge of the tub next to me. 'Go on, spill the beans. How was it?'

'It was just a quick peck before he went to London! But when Adrian kissed me, it felt all wrong. Like I was cheating on him. Then I got panicky thinking that somehow I'd end up with Adrian, in a relationship I didn't want to be in.'

'It was just a kiss, Emma. You don't have to be in anything with anyone if you don't want to be. Plus he doesn't even live in Edinburgh.'

I shake my head. 'He's thinking about moving there! It just feels like I have no control over my life, like I felt when Callum and I first got together. It all happened so fast. One minute, he was my letting agent. The next, he was my boyfriend, and I hardly knew him. I just don't want to make the same mistake again.'

Julie puts her hand on my arm. 'Callum didn't hurt you—physically, I mean?'

'No, nothing like that. He was just a smooth talker . . . very emotionally persuasive. I was flattered at the time, but now I'm thinking he liked me because he could manipulate me.'

She squeezes my arm reassuringly. 'I don't think Adrian's like Callum. Or Nathan either, for that matter.'

'How do I know that? What they show on the surface may not be the real them.'

'Any relationship is a risk. All you can do is look for clues and trust your instincts that you've made the right choice.'

'What if I can't trust anyone else because of Callum?'

'I think you'll be fine. You're strong and smart. You just got stuck with a bad apple, and look at what you've learned! There's a whole list of don'ts that you're going to be able to spot a mile off in another guy. The next relationship you have is going to be so amazing. I'll remind you of this conversation two years from now, and you won't even know yourself. It'll be like night and day.'

'Do you think so?'

'I know so.'

'I actually can't stop thinking about him,' I admit sheepishly.

'Who? Adrian . . . or Callum?'

'Nathan! But it's all fucked up.'

His parting remark lurches painfully to mind. *You need some serious counselling.*

Tears sting and I cry quietly while Julie gives me an awkward one-armed hug, not knowing what to say. Then there's a light knock on the door, and Adrian's sleepy head appears. 'Uh, is this a private conversation, or can anyone join in?'

I wipe at my cheeks with my hand and he looks away hastily. 'Sorry, didn't mean to interrupt.'

Julie rips off a length of loo roll and passes it over so I can dab my red, puffy eyes and blow my nose. 'Emma's OK. She's just dealing with a few things at the moment.'

'Ah, yes . . . not easy, break-ups.' He smiles at me sympathetically, then jigs a little. 'Um, don't suppose I can use the bathroom, though? I really need to take a piss.'

Chapter 28

DATING 101

⁂

The brothers are leaving in a couple of days. So we make the most of the time they have left—exploring the old town, dining on paella at one of the local restaurants, drinking Catalan wine, and going nightclubbing along the main strip.

It's a pressure cooker of emotion between Julie and Dex, and they're like a couple of limpets. Julie's on cloud nine, and Dex's expression reminds me of someone who's just won the lottery. It's cute, but kind of full-on too. Nevertheless, their happiness is infectious and spills onto Adrian and me, so we're enveloped in their bubble of merriment. We basically just tag along with them because what else are we supposed to do? Hang out by ourselves?

I know Julie wishes that Adrian and I were loved-up too. But even though we did have a snog that first night, I'm not feeling it, and he seems content just being friends. I also notice him surreptitiously checking out other women at the clubs, so he's definitely not enamoured with me.

On Saturday morning, we see the guys off from the hotel. Julie and Dex cling to each other in the lobby, whispering sweet nothings. Meanwhile, Adrian waits impatiently outside in the taxi, and I try not to roll my eyes.

After they've gone, inevitably, it falls on me to reassure Julie for the rest of the day that of course Dex will call or message *and* come visit her in Edinburgh. Why wouldn't he? It's perfectly obvious he's mad about her, et cetera, et cetera. I'm hoping that Dex comes through because if he doesn't, I'll personally track him down in Haworth, strangle him, and bury him in the Brontë Parsonage graveyard.

Thank God he messages her when he lands in Manchester and continues messaging her, so she's all smiles for the rest of the holiday. I have to put up with her always on her phone and the bloody thing beeping every ten minutes, but it's a small price to pay.

On Wednesday night, when we're at dinner, there's a series of beeps from Julie's phone, which is lying within easy grasp by her bowl of patatas bravas. She reads the messages and looks ecstatic.

'Oh, Em! Dex has booked a train to Edinburgh, and he's going to meet me at the airport when I get back!'

'Really?' That's keen since she's landing at 9.30 p.m. I guess he knows he's guaranteed a bed for the night. 'How long is he staying for?'

'I'm not sure. He says he wants to check out the city.'

'What about his job?' I'm not exactly sure what Dex does,

but it's something in IT, and he cycles into the nearby town of Keighley for work.

'He said he's going to quit and apply for jobs in Edinburgh. Apparently, he should be able to get something similar pretty easily.'

Wow, Dex is a fast mover. Either he's been struck by Cupid's arrow, or he's totally thinking with his pecker.

Julie starts getting philosophical. 'Thanks so much for inviting me on holiday with you, Em. God, what if I'd said no? Then I never would've met Dex!'

'You're very welcome.'

'It's like it was meant to be. I can't get over it.'

'Mmhmm.'

'He's so perfect for me!'

'That's great.'

'I really think he's the one.'

I imagine Dex and Adrian sitting in the pub in Haworth right now, with Adrian's eyes glazing over in a similar fashion to mine as he's forced to listen to Dex go on about Julie being the girl of his dreams. I take a long swallow of my sangria. I'm happy for her—truly, I am. I'm a bloody miracle worker.

Then in a few days, Julie is gone, flying back to the waiting arms of Dex and an unknown fate, but one that I'm sure will include at least a few more orgasms.

I'm relieved to have the last few days of holiday to myself.

I sleep late, head down for a leisurely breakfast, then stake my claim on a lounger by the pool. I read, and read some more, losing myself in other people's heartaches so I don't have to think about my own.

When it gets too hot, I go for a swim, enjoying the feeling of the cool water on my heated skin and the gliding weightless motion of my body. I don't talk to anyone and ignore the guys who walk past and stare at me like they want to start a conversation. I retreat into my shell to lick my Nathan-shaped wound, and no one can penetrate it.

The ice-cold wind of Edinburgh strikes me full in the face when I leave the airport on Sunday afternoon. It's just after 6 p.m. and pitch-black already. The contrast in temperature to sunny Spain shocks me to the core, and I almost turn around and book the next flight back to Barcelona. But really, it's an excuse. Inside, I'm quailing at having to face Nathan after our showdown in Stockbridge. I have my speech planned, but no idea how this is going to play out.

To my relief, the flat is dark and cold, and Nathan's nowhere in sight when I arrive. Still puffing with the effort of lugging my suitcase upstairs, I switch on all the lights and crank up the heating to a temperature equivalent to that of Spain. Thinking that Nathan might turn up soon, I get changed. Nothing too dressy, just a pair of tight white jeans and an off-the-shoulder blue cotton top that shows off my tan. I take my hair down from its ponytail and brush it. I add a touch of mascara and swish of lip gloss for a natural look. (OK, so I'm making a concerted effort to look casually hot. Sue me.)

I'm in the kitchen boiling the kettle for tea and reaching into the cupboard to get down a mug when it occurs to me: what if Nathan's moved out? My heart instantly plummets. I hadn't contemplated that possibility at all. Of course, why would he stick around? It's obviously the best solution under the circumstances. Us living together is just too awkward. I should check his room and find out for sure, but my legs seem to be made of granite, and I can't move. The thought of seeing a bunch of empty drawers and a bare closet fills me with fear. It means there's no hope for us. I may not even speak to him ever again!

Suddenly, there's the sound of a key turning in the lock and the front door opening. It startles me so much that I let out a small screech and nearly drop my mug. Hmm . . . It seems he hasn't moved out after all.

Nathan strolls into the kitchen, rugged up in a black North Face puffer jacket, black jeans, a green-and-white scarf, and a black beanie with a silver fern on it. Seeing him in the flesh after two weeks of imagining him is startling. My brain hasn't done him justice. He's gobsmackingly gorgeous.

'Hi, you're back,' he says. His eyes dart towards me, as if assessing what kind of mood I'm in. To be fair, the last time he saw me, I *was* storming off down the street.

'Oh, hi. Yes, I'm back,' I say, blushing furiously. I turn away quickly and busy myself with putting a teabag in my mug and pouring hot water on it. 'Do you want some tea?'

'Sure.'

Nathan shrugs off his jacket to hang it on the back of a chair, then removes his beanie, tossing it on the table. I notice from a sneaky peek that he's had a haircut. Is that for my benefit because he knew I was coming home today? Or has he been on a date?

I clock him giving me a subtle once-over too, and my heart rate increases.

'You look . . . rested,' he comments nonchalantly. 'Good holiday?' He turns his attention to the assortment of mail on the table and starts sifting through it, making two piles.

'Yes, thanks,' I reply brightly. 'It was very relaxing.'

I watch him out of the corner of my eye while I wait for the teas to steep, resisting the urge to ask if he's been on a date.

'Been out?' I eventually ask, trying to match his casual tone.

'Yeah, Murrayfield Stadium with a group of guys from work. All Blacks versus Scotland. All Blacks won, of course. They went out for drinks afterwards, but I . . . had some stuff to do here.'

Rugby, thank God. The muscles in my neck relax slightly.

Keep it together, Emma. Just act normal.

I finish making the teas and bring the mugs over to the table. We sit down facing each other. Nathan starts ripping open his mail with an index finger while I sip my tea and wish he was ripping off my jeans instead. Finally, he stops attacking his mail and starts drinking his tea.

'Catching up on your correspondence?' I joke.

'Yeah, I've been staying between here and Blaire's, helping with the move.'

'How's the new place?'

His eyes flick to mine, searching for a hint of sarcasm. But when he sees I'm sincere, he says, 'Beaut. It's on the other side of Stockbridge, near Dean Village. Three bedrooms. She's ordered a lot of IKEA furniture that needs putting together. Luckily, I'm good with my hands.'

I glance at his large hands cupping his mug of tea for warmth and can't resist asking, 'Are you?'

The corner of Nathan's mouth lifts in a half-smile, acknowledging the innuendo. 'You know I am.'

'Your IKEA dresser was delivered ready-made, remember? So I've seen the artist, but not the construction worker.'

He flicks a corner of an envelope with his finger. 'Yeah, well, I'm hoping to be more one than the other soon. I want to enrol in a BA in art at uni as a mature student.'

'Wow, really? That's great.'

'Yeah, I meet the basic entry requirements but need to

submit a mini portfolio to get an offer. Since my previous artwork is, er, unusable, I've set up the lounge as a studio. I hope you don't mind. It won't be for long, a few weeks at the most.'

I raise my eyebrows. 'Right.'

Nathan clears his throat. 'Look, I don't know if you've been thinking of turfing me out. But I just want to say I'm sorry you got mixed up in all that with Blaire. You're right, I didn't know what to do, so I did nothing. It was a shitty position to be in. But if I'd known you were going over to the open home to catch them out, I would've stopped you. And despite what you think, I hated seeing you in pain.'

'Is that why you kept saying I could talk to you?'

He nods. 'All I could do was be there for you, and listen.'

'But you think I need some serious counselling?'

'Ah, that came out harsher than I intended. I was a bit pissed off. I didn't mean it to sound like that.'

'So you don't think I'm a psycho?'

'Of course not. I had a few counselling sessions myself after I found out about Katie. It helps to talk to someone objective.'

'Well, I'll think about it.'

'You can still talk to me too. I'm here for you.'

The way he's looking at me is making me feel very hot and bothered all of a sudden. I think I may need to talk to a counsellor about Nathan rather than Callum.

I take a deep breath and get ready to recite my speech. 'Since we're having a heart-to-heart, I'm sorry too, for the way I reacted and what I said. I've had time to think about it and I get why you couldn't tell me about Blaire. You were being loyal. I was just hell-bent on finding a reason not to trust you. I was convinced you had a secret love nest in Stockbridge.'

What? OK, that came out wrong. I definitely wasn't going to mention the secret love nest!

Nathan arches an eyebrow. 'Really?'

I force a laugh. 'I feel a bit stupid now. I mean, obviously, I got the wrong end of the stick.'

His eyes lock on mine, and he smiles slowly. 'Yeah, I don't think I'm capable of being in love with two women at once. One is enough.'

I jolt upright in my chair. Did he seriously just say that? He must be kidding, surely. Nathan shifts his eyes away and sips his tea, unperturbed. He doesn't seem to be waiting for me to say anything. So maybe it was just a throwaway comment, and I'm reading more into it than I should?

Feeling more and more awkward, eventually, I say, 'Um, perhaps I'll just go and have a look at the lounge and see what you've done to it.'

Nathan grins. 'I thought you might.'

I get up, leaving my mug of tea unfinished, and go into the lounge, still reeling from what I think I heard him say.

He's put a white sheet over the floor (I don't have white sheets, so it must be an old one of Blaire's she didn't want). On it, there's a stool, a wooden easel, and a large sketch pad set up facing the window seat. A bunch of pencils, charcoals, and pastels are sitting on a pull-out tray underneath. He comes into the room behind me.

'What have you been drawing?'

'Nothing too exciting. I went for a walk around and took some photos of various things that caught my eye. But I don't know . . . What do you think?'

He goes over to the easel and starts flicking over the pages, revealing a montage of buildings from the Old Town. The ones at the beginning are entirely in charcoal, which are quite sombre. But as he flicks through, splashes of pastel colours start appearing, which lift the mood completely. Jesus, he's a good artist. If I could draw like that, I'd make a fortune on Etsy.

'Wow, you've been busy. These look pretty amazing to me.'

'What I really need is a life model,' Nathan comments. 'I'm more inspired by people than buildings.'

'So I should expect random women buzzing the flat at all hours and wandering around starkers then?'

'Well, I was kind of hoping you might be able to help me out with a few sessions since your other gig may have fallen through?' he says carefully. 'I'll cook you dinner to say thanks afterwards. No pressure, though.'

I gulp. 'Seriously?'

He nods.

I stare at him, and he looks back at me steadily. Is this a come-on? Or is he truly after my professional modelling services? I can't tell from his expression, but I know which I want it to be. God, the sexual tension between us is bad enough with clothes on, let alone with me naked. Would he even be able to concentrate enough to draw something decent? I could end up ruining his chances of getting into the degree.

'I'll model for you, but fully clothed,' I concede at last. 'I'm still traumatised from the Callum incident.'

'I get it. I'm still traumatised by what he did to my artwork.'

I smile at that. 'OK, it's a deal then.'

'Thanks, Emma.' He gives me a grin. 'I appreciate it. And I'm glad that you're not kicking me out.'

'Hmm, you might have to go on flat cleaning duty for the next month to make it up to me,' I tease.

Nathan laughs. 'All good. I'm prepared to don the pink rubber gloves.'

He takes a step forward and I sense that he's going to hug me because everything's OK between us now. But then he changes his mind and ends up hovering awkwardly like he's not sure what to do with his arms.

I giggle nervously and edge towards the door. 'Well, I should go and unpack and do some washing. That's always the worst part about coming back from a holiday.'

In my bedroom, I close my door and lean against it, breathing heavily like I've just run a marathon. All things considered, that actually went quite well. I've realised I'm capable of talking and acting in a civilised manner with Nathan and that I don't have to let past events spoil our current living situation.

Who am I kidding? There's only one thing I've realised in the last half an hour: I've got it so bad for him I can hardly think straight.

Nathan stays over at Blaire and Sian's place on Monday night because he's assembling yet more IKEA furniture. So I have the flat to myself. It's nice to have some space from the 'situation'. Otherwise, I know I'll feel strung out wondering if he's going to make a move. And if so, when?

Julie messages me with lots of exclamation marks and smiley face emojis, saying that things are going well with Dex. He's staying at her flat and has started applying for jobs. I can't believe how quickly that's happening. A couple of weeks ago, she didn't even know he existed! There's no mention of Adrian. I guess he's decided to stick it out in Haworth.

On Tuesday afternoon, I get home from work full of anticipation, and . . . Nathan's not there. I don't know if he's coming back tonight or not. Maybe he's letting things between us breathe a bit more.

Late-afternoon sunlight is bathing the window seat, so I don't bother changing out of my pencil skirt and blouse in case it disappears in the time that I do. Taking off my heels and releasing my hair from its bun so it flows down over my shoulders, I stretch out languidly on my back in the warmth, pretending I'm back in Lloret de Mar.

I'm lying there with my legs crossed at the ankles and absent-mindedly twirling my long strand of pearls when I hear a movement. Nathan is standing in the doorway, looking at me. I turn my head towards him and smile. 'Hi, I didn't hear you come in.'

'Hi,' he murmurs. He doesn't take his gaze away from me, just kicks off his work boots and pushes up the sleeves of his sweatshirt. His eyes rove over my body with laser-like focus. Then he sits down at the easel and flips over the paper to a clean sheet. 'Just ignore me for a bit. But can you keep your head turned towards me like that?' The intensity of his stare is making it quite difficult to ignore him. Nathan in artistic mode is so bloody sexy. So that I don't have to look at him, I close my eyes instead and zone out.

All I hear for a while is his charcoal pencil scritch-scratching, with the odd intermission of his finger smudging lines on paper. I can feel the sunlight starting to fade, and I'm getting sleepy.

'So did you meet anyone in Spain?' Nathan asks out of the blue. The sound of his voice jerks me awake. I glance over and see a grey-green eye staring at me intently from behind the easel.

'Ah, no,' I reply. 'But Julie did.'

'Oh?' His eye disappears and the scritch-scratching resumes.

'Yes, a guy called Dex. They hooked up. It was pretty full-on,' I say with a laugh. 'He's actually here in Edinburgh now, looking for jobs. Talk about a whirlwind romance!'

'So you were the third wheel?'

'Yes, me and his brother, Adrian.'

The scritch-scratching stops, and there's a silence, as if Nathan is searching for the right words. 'What was he like?'

I shrug. 'He was OK, not really my type. We were kind of lumped together because of the lovebirds. It was nice having people to hang out with. But to be honest, I was glad when they all left, and I had some time to myself.'

The scritch-scratching resumes. 'Well, you did go there to chill out,' he says neutrally.

'What about you? How's things with your flat in London?'

'It's on the market, and we're just waiting for it to be sold.'

'And Naomi's OK with everything? You being up here, I mean?'

'Yes, she's happy. Nicholas is on the scene now. She decided that he should know about Katie. Luckily, he wants to be a part of her life. He is her real father, after all. But I'll visit whenever I can, so she'll have two doting dads.'

'That's nice. Two dads are definitely better than no dad.' I've been pretty tight-lipped about my family up until now. So if Nathan wants me to 'talk to him', this is his chance.

Sure enough, he takes the bait and immediately asks, 'What's the deal with your dad?'

'He left when I was ten and moved to Sweden.'

'Sweden? That's kind of random.'

'Not if there's a Swedish hairdresser involved. Then it all makes perfect sense.'

'He had an affair with a Swedish hairdresser?' He pokes his head out from behind the easel and stares at me.

'Yeah, he moved there to be with her and now has a whole new family. They've got two kids, a boy and a girl.'

'Have you ever met them?'

'No, I've never been invited over.'

'Well, I guess he's happy, though?'

'As far as I know. And he gets free haircuts for life!' I quip. 'I do get the odd phone call and email, so at least I know he's wondering if I'm alive.'

'What about your mum?'

'She lives in Fort William. I had a stepdad for a few years, but it didn't last.'

'How did you get on with him?'

'Not very well. He was quite strict and used to lay down the law, which turned me into a rebellious teenager. I started drinking and smoking and staying out late with my mates. Mum didn't want me turning into a no-hoper, so she got rid of him.'

'Is she with anyone now?'

I shake my head. 'She's very active in the community and has a lot of friends, so she's kept busy. She's not too bothered about men now, I think. She doted on Callum, though. So she'll be upset we broke up. I should probably ring her.'

Nathan sits up straight and stretches his hands above his head. 'She sounds nice. I'd like to meet her.'

'Oh . . . uh, sure,' I say, slightly confused. He wants to meet my mum? That's definitely not flatmate behaviour. 'So, have you finished?' I ask quickly to change the subject.

'Yeah. I dunno if it's any good. I couldn't concentrate. I'll work on it a bit more tomorrow.'

'Sorry, I shouldn't have talked so much.'

'That's OK. My lack of concentration wasn't because of you talking.'

He grins, and I notice him glance at my neckline, where a few buttons have come undone.

'Um, can I see it?' I ask, hastily doing them back up.

'Sure.'

I get up and go over to stand behind him to peer over his shoulder. I'm not sure how he's done it, but he's managed to make me look superhot. Kate Winslet, eat your heart out!

'I think you've made me more attractive than I actually am,' I say doubtfully.

Nathan laughs. 'I just draw it how I see it.'

'Well, I'm flattered.'

'I think I'll call it *The Sexy Librarian With The Pearl Necklace*,' he muses.

'Ha ha.'

Without meaning to, as I'm looking at the drawing, my hand has drifted up onto Nathan's shoulder to rest on it. Now I'm suddenly aware that his breathing has quickened and it sends my heart rate into double time. There's an awkward silence that seems to go on forever. I'm not sure what to do. Should I say something or wait for him? At last, because my left calf muscle is about to seriously cramp up, I squeeze his shoulder firmly and tell him, 'I'm just going to my bedroom for a bit.'

How much clearer can I make it?

He nods and starts putting away his pencils. Damn, perhaps I should've made it crystal clear. Maybe he thinks I've got a headache? But it's too late now.

In my room, I lie on the bed with the lights out, the curtains pulled, and my eyes closed. My heart is speeding like a freight train, my muscles are rigid and I can't relax. I think I *will* develop a headache if he doesn't come in soon. Finally, just when I think he's not going to show, there's a light tap on the door. He opens it a crack. 'Have you got a headache?'

'No,' I answer.

'I've got some paracetamol if you have.'

'I don't have a headache.'

Maybe because I sound a bit impatient, Nathan finally gets it. He says, 'Ahh.' Then comes in and closes the door. He lies down on the bed, being careful not to touch me. 'Is this what I think it is?'

'Yes.'

He lets out a breath. 'Thank God, because I'm not sure how much longer I can keep my hands off you.'

Hearing that, I start fumbling with the tiny mother-of-pearl buttons on my blouse, but my hands are shaking too much. Fuck the buttons. I rip open my blouse and chuck it on the floor (I need new work clothes anyway). The sound catapults Nathan into action. There's a rustling as he takes off his T-shirt and the bed bounces wildly as he clambers out of his jeans making me giggle. I unzip my skirt and wriggle out of it, then unhook my bra and ease down my stockings and knickers. I hear further rustling then the ping of a bedspring as he stretches out full length.

There's a quiet pause, and then he asks, 'Are you naked?'

I stifle a laugh. 'Yeah. You?'

'Yep, in my birthday suit.'

Oh God, I almost lose my nerve. Our heavy anticipatory breathing intensifies. *Yikes,* I think, *someone's going to have to make the first move.* Well, it's not going to be me. It most certainly will *not* be me.

Finally, out of sheer sexual frustration, I reach over a hand, unsure of what I'll touch. It meets warm, smooth, muscled flesh. His arm, thank goodness. I do some more exploring, running my fingers over his shoulders, chest, and abs. Mmm, beautiful Nathan, he feels perfect under my hand. Then he whispers my name and his hand snakes around my waist pulling me closer to him. The heat radiating from his body is like a furnace. He kisses my neck and I bury my face in his sweet coconut-smelling hair; does he use Jamaican Delight as shampoo too? I open my mouth to ask him but Nathan's lips are suddenly on mine and we're kissing, properly this time, with tongues exploring; it's heavenly and seriously arousing. The kissing becomes deeper and sloppier as passion takes over from technique. I can't help moaning as he runs a hand over my breasts, cupping them and feeling my nipples, and then down to squeeze my backside.

'Are you turned on?' he murmurs in my ear.

'Yeah,' I murmur back dazedly.

'Hmm, let me check.' His hand moves between my legs, and I sigh at the stroking touch of his nimble fingers. I open wider as pleasure builds. Mmm, God, *yes*.

'What about you?' I ask. (Well, if we're playing that game.) I do a little stroking of my own, and he makes a sound somewhere between a gasp and a groan—he's incredibly hard.

'Uhhh, yeah. But we can take it slow,' he says softly, nuzzling my neck. 'If you need more time. If you're not sure about me.'

Wow, he's gagging for it, and he's worrying about how I feel instead. My heart smoulders. 'Nathan, stop a minute.' I stay his hand between my legs.

'Is something wrong?' he says immediately.

'No . . . I just . . . need to see you.'

I reach over and turn on the bedside light and we duck our heads and wince as it sears our retinas. I stare into his eyes, which have gone all squinty from the sudden brightness. 'I just wanted to say that I *am* sure about you. I've never been surer of anyone in my life. You're . . .'—I take a deep breath—'absolutely amazing.'

Nathan doesn't say anything. I hold my breath, hoping he gets my meaning. At last, he says, 'So, just to be *really* clear, because I'm a bit thick. Are you saying you love me?'

I nod vigorously and the smile he gives me is so dazzling it overshadows the bedside light. 'I love you too,' he says and gives me such a passionate kiss it would've knocked my knee-high socks off, if I were wearing any.

'I knew you did,' I say, breathlessly when we come up for

air.

'Well, I did mention it in the kitchen the other day.'

'I know. But I thought you were joking.'

'I'd never joke about that.' He shakes his head.

'I loved you the first moment I saw you.'

'Yep, me too. When you opened the door.'

Nathan and I grin at each other like happy fools.

Whether it was lust or love, I don't care. It feels right to say it. There *was* something there from the start, I couldn't take my eyes off him.

Then I realise we're happy *naked* fools since the light's now on and we're totally in the buff. I'm kind of used to lying around with my clothes off but he may not want certain parts of his body to be under scrutiny.

'Uh, do you want to get under the duvet?' I suggest, trying not to gawk.

Nathan follows the line of my gaze. 'Nah, I'm OK.'

'Very OK,' I murmur, arching an eyebrow. 'If you ever decide to do life modelling, I'm pretty sure your sessions will be booked out with a waiting list.'

His eyes glint mischievously. 'Speaking of life modelling, how would you feel about an up close and personal inspection? Purely for artistic purposes, of course.'

He draws a finger down my neck, trails it round the underside of my breasts and up over the top to gently tease my nipples, which are hard and aching. I groan and pull him over to kiss me again. The length of his body presses against mine, causing an urgent need between my thighs. As he kisses my breasts and his fingers explore me, I'm engulfed with it. All I can think is *Oh God, I want him—on top of me, in me, doing everything to me. And it's actually going to happen—right now.*

It seems I have to wait a bit longer though; wonder of wonders, Nathan enjoys lengthy foreplay. So I relax and savour the experience of being with a man who loves me and who wants to take his time. There's no Apple Watch, no schedule to keep, no contract that's more important than what's happening between us right now.

Eventually, I wrap my legs around his waist and in the soft glow of the lamplight, Nathan hovers above me, taking the brunt of his weight on his forearms. I let out a small moan of rapture as he enters me; an indescribable pleasure better than any fantasy. Fire takes over and we move together in perfect unison, breathing as one, like we were made for each other.

Epilogue

CALLUM'S NEW TOWN OFFICE

⁂

Six weeks later, on a Monday after work, I find myself in Duncan Stratt sitting across from the letting agent Shona McPherson. We're in Callum's old office—the one where he and I met. It's the last place on earth I want to be right now, and if I could've avoided it, trust me, I would've. But Nathan and I just moved to a gorgeous two-bedroom third-floor flat in Marchmont. So I'm here to drop off the keys for Bruntsfield and to sign some paperwork.

The new flat is in a great location, directly across from the Meadows, and there's a small grocery shop and a bus stop right outside. We've converted the spare room into a studio slash library. Nathan says it's perfect for capturing the afternoon light, and it has a window seat that looks right over the Meadows where I can curl up and read.

I was upset at leaving my old flat, yet we wanted a fresh start as a couple. Also, Callum still has a key. It was making us paranoid that he might come in and tear up more artwork, especially if he saw me in it.

Anyway, I'm praying that I don't bump into him. Thankfully, his new office is at the other end of the hallway from Shona's, and her door is shut. Unless he walks by and peers in the window, I should be safe.

'Thanks, Emma. That's all we need,' says Shona as I hand back the bit of paper I've just signed. It's some kind of declaration to say I haven't done anything illegal in the flat or hired a dodgy electrician to rewire the place without Duncan Stratt's knowledge—basically them covering their arses.

So it seems everything's in order, and I'm free to go. But just as I give her the keys and get up to leave, Shona's landline rings. She answers it with a 'Hello?' She listens for a bit, then looks at me. 'Yes, she's here.'

Oh no, it's not who I think it is. She hangs up. 'Callum would like to have a word with you.' Fuck. I really don't want to talk to him. Shona sees my wary expression and smiles kindly. 'Och, it's OK. He won't bite.'

Not much for a shark, I think.

Feeling like lead weights are attached to my feet, I make my way down the hallway to his office. He must've known I was here the whole time. He's like a predator with a sixth sense. Either that, or Shona told him I was coming in.

The door to his office is ajar, so I push it open and stand in the doorway. Callum's sitting behind his desk. He's wearing a crisp white business shirt and gold cufflinks I haven't seen before. He has on his blue silk tie, the one that matches his eyes. His hair is as immaculate as ever. The only mar on his chiselled face is a slight pinkish scar on his forehead. He still has the capacity to make me feel like all the air in the room has been sucked out. I take a deep breath to steady myself.

'Ms McTavish,' he drawls, then leans back in his chair and gives me a lingering look. 'Come in and have a seat.' He nods towards the chair opposite him.

I feel like I'm being invited into the wolf's lair.

'I'll stand, thanks,' I say, leaning with my back against the closed door so I can make a quick getaway. 'What do you want?'

'I heard you've left your flat.'

'You heard right.'

'Whereabouts are you now?'

'I don't think that's any of your business. By the way, you need to hand back the spare key to Shona. She asked me for it.'

Callum shrugs. 'Fine, I'll give it to her . . . I take it you're still living with lover boy?'

I don't say anything, and he chuckles. 'That's a yes. I already know you're fucking him, so it's not news. You didn't waste any time, did you?'

A flash of annoyance shoots through me, and I stiffen, ready to retaliate. Then I see the amused glint in Callum's eye. Let it go, Emma. He's just trying to get a rise out of you.

'I could say the same about you,' I reply flatly. 'Does Davita know about your "hobby" yet?'

He frowns. 'There's nothing to tell her. I haven't been to'—he lowers his voice—'that place for months now. Not since I was made to see the error of my ways.'

God, don't tell me he's become a born-again Christian. Not likely.

'You should tell Davita about it, Callum,' I state abruptly. 'Or I will.'

It's an idle threat. Davita and I haven't spoken for ages, but I know they've shacked up together in his West End flat. If she was having problems with him, I'd tell her in a heartbeat what he did to me. I'd hate for her to have to experience what I've been through.

'I don't want you talking to her about that. Things are different now, and she's not adverse to certain parts of it,' he says, avoiding my eyes.

Ah, OK, I take that to mean that Davita has been satisfying his desires to some extent. More than I could anyway. Or more than he let me. I nod, not wanting to hear anything else about it.

But then he adds softly, 'She's not you, though, Em.' This surprises me somewhat. I didn't think he'd be missing me. 'Maybe we can work it out,' he continues. 'If I'm OK with your life modelling and now that you know about my . . . needs. We had some good times, didn't we?'

I'm confused. Surely he's not trying to get back together with me after everything that's happened? He's got a nerve.

'No, we can't. I'm with Nathan.'

'But that's not serious, surely?' he questions, frowning.

I take a deep breath; he's going to have to hear it whether

he likes it or not. 'I love him.' *So much.*

A flicker crosses Callum's face, and his jaw clenches. *What is it?* I wonder. *Anger? Regret that he's truly lost me? Indigestion?* Whatever he's feeling, my words have had some effect on him.

I press on. 'I was never entirely happy in our relationship. And neither were you, it seems, since you cheated on me for months. You don't seem to realise that I can never trust you again. Ever. As for your needs, to be honest, I'm glad I don't have to wear BDSM lingerie anymore to feel desirable. You need to move on with your life, like I have.'

Callum shrugs, and his face smooths of any emotion. 'Fair enough. You can't blame me for trying,' he says offhandedly. It sounds like something he'd say if he hadn't quite managed to convince a buyer to put in an extra ten thousand to secure a property.

I twist the door handle behind me and turn to leave.

'Emma.'

I look back at him. 'What?'

'You were fucking hot in that black strappy number.' He gazes at me contemplatively and fingers his blue silk tie. Oh for God's sake. Don't tell me that's what he's missing—having sex on my kitchen table amongst a chicken curry takeaway!

I'm not sure how I do it without laughing, but I manage to look him dead in the eye, lift up my chin, and say in a sultry Florida drawl, 'Why thank ya darlin', Mervin thinks so too.'

I don't wait for Callum's reaction, just yank open the door and walk out of his office without looking back. I'm going to *burn* that particular item of lingerie. I'm pretty sure I won't be wearing it again. Nathan is definitely a 'lace and bows' kind of guy.

Actually, amend that to an *au naturel* kind of guy.

On Saturday, I'm lying on the window seat in Nathan's studio, bathed in afternoon sun, and wearing only my grandmother's pearl necklace. I finally agreed to do a proper life modelling session to help him out with his portfolio for uni. He says he's trying to depict the two states of the human form, dressed and undressed. But from the way he keeps poking his head out from behind the easel to perve at me, I get the feeling he's going to be spending more time working on the undressed state.

Not that I'm any better—Nathan naked is extremely distracting. I felt nervous about posing, so he decided to wear his birthday suit to keep me company.

'You're starting to look a lot like the guy in Jack's painting,' I comment, eyeing his delectable lower half underneath the easel. The fact that I'm turning him on is starting to make me feel very aroused.

Nathan crosses his legs and bends over slightly.

'Are you blushing, Mr Ellington?'

'Nup.'

'I think you are.'

'Just hold still,' he says gruffly. 'You're making things difficult.'

'I'm making things difficult and *hard*,' I say breathily, twirling my pearls with one hand and running the other seductively over my breasts.

'Huh?' Nathan pokes his head around the easel, a studious frown on his face, but then a lopsided grin appears when he sees what I'm doing.

'So very *hard*.'

By this point he seems to have given up drawing and is more interested in watching me. I arch my back, groaning suggestively, and my hand dives down between my legs.

Before I know what's happening, Nathan's throwing down his charcoal and shoving aside the easel. He's striding over in a manly fashion, and well . . . let's just say, I was wrong about the kitchen table. Making love with Nathan on a window seat, in full view of the Meadows (and possibly the bus stop) is *way* hotter.

And, surprisingly, there's no argument from either side of my personality about it. For the first time in my life, it appears they're both completely in agreement.

The End

Thank you so much for reading this book! I hope you enjoyed it and if you have, I'd be thrilled if you left a review or star rating on Amazon / Goodreads.

Keep Reading

If you enjoyed *My Double Life*,
check out my enemies to lovers rom-com
The House of Dating Disasters.

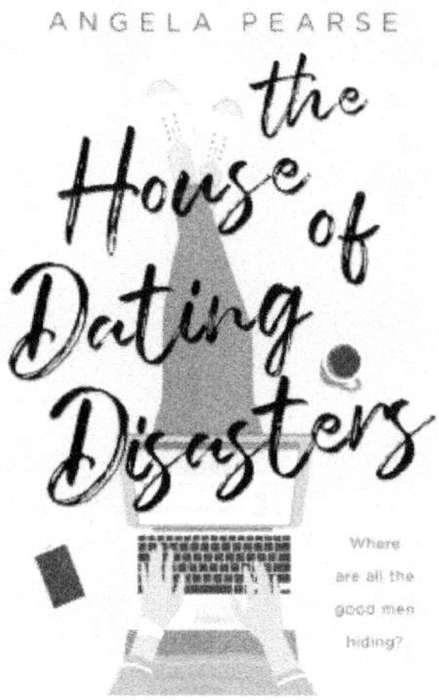

Aster's been on more dates than she's had hot dinners, from players to weirdos, she's met them all.
So when flatmate and fellow dater Edie suggests a new approach to weed out the undesirables, she's right on board.
Then Edie gets together with her physiotherapist and Aster has to face the uncomfortable truth—her best friend is dating the guy she's been looking for.

Available on Amazon and Kindle Unlimited

Also by Angela

You Had Me at Ice Cream

Zara isn't what Oliver expects when he enlists a personal trainer named "Zee" to shed his excess kilos.

I'll Meet You in Florence

House sitter Jenna falls for the owner's stepson who lives in the back garden, and gets a surprise when he follows her to Florence.

The House of Dating Disasters

Serial dater Aster gets into love triangle trouble with her best friend Dee.

Travel & Mayhem

Frustrated receptionist Jane escapes to Europe with a sexy, but emotionally unavailable, Scotsman to be a digital nomad.

All books available on Amazon and Kindle Unlimited

Acknowledgements

Many thanks to my beta readers: Katie Griffin, Aimee Ferro, Kylo Kotze, Ellie Race and Lauryn Lambert. I'd also like to thank Peachy Yap for her copy editing, Anita Saunders for her proofreading, and My Lan Khuc Valle for her gorgeous cover art. Thanks to my partner Chris Lambert for his patience, support and scrambled eggs. This one's for you!

Angela Xx

About the author

ANGELA PEARSE writes quirky romantic comedies which capture the humour of everyday life. A freelance copywriter with an MA in English, Angela enjoys travelling, hiking, cooking, binge-watching Netflix, and reading copious amounts of chick lit. Originally from New Zealand, Angela currently lives in Edinburgh.

To receive alerts about new releases,
sign up to her newsletter at:

➔ angelapearse.pub

Printed in Great Britain
by Amazon

26868471R00212